The Valkyrie of Vanaheim

Phil Parker

"In Vanaheim wise powers him created, and to the gods a hostage gave.
At the world's dissolution, he will return to the wise Vanir."

Extract from The Elder Edda of Saemund Sigfusson,
(translated by Benjamin Thorpe 1866.)

Contents

CHAPTER 1

CHAPTER 2

CHAPTER 3

CHAPTER 4

CHAPTER 5

CHAPTER 6

CHAPTER 7

CHAPTER 8

CHAPTER 9

CHAPTER 10

CHAPTER 11

CHAPTER 12

CHAPTER 13

CHAPTER 14

CHAPTER 15

CHAPTER 16

CHAPTER 17

CHAPTER 18

CHAPTER 19

CHAPTER 20

CHAPTER 21

CHAPTER 22

CODA

ACKNOWLEDGEMENTS

Chapter 1

'The invasion by the fae was no accident of timing. They'd waited for global warming to raise sea levels and erode civilisation. A weakened humanity couldn't resist the onslaught from interdimensional doorways they knew nothing about. The decade-long war that followed was both brutal and bitter.'

Preface of 'When the Fairies Came' by Professor Clifton Montgomery

The stench of dragon breath woke Frida and made her senses tingle.

It summoned unwanted memories of the war; she pushed them away, stumbling out of bed, blurred by sleep. It took a moment for her brain to catch up with her surroundings. This wasn't her bedroom. It was tiny, just enough room for the bed, a chair and a wardrobe the size of a matchbox. Shafts of moonlight lit up the wooden floorboards through rags masquerading as curtains.

Their hotel. She'd been billeted there with the rest of the expedition team. There'd been drinks the night before. A lot of them. For someone who'd hardly encountered alcohol, she'd escaped to her room before things got out of hand. She couldn't be around a bunch of rowdy soldiers, certainly not with the attitude they'd already displayed toward her. A situation aggravated by Bloody Mike.

As she opened the door, the smell intensified. Of course, it wasn't dragon breath. Those creatures withdrew with the rest of the fae's invasion force. It was smoke. Common or garden smoke. Just too much of it to be good news.

She stared down the stairwell from her second-storey eyrie, but it was too dark to see anything. Frida hesitated. Should she shout a warning? If it turned out the smoke came from the fireplace in reception, her panic would cause them to think even less of her. If that was possible.

Except the smell was too strong to reach this far from the fireplace. She extended her senses into the velvet darkness but felt nothing. Not at first. She frowned for the millionth time and wished her training had extended beyond the capability of a child. At eighteen, it should've been second nature by now. She gripped the banister, white knuckled with frustration, and pushed out into the darkness again. She closed her eyes; it helped her focus sometimes.

There was movement downstairs. A sense of apprehension, but also determination. But something else. She could sense it, just beyond the boundary of her expertise.

Frida tried desperately to remember her mother's advice, dimmed by the years now, something about closing down the rest of the body and turning the mind into a funnel. Sometimes it worked, but mostly it didn't. What didn't help, the increased smoke that tickled her nostrils now. She closed her eyes again, concentrated as hard as she could, furrowing her brow with the effort. Like a candle's flame in the darkness, guttering and small, she snagged it. The intent. Someone planned to do something terrible, wicked.

And now.

It was the surge of conviction which registered in her poorly disciplined mind.

'Fire!' she yelled at the top of her voice. 'Fire!'

Except her second warning was lost in the thunder of an explosion. The walls, staircase, even the roof above her, shuddered. Without her firm grip on the banister, she'd have been catapulted down the staircase. With the same roar as a strafing dragon, heat and flame swept toward her. Frida threw herself backward in panic as air vanished and heat enveloped her. She curled up into a ball, knees pressed hard against her face, and whimpered.

The furnace-like heat vanished as quickly as it had arrived, but the crackling of flames below told her all she needed to know. There'd been an explosion, deliberately detonated. She was certain. As certain as her limited psychic talent could tell. Screams and coughing filled the choking air, and people called out for help or to give instructions. Frida struggled to her feet. She had to get downstairs to safety.

A goal which looked unlikely. Flames licked hungrily at the ancient woodwork, running up the walls like orange mice as people on the floor below scurried to escape. She shouted for help just as another explosion shook the building, even worse than before. The floor lurched. Frida lost her balance and collided with the wall. For a moment confusion addled her mind; she stared at the peeling wallpaper in bewilderment.

Someone called her name. At the foot of the staircase, amidst the smoke, she could just make out the figure of a woman. Layla Quinn. The history woman.

A loud cracking, the sound of a whip amplified a hundred times.

The floor lurched again, followed instantly by an ear-splitting crash. The first-floor corridor disappeared, dropping into a pit of flames which billowed upwards in thanks for the additional fuel. The woman at the bottom of the staircase screamed. She clung to its steps, an inferno waiting for her below.

Like a snake, Frida crawled down the staircase on her belly. The other woman sobbed, unable to take her eyes off the fiery pit, waiting to consume her.

'Layla, take my hand!'

There was something in how she clung to the wooden step, a weird, lop-sided way that showed something was wrong. The other woman looked up at her, pain and panic scrawled across her face.

'It's my leg.'

'Take my hand, I'll drag you toward me.'

What they'd do after that was a mystery. There was nowhere to go. But that problem could wait. Deal with one challenge at a time – one of the many tips her mother had given her as a little girl.

Layla grabbed her hand, slick with sweat. Frida gripped the wrist and pulled. The woman grunted in pain, screwed her face up, and bit her lip. Slowly, far too slowly for her liking, Frida hauled the woman toward her.

A loud *whoomph* and fire surged below them. The air vanished briefly, and when it returned, so did the cracks, pops and crunches of things breaking and collapsing. The hotel had looked like it wouldn't withstand partying soldiers, so it was never going to survive the explosion. Frida was no architect, but she knew she had only moments before the hotel became a demolition site.

With a final surge of effort, which promised to pull her arm from its shoulder socket, the woman fell on top of her. She groaned and passed out.

The second-floor landing, with its one room, was no more than a square of bare floorboards that were already warm to the touch. Frida ran into her room, shoved her feet into her shoes, and hurried to the small window. It looked out onto a flat roof at the back of the hotel. Clambering out the narrow window with Layla's unconscious body was out of the question. She had one option. It was unlikely anyone would see them at the rear of the building, but she had to take the risk.

Frida stepped back and focused her mind, then straightened her arms and fingers and let rip. Incandescent energy leapt from her fingertips, broad beams of destruction that struck the wall and blew it outwards. Frida grinned.

She rushed back to the unconscious woman, picked her up, and hung her around her broad shoulders. She was lighter than she looked – Frida had carried heavier bags of grain. The life of a farm labourer hadn't just offered her a bed and food, it had made her strong. Correction. Stronger. She'd always been strong. How could she not be? Looking like she did?

She jumped, and landed on the flat roof below. Its pitch waterproofing already smouldered from the heat of the fire and tiny spirals of smoke rose from it. She sprinted the length of the roof and scrambled onto an old oil drum to the abandoned carpark where Nature was busy reclaiming the rotted tarmac with tufts of grass and weeds. She laid Layla's unconscious body on the ground and sat down heavily next to her. The adrenalin wasted no time in abandoning her and exhaustion claimed its place.

8

A loud crash filled the night. Flames and sparks leapt into the air, performing feats of aerial ballet, before falling back into the inferno below. Like a pack of cards, the walls and roof of the hotel collapsed inward and the fiery choreography began again.

On the main road a short distance away, a fire tender arrived. Its crew went to work instantly, hauling out battered hose to douse the flames to rescue the other buildings. The hotel was gone.

The other woman was still unconscious. Frida struggled to her feet, exhausted, her throat burning from the smoke and effort. She could make out a group of soldiers directing activity, a likely source of help. A young man, sweating and soot-stained, called out orders. Frida vaguely recognised him as a lieutenant she'd met a day or two earlier. He turned a kind face toward her as she coughed and gasped her need for someone to help the other woman. He barked an order for a younger soldier to accompany them, a lad probably no older than Frida, his anxious face covered with freckles.

The lieutenant assessed the woman with agile fingers and the confidence born of experience.

'It's her leg. Don't think it's broken, but she's damaged it somehow.' He looked up into Frida's exhausted face and frowned. 'How did you two get out?'

Frida explained, minus any mention of blasting walls.

The young lieutenant shook his head in disbelief and turned to the young soldier. 'Corporal Frears, fetch my jeep and get them to the hospital.'

The young man saluted and ran, hare-like, into the night.

The lieutenant stood up, still watching Frida carefully. She felt herself blush. His good looks intimidated her.

'I'm Lieutenant Tristan Wheeler. I've seen you before. You're part of the expedition team, aren't you?'

She nodded awkwardly, uncertain how to react to his question, even more anxious when it came to dealing with men. Usually, they noticed her powerful physique and treated her as an asset, a body capable of heavy manual labour, no different to a man. Occasionally some saw her gender as a vulnerability, but they usually backed off once she proved how wrong they were. The young lieutenant's smile unnerved her, leading her into unfamiliar territory.

'What's your name, miss?'

'Frida. Frida Ranson.'

'Did you really carry her out?'

Another terse nod.

'That's amazing. You saved her life. That's more than can be said for most of your team, I'm afraid.'

Frida looked into the young man's face and found sympathy waiting for her. 'How many survived?'

'A handful got out but they're all in bad shape, badly burned while trying to get their comrades out.'

She didn't want to ask the question but she had to know. Even if the news was bad. Not knowing was even worse. 'What about Elsa? Colonel Olsen. She's OK, isn't she?'

His sad smile and shake of the head were enough. 'No sign of her, I'm afraid. Her room was close to where the explosion happened. It's why we think it's probably an act of terrorism.'

She nodded. An automatic response. There could be no other. It was like the fire had burned away all her feelings, left her numb, empty. Elsa had been a second mother to her, found her, saved her. She couldn't be dead. Couldn't.

'Did you know her well?'

Another nod. How could someone she'd known for just a year, twelve amazing months, be so important to her? Just as importantly, as reality hit, what would she do now? Elsa commanded the expedition. With most of the team gone, it would be over. Over before it began. What would she do now?

Tears burned and threatened to breach the dam she'd built so carefully after her mother's death. She couldn't let this handsome young man see her so upset. She knew men used it for their own advantage.

She took a deep breath and stared at him, hard. 'Don't let me keep you. There will be others who need help.'

He frowned. 'If you're sure. Billy will be here shortly. He'll take the two of you to hospital.'

'I'm fine.'

He stopped mid-turn. 'I think you ought to get checked out, just to be sure.'

'I said, I'm fine.' It came out harsher than she'd intended.

He shrugged his broad shoulders. 'Don't you want to go with your friend? Make sure she's all right. Tell them what happened. That sort of thing?'

He strode off to re-join the chaos before she could reply. He was right, of course. She'd made a mess of that conversation, as usual. A jeep bumped and swayed its way to screech to a halt in front of her. The freckled-faced corporal flung himself out of the vehicle and grinned at her. Clearly, he'd enjoyed himself. He bent down to pick the woman up and then had second thoughts.

He blushed as he looked up at Frida. 'Sorry, miss. Could you give me a hand ...?'

She told him she could. She could handle this young man easily, too. It was the older ones, those who thought age and experience mattered, that caused trouble. Unless you faced a gang of youths. She'd done that a couple of times.

She jerked a thumb at the jeep. 'You open the door, I'll put her in the front.'

He stared, slack-jawed, at the ease with which she picked up the unconscious woman and laid her on the front seat.

She jumped in the back. 'You'd better drive a lot more carefully this time!'

He grinned at her and promised he would. He reversed back up the lane, behind the embers of the hotel, to reach the road. As he slowed the jeep to signal to the young lieutenant, Frida spotted a figure in the shadows. He stood apart from the local people, whose sleep had been disturbed by the night's drama, his cloak drawing her attention. No one wore cloaks. She craned her neck out of the jeep's window to get a better look. Their eyes met.

Almond-shaped eyes, along with higher-than-normal eyebrows and a domed forehead. As much by instinct as anything, her senses reached out toward him.

12

As though he knew what she was doing, he stepped backward and faded into the darkness.

The jeep took off again.

'Do they have any suspicions who might be behind this attack?' she asked.

The young man shook his head, ginger hair sprouting from beneath his cap. 'Probably Humanity First, miss. They threatened to take action, unless your expedition was cancelled.'

'It wasn't my expedition. I was just helping out.'

Elsa's face swam into her memory: her engaging smile that she used like a weapon to charm everyone she met, persuading them to agree to her requests. Tears made their second attempt to escape, and she fought them back.

'Sorry, miss. Didn't mean anything by it.'

Her terse reply had managed to offend someone else. Well done, Frida. Partly to show she could be friendly, she made a supreme effort and tried another approach.

'Any possibility it might be an attack by the fae?'

The young corporal turned to look at her over his shoulder, his freckles screwed up into a frown. 'They've retreated back to where the bastards came from. Why would the bloody fairies bomb a hotel?'

She didn't have an answer either. 'To stop the expedition?'

'Why would they care? We might be using the same portals they used to invade us, but the government told them what we were doing. Nah, far more likely that Humanity First bombed the place because they don't want the expedition to happen. I mean, they've succeeded, haven't they? I think they even killed the woman who was leading it. Nah, it's Humanity First. Don't know why you'd think it was the bloody fairies.'

They sped through the silent streets of York, Frida staring out at the empty buildings, their vacant windows like eyes, watching her. The corporal might be right but, it didn't explain why a member of the fae had stood and watched the hotel burn. Or recognised her. Why else would he shrink away from her attempt to penetrate his mind?

It didn't make sense.

It irritated her. As they pulled up outside the hospital, she made a decision. She owed it to Elsa to find out who was responsible for her murder. And pay them back. Pay them back in blood.

Chapter 2

*'We called them Fae Portals at the start, in
recognition of how the enemy had used these
interdimensional doorways to infiltrate our world. After
the war, the name remained though their relevance
changed. Here we were, in the twenty-first century, with
the means to flee our tortured world for somewhere
which offered promise of a brighter future without using
spaceflight.'*

'Norse Mythology and its Reality' by Dr. Layla Quinn

'I'm not a hero, Layla!'

No matter how many times she said it, Frida
couldn't stop the other woman from proclaiming the word
to everyone. She'd had no choice but to stay with her. The
staff in the small hospital were struggling to cope with the
influx of injuries from the fire and, after six hours, only one
doctor had given Layla's leg a cursory glance and declared
it to be a likely sprained ligament. It required an ice pack
and painkillers so it wasn't urgent. The burned and the
dying were.

Frida sat on an uncomfortable plastic chair that
tormented her aching muscles. The hospital ward was no
different: basic, utilitarian and comfortless. During the
hardships of a decade-long war, every form of luxury and
relaxation had been abandoned. Money was in short
supply, and healthcare was not exempt from those
shortages. The whole place smacked of desperation and it
didn't help Frida's dark mood. Elsa wouldn't leave her
thoughts. She wasn't going to turn into some blubbering

lump in front of a woman she hardly knew her. Truth be told, she resented her. She'd known Elsa longer; they had been good friends and the joint instigators of the expedition.

She sensed the other woman's scrutiny and glanced over at her. It earned a smile.

'You really liked Elsa, didn't you?'

The sudden arrival of a tight throat and her tears bursting through their dam meant Frida could only nod.

The other woman took her hand and squeezed it. 'She really was something, wasn't she? I'm going to be lost without her.'

Tears formed in the older woman's eyes, magnifying her unusual olive-coloured irises. The small lines around her eyes suggested the woman's age might be greater than she looked, even though her skin was smooth. Flawless, in fact. The same lines formed at the edges of her mouth and hinted at a readiness to smile but there was no sign of that now. Layla Quinn displayed the same level of grief as Frida and it surprised her.

'I'd only known her a couple of years. I met her during the war. I was in Lincoln doing some research when the fae invaded. She commanded the nearest battalion.'

'I thought Lincoln was one of their entry points. It had a portal like the one here in York Minster, didn't it?'

'Yeah, but they didn't stay in the city. They left a small force to protect the portal, then fanned out to ransack the eastern parts of the country, from the Humber down to the Wash. Their mistake was to spread themselves too thin. Elsa once told me they had underestimated humanity's progress since their last visit.'

Frida shrugged. She felt uncomfortable talking about the fae. It made her anxious. It was almost a relief when the conversation moved back to Elsa.

'Elsa's soldiers finished off the fae who'd been left behind then set about protecting the city. I used to marvel at how she issued commands and everyone instantly did as she said, since she was such a quiet, kind and sensitive person at other times. I think it was a mixture of respect and charm.'

Frida nodded. She'd have used the same words.

'How did you meet?' Layla asked.

Anxiety spiked Frida's pulse rate instantly. She wasn't in the military so it prompted questions about the inclusion of the strange young woman with the jade green eyes, silver hair and musculature of a man.

A freak.

'You know what Elsa was like. Picked up people because she thought they might be useful. I never understood what she saw in me, but she kept saying how I needed to join her on the expedition. In the end her pestering paid off.'

It prompted a quiet snigger. 'Yeah, that was Elsa. She used her charm, and when that didn't work, she'd keep nagging you until she got her way.'

The memory made Frida chuckle too. It faded almost straight away. Laughing felt wrong when grief was so raw. They lapsed into silence. Elsa's sudden departure from their lives left an emptiness only memories could fill, and they weren't enough. She might have been small in stature but her part in their lives had been huge.

17

'I don't suppose the expedition will go ahead now. Not unless I can find someone else to lead it.'

The admission brought Frida up short. 'I thought it was Elsa's idea? Her mission?'

The other woman shrugged casually. 'Technically. It was my research, my curiosity that inspired Elsa to make it happen.'

'What research?'

It triggered a huge sigh, and Frida wondered if she'd upset the woman who now stared blankly at the window opposite her bed.

'The fae invasion introduced us to interdimensional portals. Their entry points were always in historic locations, long associated with myths and legends. Places of worship were common because Christianity built on pagan places of worship. Elsewhere, they were found in standing stones and Stone Age fortifications.'

Frida did her best to concentrate under the woman's gaze, though she already knew that part of the story.

'It got me wondering if these portals might be connected to other locations of legend. Medieval man couldn't differentiate between races that weren't human, so that's why they came up with the collective term of fae. Every creature they encountered was a fairy. Or a god. Our encounter with the fae showed us how similar we were in many ways. They are just a lot older. We're infants in comparison.'

'And your research?' Frida asked, eager to move things away from the fae.

'There are portals all over the world. The war proved that. Therefore, it seemed likely different locations in Britain might lead to different realms. The Vikings believed there were nine realms, including ours. The same is true for all the major early civilisations, like the Egyptians, Greeks and Mayan. That couldn't be a coincidence.'

She took a breath. Her enthusiasm caused her to speak faster, with greater passion and energy, which must have also hooked Elsa into this story.

'Here in the north of England, where the Vikings dominated, I posed the theory that the fae's portals could take us to the Norse realms. If they did, we could find other worlds to colonise. New gardens of Eden where we could start again, without needing to fly rockets through space to get there.'

'Elsa had explained some of that but I hadn't realised it was your idea. So why Vanaheim?'

'Most of the Norse realms are inhospitable. The Vikings believed Muspelheim to be a volcanic world, Nifleheim an artic wilderness and Svartlefheim a cavernous realm within mountains. Helheim was their version of Hell, ruled by the tyrannical Hel and Jotunheim another snowy wilderness full of giants. When you remember Midgard is our world, two remain. There's Alfheim, which we now believe to be the world of the fae, and where we get the term elf. That leaves Vanaheim. A world of mystery. The Norse have few records of it, unlike all the others.'

Layla's excitement radiated from her handsome features. 'Elsa and I wanted our expedition to find out if it might sustain a large-scale migration of humanity. For it to become our new Eden.' She turned her gaze back to the window. 'The fae war brought us all kinds of problems. People died in their thousands. Yet it also brought new discoveries, such as the portals. A number of countries are attempting to use theirs for colonisation.'

That was news to Frida. 'Do you think another country might be responsible for the destruction of the hotel? To eliminate us from the race?'

Layla opened her mouth to reply and snapped it shut. 'You can ask that question of this man marching toward us now.'

Frida looked over her shoulder. The handsome Lieutenant Wheeler strode through the hospital ward toward them. At his side, an older man, flame-haired and bearded with gimlet eyes and an expression of someone who'd sucked too many lemons.

'Don't leave me!' Layla hissed and grabbed Frida's hand and held it like a vice.

'Good morning, Doctor Quinn. I hope you are recovering from your ordeal.'

The grizzled soldier didn't give her chance to answer; it couldn't have been more obvious he wasn't interested. He fixed his gaze on Frida, though he spoke to the young man stood to attention at his side. 'This her?'

Treating her as though she was invisible made Frida grit her teeth but she remained silent. This man was no different to most of the soldiers she'd met.

'Yes sir. Frida Ranson,' replied the young man and gestured to his superior. 'This is Major Sven Olsen.'

The name caused Frida to catch her breath. 'Olsen?'

'Yes. Elsa was my wife.'

20

'I'm very sorry. Elsa was a wonderful ...'

'Yes, yes.'

Frida didn't like being shut down either. Instead she decided it was his manly way of dealing with grief.

'I'm informed you were the only person, either military or civilian, to escape the hotel unharmed. Is that correct?'

Frida shrugged, not liking where this conversation was going. Suspicion hovered around her, like persistent flies around bad meat.

Her gesture made the red-haired man's eyes narrow. 'How did you get out, Miss Ranson? When none of the trained military personnel in that building could?'

Layla watched her with sympathy, for all the help it gave. She was on her own. There was nothing new there. She'd spent a third of her life explaining away things normal people wouldn't believe. With the simple farming folk she'd lived with over the last few years, it was never that difficult. This time was different. This bastard wanted to blame her for the explosion.

Frida took a breath. 'Your highly-trained soldiers didn't escape because they were pissed out of their heads. I left early and didn't drink myself into oblivion. Most of them wouldn't have woken if the entire world had blown up. Don't accuse me of anything unless you've got evidence as hard as your head.'

Out of the corners of her eyes, she saw Layla and Lieutenant Wheeler stare in wide-eyed shock, the young man glancing nervously at his commanding officer. His apprehension grew when the other man, whose face was now as red as his beard, turned to him.

'Who sanctioned the alcohol?' It was little more than a snarl.

'I don't know, sir. Your ... Colonel Olsen had been taken ill, I understand. She was instructed to go to bed by the army medic, sir.'

Frida and Layla glanced at each other at this new information.

The young man cleared his throat. 'I think there was a collective decision to raid the hotel's bar and beer cellar, sir.'

The Major's blue eyes turned into orbs of ice as he turned from the young man to Frida, glaring at her in sullen silence for just a little too long.

'Are you deciding how to word your apology, Major?'

'My apologies, Miss Ranson.'

She bowed her head ever so slightly. She wasn't going to get anything more, but she'd made him think twice about picking a fight with her. Standing a pace behind the Major, the young lieutenant gave her the slightest of smiles. She felt her face and neck flush and turned her attention to Layla who was doing her best not to laugh.

'Frida and I were discussing who might be behind the explosion, Major. We couldn't decide if it was Humanity First or another a competing nation, eager to claim Vanaheim for themselves.'

The man looked grateful for the distraction. He huffed and sounded like a horse. 'Bloody Humanity First, they're crazy and desperate enough to pull a stunt like this. They threatened Elsa ... Colonel Olsen ... a few weeks earlier in London. I believe you were present, Dr Quinn?'

The woman gave a tight nod. Frida didn't know about that either. It was becoming obvious she'd not asked enough questions of anybody.

'They reject our use of the fairy doorways ... portals ... call them what you like. And the likelihood of working with the fae to find a route to new worlds.'

'Working with the fae?' Frida squeaked. She really hadn't been paying attention.

The Major hardly looked at her but directed his answer at Layla instead. 'The national government has been working through diplomatic circles to arrange communication and help. I understand we are close to establishing an ongoing liaison.'

Frida could hardly believe what she was hearing. Barely a year after the cessation of hostilities and the signing of the armistice, the fae had turned into allies. She understood the popularity of Humanity First, if the rumours were true.

'But we've been at war with them!' she blurted out. 'How can ...'

Olsen dismissed her with a wave of a hand.

'When you've seen as much conflict as I, Miss Ranson, you come to realise political alliances change with the wind. I've fought alongside men who, a month later, turned into my enemies. Such is life.'

Frida shook her head. How could things be so easily explained? It wasn't that she felt any animosity toward the fae. That wasn't the issue. Their return, in any form, presented a real danger for her. It increased the risk of her connection being discovered.

'Anyway, Dr Quinn, I came to tell you the government has commissioned me to take over the leadership of the expedition. I would deem it an honour if you would accompany me, as you agreed to do for my wife.'

Layla beamed. 'Of course, Major. I'd like nothing better.'

'Good. Liaise with Lieutenant Wheeler here, he'll arrange whatever you need.'

He turned sharply as Layla called over to him. He paused but didn't turn round.

'I hope you will extend your invitation to Frida, as well, Major?'

Now he turned, with a face like thunder.

Layla smiled at him. 'Elsa was insistent on her being on the team. Don't renege on her wishes. Please?'

Ice-cold blue eyes swivelled toward Frida. 'If you wish.'

He spun on his heel and marched out of the room with such speed Lieutenant Wheeler had to run to keep up with him.

'Why did you do that?' Frida asked.

Layla lowered her voice to little more than a whisper. 'Both of us want to find out who was responsible for Elsa's death and complete this mission in her honour, don't we?'

Frida nodded. She saw the same grim determination in Layla's face as she imagined the woman saw in hers.

After admitting she felt sleepy, Frida left Layla and the hospital. She urgently needed somewhere to stay as well as clothes. She didn't know anyone in York, no one took in lodgers these days and the army wouldn't help.

She had to look after herself, as usual.

The city of York had suffered terribly during the war, mainly down to the dragons. It had been the site of an early battle, when the fae equivalent to electromagnetic pulse amplification rendered the army's twenty-first century technology useless. The dragons burned parts of the city into heaps of charred carbon. The army's attempts to regain the city only made things worse.

Everywhere she looked, buildings were in the process of renovation or demolition. The only one to avoid any damage was the Minster. It provided the way home for the fae and religious significance for human beings. Frida headed in its direction, its gothic towers visible over the nearby rooftops. Agnes would be there. She didn't know the girl all that well but she might have some suggestions. It was the expedition's hub, and she might be able to stay there for tonight at least.

The moment she arrived on the street, Frida's brain crackled with alarm. She had no idea how it worked, except that it paid to react to the warning. The street was a bustling mass of people going about their daily routines. Local farmers had taken to selling their produce on stalls along one side of the street. With the absence of fuel, the only traffic was the horse and cart. Everything looked normal.

The fizzing sensation in her head told her otherwise.

She was the only survivor of the attack on the hotel, apart from Layla. It made her wonder if the Humanity First terrorists wanted a hundred percent success rate in killing the expedition team. If the government were so intent on the mission, to the degree they were talking to the fae, then killing a few dozen soldiers wouldn't stop them. Major Olsen might be happy with that theory. Frida wasn't. She didn't know why; it just felt wrong. Over the years, she'd learned to listen to her instincts. They rarely misled her.

She needed to find safety and it wasn't in a street doorway. As if to reinforce the point, a crossbow bolt thudded into the doorframe so close to the side of her head she heard it vibrate in the wood.

She ran.

Chapter 3

"Dragons rained fire every day for a week. We were powerless to do anything but hide and hope something would stop them."

Eye-witness accounts from the Battle of York assembled by Roger Denham

Frida's decision to run meant dodging farmers delivering produce to market stalls and disgruntled women buying their wares. It quickly expanded into sidestepping screaming shoppers as more crossbow bolts thwacked into carts, barrels and a wooden sign proclaiming the cheapest meat in the city. Frantic glances over her shoulder told Frida the archer wasn't human. He had to be fae and didn't care who knew it. Townspeople, demoralised and exhausted, shook fists and cursed but none of them attempted to stop him. He had to be a professional assassin, one who didn't go in for subtlety.

Staying alive meant swerving and jinking through the narrow streets and alleys of York, a place Frida didn't know. She fled without any plan other than to avoid other people, lose her attacker and put some distance between them so she could think. She dodged around corners, sprinted through courtyards and dark alleyways, searching for somewhere to hide.

In a large yard, broken furniture provided convenient steps onto the roof of an abandoned garage. As she clambered upward, she snatched up a length of timber and hid behind a small retaining wall which connected the garage to a taller house. She waited, desperately holding her breath so as not to give herself away, but her lungs were having none of it. They burned, her heart pounded like a drum, loud enough for the whole city to hear.

She ducked behind the wall as her fae attacker burst into the yard, his heavy breathing and footsteps echoing from brick walls and uneven cobblestones. He stopped. She clamped her mouth shut and held her breath, her lungs objected but he was close enough to hear the slightest of sounds. His footsteps took him farther away, enough for her to peek around the wall. He searched amidst the rotting furniture, crossbow at the ready. He was undoubtedly fae. His simple cotton clothes, a smock and leggings, were typical of the working class. His long, blonde hair fell down over broad shoulders. He had powerful biceps and thighs – this man was a fighter as well as an archer.

She could blast him. It wouldn't be all that difficult, since he had his back to her. She considered the idea briefly but dismissed it. It was a last-ditch option. She hadn't taken a life before, at least not in cold blood like this. He might be trying to kill her but she wasn't a murderer. Not yet. Besides, if she could incapacitate him somehow, she could find out why he was hunting her. Find out if it was connected to the destruction of the hotel.

The archer turned, and she shrank back behind the wall. Her plank of wood wasn't much of a weapon, but it could be if she could jump on him and hit him as she dropped. It might be enough to overpower him and, with luck, cause him to drop his crossbow. There was no one around to see her, a warning blast could be enough to make him talk.

She waited, calming herself like her mother trained her. She listened and reached out with her senses. She felt his determination to complete his mission and a strong dislike of being in the human realm with its deprivation and filthy air.

Footsteps drew closer. He kicked at something that clattered, and scuttling sounds followed. He cursed. He moved toward the only other way out from the yard, his mind telling her he'd concluded she wasn't there. He wouldn't expect an attack.

She ran along the roof, plank held aloft, and leapt. Her landing was awkward, one ankle buckling slightly on the cobblestones, but she quickly regained her balance. Her awkward landing robbed her of surprise and momentum, and he turned, wide-eyed, as she swung the length of timber with every bit of strength she possessed. It hit his arm, he staggered sideways to collide with the alley wall, and grunted with the pain. She raised the length of wood a second time but he was quick to recover. Frida shifted her position, faced the man head on, and levelled the length of wood at his throat. He spotted her intention as she jabbed at him, dodging sideways, just not quite fast enough. The end of the plank scraped the side of his head, taking his ear with it. He screamed and tried to do two things at once. He brought up one hand to stem the blood pouring down his neck while bringing up his crossbow with his other hand.

The forward thrust of the plank had brought her close enough to see his almond shaped eyes and broad forehead. She'd dealt with other men who thought they could subdue her; she knew what to do next. She threw herself at him, grabbed his shoulder and brought her knee up hard into his groin. He screamed as he doubled up, but only for a second. He snatched up his crossbow and released a bolt. Frida pivoted on one foot, like a dancer, smacking his bloody ear with a fist as she side-stepped him. The bolt smacked into a wall by her leg.

She wouldn't defeat this man easily, despite his injuries. He was too strong, too determined. He held onto his weapon as though his life depended on it. She abandoned her plan and ran, hoping his bruised testicles would slow him down.

Frida sprinted through a narrow alleyway, angry at herself for failing to thwart the assassin's attack. Quick glances over her shoulder told her all she'd done was make him even angrier. Her only reassurance lay in the way he kept shaking his head. It hinted at a concussion or problems with his vision. There'd been no more attempts to shoot her either, that reinforced her theory. If only she had time to think, to plan and not have to react all the time. She ran even faster.

Hope blossomed as the Minster loomed up into the early morning sky in front of her. The army had commandeered the place as their research centre, led by Layla and Agnes Hall, the young archivist. There'd be a couple of armed guards to offer protection. She'd be safe.

She glanced over her shoulder one last time to gesture her victory over her attacker. She stopped. He'd vanished. Frantic, she scanned the area. Once this part of the city, with its proximity to the Minster, offered safety and prestige. A few grand houses had been built nearby for its powerful clerics as well as a line of cottages for their servants. Now they were blackened, burned-out shells. Ideal places from which to snipe.

'Frida! Hi!'

Startled, she turned on her heel, hands poised to defend herself. Agnes strolled toward her, smiling and waving, oblivious. The young woman, dressed stylishly, wore makeup and came from an affluent background. Danger wasn't the constant companion to her as it was to Frida.

A crossbow bolt thudded into a blackened timber behind the woman. Her mental warning, fizzing in Frida's ears, made her duck her head in time. Agnes screamed, threw her hand to her mouth to stifle the sound and looked around in confusion, making herself an easy target.

'Take cover!' Frida yelled.

Except there wasn't any. An open street and the derelict remnants of a line of cottages. She grabbed the girl by an arm and dragged her to a doorway, pushed her to the ground and squatted in front of her, hands once again raised in defence. Ethical considerations evaporated. Agnes' inability to defend herself meant something. This assassin could take his pot shots at her – she could defend herself, to some degree. Innocent and helpless young women were a different thing entirely. Her top lip curled and her pulse increased, signs she knew all too well. Her breathing calmed and her vision sharpened, more by instinct than anything, and her mind reached out. She sensed him instantly, the grim determination now sharpened by his anger and pain. He was muddled too, likely his concussion. The qualities liable to force him into making a mistake.

Right on cue, he appeared from behind the remnants of a wall in the string of derelict cottages, crossbow ready. Frida didn't hesitate, didn't even think. Her reaction was pure instinct.

Incandescent white energy launched from her fingertips, blindingly bright, flaring the width of the street and striking the burned-out remnants of the building. In her later childhood, once her ability to manipulate energy had manifested, her training had centred on accuracy and intensity. Where the latter was concerned, her mother said it would take time and experience. Accuracy could be achieved quickly.

Unless the woman destined to train you died.

Panic and adrenalin fuelled the blast. She could tell the moment the energy left her fingertips she'd over-compensated. She halted it instantly; a second or two of her power would be enough. The building exploded, like a bomb had detonated within it. Fire shot up into the sky, bricks and timbers followed, to fall back to earth a second later and join the inferno she'd created.

The cottages' previous experiences with fire meant there was little to sustain its intensity for long. Within a minute, flames diminished as the blackened timbers gave up the last of their fuel, leaving just the normal cracks and pops of burning wood.

Frida stood. Behind her, she sensed the other woman's mind. She couldn't help it. Like a deluge, it poured over her, the fear and uncertainty. Followed quickly by shock.

There was no hiding her secret now, no way to pretend something else had happened. And Agnes was a gossip. Like many of the young women Frida had encountered, the urge to share her experiences meant everything. She wouldn't hold back on what she'd witnessed, no matter how much Frida begged.

She turned to look at her, waiting for the interrogation. It would have only one outcome, one consequence. The need to escape, to hide again, to prevent people finding out the truth.

'Who was he?' Agnes asked.

She stared, transfixed, at the burning heap and slowly shook her head. 'I don't know. I think he was a fairy.'

Wide, fear-filled eyes found hers. 'I thought they had all left?'

Frida could only shrug. Thanks to her over-reaction, she wouldn't find one either. Agnes continued to scrutinise her. Her gaze eventually shifted to Frida's hands, hanging limply at her side.

'How did you do that? Does it hurt?'

Not the reaction she'd expected. Normally there were accusations.

'No.'

She'd learned to keep answers short, not give away too much. Agnes' eyes found her face again, searching it carefully.

'Is this connected to what happened at the hotel?'

'I don't know. Why do you ask?'

Her question earned a shrug. Frida didn't know Agnes all that well, and their paths had seldom crossed since arriving in the city with Elsa. She didn't share the girl's interest in old books and ancient musty-smelling documents. They came from different worlds. But she'd quickly discovered one thing about this girl, who was roughly her age. She was curious. Not surprising for an archivist but her investigative skills posed a threat now.

Her question showed she'd reached the same conclusions as Major Olsen.

'The deaths of the expedition team suggest someone is eager for the project to be abandoned. The current theory is that it's Humanity First. What if it's not? You're the only survivor and hours later you're being hunted by a fairy. That can't be coincidence.'

'No.'

They hadn't moved. Both young women gazed at each other and frowned. The sounds of approaching people, no doubt ready to confront more devastation in their city, made them both react. Agnes hurriedly made her way along a narrow alley and into the open square in front of the Minster. Frida followed, uncertain of the girl's motives but eager to escape the devastation and any connection to it. Agnes headed toward two soldiers on duty at the main entrance to the building. They grinned at the young woman as she approached, giving her the look of appreciation that normally made Frida jealous.

'Morning! What caused that explosion? Do you know?'

Both men shook their heads.

The girl shrugged nonchalantly. 'Perhaps they're demolishing more buildings. We'll bring you out a cup of tea in a minute, won't we Frida?'

Bewildered, she nodded, astonished at the young woman's ability to lie so convincingly. She followed Agnes into the building, along its nave and down a staircase into the crypt, where the expedition stored its research materials. It was a place of low ceilings and vaulted stone arches, dwarfed by a huge table in the centre. Books, papers, manuscripts and the paraphernalia only researchers would recognise littered its surface. In one corner, near an electric socket, stood a small table with mugs and a kettle. Agnes flicked it on then turned to Frida with a smile.

'Now we can talk. Let's start with what you just did.'

It wasn't a threat or an accusation but a simple statement of curiosity.

'I can't. Sorry.'

The slightest of nods. 'I get that. You don't know me. You can't trust me.'

This wasn't the fear-filled reaction Frida normally received.

The girl still smiled. 'Listen, I've spent my career investigating Norse mythology, it's how I got on to the team. I maintain I know a lot more than our highly esteemed Dr Quinn. I don't have her fame though.'

She hurled teabags into mugs.

'A good researcher needs to be open-minded. You discover legends are always based on some truth, events misreported and exaggerated over time. An archivist learns to make sense of their source materials, to search for explanations. When the fae invaded, it forced human beings to accept we were not alone. There were other species, capable of doing things we'd thought impossible. We used to think fairies had magical abilities, remember?'

The kettle boiled and she poured its steaming contents into the mugs.

She looked over at Frida and smiled again. 'I'm saying that, when you're ready, I'll be open to your story. I won't judge. I'm sure you must be scared of how people

35

will react to you. I'm not like them. I have a feeling you might have something to contribute to the expedition. I think Elsa knew that.'

She turned back to the mugs of tea, spooned out the tea bags and added milk, and handed one over to the bewildered Frida.

'When you're ready? OK? Just don't keep me waiting too long.'

She left the room with the promised mugs of tea for the soldiers outside. It left Frida reeling as she tried to work out what to say or do next. She'd never encountered this open-mindedness before and didn't know how to react to it. Agnes' reasons made sense but that wasn't the point. From the earliest of times, her mother had instilled the need for secrecy of the family's heritage. Explaining her ability to manipulate energy was one thing but it would only lead Agnes to ask more questions. That was a massive risk.

Agnes returned, still smiling, but said nothing more. She busied herself with documents on the table. It was deliberate, an act of someone trying to prove her willingness to wait.

'I'm going to get some fresh air, I need to think,' Frida said.

She climbed the steps to return to the Minster's nave. Before the war, the crypt had been a gift shop, accessed by a staircase made from Perspex and wood. It bore the scars of a battalion of fae soldiers departing the portal in the Minster's subterranean vaults. The scars represented something more than the traces of an unexpected invasion, they illustrated the danger she still faced. She'd spent the war living in fear of her secret

36

getting out. Suspicion and paranoia still existed, Major Olsen's doubts about her escape from the hotel proved it. If they found out the truth, she'd be accused of being a fae spy and that would be it.

Deep in thought, Frida strolled past the two soldiers who ignored her. The morning sun bathed Minster Yard in warmth, it penetrated her tense muscles, like it used to do in the fields during harvest. So much had happened in the last few hours, she needed a moment to make sense of it all. She ambled over to the bronze statue of Constantine the Great, sat on its stone steps.

She liked Agnes, she realised. Sure, they'd led very different lives but the young woman was friendly and that was a rare thing these days. Elsa had repeatedly encouraged her to make friends, pointing out she couldn't live the life of a hermit forever. Perhaps Agnes was someone who might provide answers. She wasn't going to find any otherwise. Certainly not when she killed anyone who might qualify.

Movement out of the corner of her eye distracted Frida. On the corner of Stonegate, in the shade of one of its remaining buildings, stood her caped figure, watching.

She'd assumed he'd been the assassin. Now, it appeared, there were two members of the fae in the city. She stood up and walked as casually as she could toward the figure. He stepped out of the shadows, still watching her carefully.

Off to the side of the Minster, at the main entrance she heard a muffled cry and something clattering to the ground. The two soldiers had vanished. The caped figure watched her. She threw up her arms in frustration and hurried to the main entrance of the Minster. There was blood on the floor.

Chapter 4

"As an archivist you need to keep an open mind, you question and challenge every source of information. Looking back, I suppose I'd been sheltered from the fear and prejudice which influenced the actions of those who had suffered."

Extract from an interview with Agnes Hall, Celebrity Magazine

Frida found the unconscious soldiers in a heap at the side of the main entrance and a trail of blood leading to the crypt. It looked like there'd been a scuffle, injuring the attacker in the process but not stopping him from getting to the crypt. And Agnes. Frida followed the trail and hoped it wasn't another assassin with the strength and determination of the last.

An attack on the crypt made sense. After killing most of the original expedition team the logical next step was to destroy the research which informed the mission. That placed Agnes in danger.

Frida halted at the top of the staircase, she could hear Agnes pleading, not for her life but for the protection of her research. A quick peak around the corner of the stairwell showed her tied to a chair. She couldn't see the assailant. Frida crept down the steps that circled a pillar to give her a better view of the room.

The attacker was on his own. Good. He wasn't as muscular but undoubtedly another fae, his clothes giving him away instantly. He gathered the papers, books and manuscripts into a pile on the table with the intention of burning them. He didn't appear to pose a threat to Agnes, therefore keeping him alive to provide answers was vital. The fact he was smaller, less muscular than the other man, should make him easier to overcome too, so long as she caught him by surprise.

Frida waited as her target circled the table then launched herself onto his back. The combination of her weight, the force of her jump and the surprise, drove them to the floor. Her opponent quickly recovered but she had the strength and the position. She pinned him to the ground as he bucked and writhed. The blood he'd lost came from his injured nose. She head-butted him hard, heard the crunch and the guy squealed in pain. He stopped wriggling.

He was younger than she'd realised, no more than a kid. His facial features and hair colour gave him away, he had to be related to the assassin. They must have been working in partnership. Chances were that this one didn't know what had befallen his comrade.

She stared into his eyes. Hers were resolute and fearless, his full of panic.

'Listen to me,' she said. 'If you want to live, you need to answer my questions.'

She hadn't been certain he would understand. Not all fae were well educated, but the contempt displayed in his curled lip told her this one was and he had no intention of cooperating.

'If you don't help me, I'll kill you, like I did your friend.'

He couldn't hide his horror at her statement. Tears quickly filled his eyes as he stared up at her, and his contempt turned to hatred. In the darkest days of the war, she'd watched similar scenes of interrogation, particularly unpleasant ones still inhabited her nightmares. Fear acted as the lever when it came to confessions and, though the boy hated her for what she'd done, his fear could trump that. She hated herself for what she was about to do.

She moved her hand that gripped the boy's wrist so it pressed against his neck. He winced with pain. The technique had been part of her training years ago, her introduction to the darkness of her mother's activities. Its shadows had alienated them for a while. It had meant confronting a murky world and a role she didn't want. There'd never been any reason to use the technique since and she hoped her lack of experience wouldn't lead to blowing the kid's head off his shoulders. She allowed her energy to slowly build in her fingertips, the boy's expression telling her he could feel the heat.

'I brought a house down on top of your friend with these fingers. If I want, I can blow your head apart. It'll be messy, blood and brains everywhere, but you won't care. You'll be dead. Is that what you want?'

He glared at her. She increased the heat.

'You want to be a martyr? Die for some stupid cause?'

The concentration she needed meant she couldn't sustain the lack of release for very long. It was like holding back a sneeze. She increased the energy and gritted her teeth. The skin on the boy's neck turned red where it met her fingers. He whimpered.

'Last chance. Do you want to die?'

His tear-filled eyes stared into hers. She felt cruel and heartless, but it was necessary, she told herself.

'All right. I gave you a choice.'

40

'Don't! Please. I'll tell you.'

His name was Johl and fear drove his collapse. He started to cry like a little kid, chest heaving as he tried to suck in air to sustain his sobs. He didn't pose a threat, that was obvious. He was out of his depth and all alone. Frida stood up and kept her fingers trained on him as he staggered to his feet. He didn't take his eyes off her the whole time, even while he untied Agnes. She smiled sympathetically at the boy, the threat to her precious research forgotten. She really must have been sheltered during the war, Frida decided, if she forgave so readily.

'Who sent you? Frida asked.

The lad stared at her, like a little kid caught doing something he shouldn't. She'd wanted to tie him up but Agnes was against it. He was too frightened and she thought her warmth might obtain more answers. She sat him down on the chair she'd vacated and knelt in front of him, holding his hand and smiling. He directed his reply to her.

'Yissen made all the arrangements.'

That turned out to be his brother.

'He said I had to come along to burn papers. It would be easy.'

The lad sniffed as his breathing turned ragged. Agnes squeezed his hand, increased the warmth of her smile and told him he was being brave. He gave her a look of abject sorrow but his eyes never left hers. She was a good-looking young woman and the lad was clearly smitten, despite everything.

'Who sent your brother, Johl?'

More sniffing. 'The Order of Freyja. Yissen joined them when he returned from the war. He was angry, said the fae had been betrayed. He was different when he came back. So angry.'

The boy dissolved into tears again.

'Freyja did you say?'

Agnes's expression had changed. Some of her warmth traded for curiosity, her eyes burned with it. The kid just nodded.

'What can you tell me about this Order? Who are they?'

With a shrug and a shake of the head the lad lapsed into silence.

'Are they fae, this Order?'

He looked at her as though her question was ridiculous and nodded again.

'Why do they want to sabotage our expedition?'

His red, tear-stained eyes looked at her for a couple of seconds as he struggled to decide how much to confide. 'If they find out I've said anything …' he said.

Agnes took his hand, squeezed it and smiled again. 'We'll keep you safe.'

She half-turned to Frida as though making an agreement.

The boy swallowed. 'They're pledged to protect a special place, no one is allowed to go there. It's forbidden.'

Agnes nodded. 'Is that place called Vanaheim?'

'Something like that, I think. I'm not sure.'

'That's why you had to destroy these documents,' Agnes said with a sweep of one hand over the table.

The boy nodded.

'Why was your brother trying to kill me?' Frida asked.

As he looked up at her, she could tell he didn't know. She'd been sensing his reactions the whole time, everything he said was genuine but he clearly knew very little. He'd been dragged along by his brother's obsession.

Barked commands in the nave of the Minster startled all three of them. The boy leapt up like a frightened rabbit searching for escape. Frida recognised the voice. Major Olsen.

The stomp of boots grew closer. The young fae boy rushed toward Agnes, took her arm as though she offered sanctuary just as the ginger-headed warrior appeared on the staircase, gun in hand.

'Get away from her, you fairy bastard!' he yelled.

The boy looked ready to bolt as he raised his hands in the traditional gesture of surrender. Olsen fired his gun and the boy collapsed in a heap, a red hole blossoming in his forehead, his eyes already glazed. Agnes screamed.

Olsen bellowed over his shoulder as more soldiers appeared behind him, brandishing guns and bayonets.

'Assailant down!' he yelled. He strode down the staircase, stood over the body and sneered. 'Fucking fairy bastard!'

Frida's fury turned her fingertips white hot. The urge to release the energy was almost too much to bear as her heart pounded in her chest.

'He was cooperating!' she shouted. 'He was answering our questions. You didn't need to kill him.'

Olsen glanced at her for a second before turning to the soldiers waiting on the staircase. 'Get that mess out of here and dispose of it.'

He was talking as though the boy was dirt and yet it was a life he'd thoughtlessly snuffed out without any regret. The urge to blast him boiled inside Frida's chest.

'He attacked two of my men. He's a fucking spy. We shoot spies, Miss Ranson.'

He turned smartly on his heel and marched up the staircase, scattering his soldiers in the process. She let him go; an argument wouldn't achieve anything but make him more of an enemy. The man's departure meant Agnes' look of horror turned into a flood of tears. Frida knew what her friend needed, someone to make her feel better. Except that wasn't anything she could do, she never knew what to say in situations like these.

Self-consciously she knelt at the girl's side and placed a hesitant hand on her shoulder. 'Are you all right?'

A stupid question, she hoped she wouldn't need to say anything more.

'He didn't need to shoot him, Frida. He was helping us. And he was only a boy. Just following his bully of a brother. Poor kid.'

They watched in silence as three soldiers picked up the body like a sack of potatoes. They ignored Agnes' complaints with a sneer – she'd never witnessed what happened when a fae soldier was captured. The boy had got off lightly. People could be sadistic bastards when there would be no recriminations.

Agnes stood up, gripped the edge of the table as though it was the only thing holding her up. She kept repeating, 'So unfair!' under her breath. It was obvious to

Frida this was the first death she'd witnessed. Once again, the need for comfort and sympathy beckoned. The distraction option seemed preferable.

'You reacted to the name the boy mentioned. Did it mean something?'

Tearful eyes turned toward her. She got a nod and a shaky intake of breath. 'I've read it a few times. In Norse mythology, Freyja was one of the Vanir, exiled by Odin after the civil war in Asgard.'

'I see.' She really didn't, but the discussion had already aroused Agnes' curiosity and shifted her attention from the boy's death. 'Could that be important?'

It provoked a search of the jumble of documents on the table. For a moment, the only sound in the room was the shuffling of papers and turning of pages, giving Frida the chance to indulge her rapidly developing hatred of Elsa's husband. She'd met his kind before, lots of times. A bloody war drove people to desperate acts of violence when food was short, they had no money and felt abandoned. Ruthless self-protection meant sacrificing lives without a care for the rule of law.

It was a rule Frida had learned quickly after her mother's death. Survival meant never trusting anyone and being ready to do whatever was necessary to stay alive. The young woman holding up a sheet of handwritten notes clearly had a very different experience.

'Found it!' Her satisfied smile. 'My notes from the *Prose Edda*, a collection of thirteenth century poems compiled from Scandinavian sources. These are sources which describe a war between the Aesir, the Viking gods ruled by Odin, and the Vanir, led by someone called Njord.

Freyr and his wife Freyja were his allies, banished to another realm, to Vanaheim.'

'Are these people supposed to have existed then?' Frida asked. The whole idea of gods being around long ago was ridiculous.

Agnes leaned against the table with a sigh, clearly this was a topic she'd covered with other people in the past. 'More than two thousand years ago, how would people have reacted if they met the fae, who appeared out of thin air, with equipment and abilities they didn't understand. What would human beings call it? Magic, perhaps?'

It was obvious where this was leading and that made Frida nervous. She gave a non-committal shrug.

'Throughout the Middle Ages, human beings labelled anything they didn't understand magic, or witchcraft. Fairies were creatures that abused human beings, stole their children, enslaved them sometimes. Their leaders, as far as our pagan ancestors were concerned, would be considered gods.'

'You're saying the Norse gods were really the fae?'

'I believe so. The war proved the existence of the portals across the globe. We know the fae are long-lived. Isn't it likely the Vikings would have considered them gods?'

'What is this Order of Freyja then?'

Agnes paused and took a deep breath. The mention was enough to remind her of the boy's death, and sadness spread across her face rapidly. 'I wonder if there are fae who don't want us to go to Vanaheim for some reason. They might be like Humanity First, opposed to any interspecies cooperation and eager to scupper our government's negotiations.'

Frida could only nod her agreement. The thought brought back the image of the fae man standing at the corner of Stonegate. That couldn't be coincidence. Was he another member of this secret order?

It was time to find out, time to be the one to do the hunting.

As Agnes continued searching for more information about the enigmatic Freyja, Frida slipped out of the crypt and along the nave. Two more soldiers stood guard on the main entrance with stern expressions which they turned on her. She didn't care. The military mind was an oxymoron. It suggested a capability for reasoned thought, whereas in reality, they instinctively killed and destroyed anything that didn't fit into their definition of Right and Proper.

She might not care about the guards but Olsen's killing of an innocent kid stubbornly refused to go away. It added to her anger and made her wonder how Elsa, a woman she respected and admired, could have married such a bastard. She strode along Stonegate lost in spiralling resentment that made her fingertips throb. With intense concentration, she forced the rage into a small and dark compartment in her head and the throbbing eased. Even then she couldn't be certain how she'd react the next time they met.

A flash of cape drew her attention back to the here and now. The street was narrow and cobbled, busy with people buying what provisions were available and irritated by what wasn't. Everyone frowned these days. She dodged gossiping groups and unhappy shoppers arguing over prices as she tried to keep the shadowy figure in sight.

At each corner he turned left, it made no sense until she worked out that perhaps he was circling back to the Minster. He clearly wasn't trying to lose her either. His actions only sharpened her suspicions. With the towers of the Minster peeking over the rooftops of buildings once again, the figure darted into a narrow alley. An ideal place for an attack. She stopped; the path was empty. With fingers splayed, ready to incinerate anything that stepped in front of her, she slowly made her way forward. She peeked around the corner of an abandoned shop to another alley, empty now. Ready for an attack, expecting her brain to sound its warning with every step, she crept forward. Frida arrived at a lawned area with a large copper beech tree, its crimson leaves glistening in the morning sun.

Her target leaned against its trunk with a casual demeanour that infuriated her. He didn't appear to have a weapon, though it was probably hidden in the folds of his bloody stupid cloak. Her irritation, provoked by Olsen, demanded release. It took all her concentration to hold it back, at least until she'd established if this trickster was friend or foe. She stomped over to him, silently daring him to challenge her.

He smiled with enough power to eclipse the sun.

Frida's fingertips pulsed at his arrogance. She needed to teach him a lesson.

Chapter 5

*'Fae society could best be defined by its strict formality.
For the human mind it mirrors the Georgian era, when
honour and integrity defined a person. Manners meant
everything. Obligations even more so.'*

An Insight into Fae Society by Professor Sarah Malcolm

Her first thought was that the enigmatic fae stranger wore
a glamour; no one could be that good looking. Glamours
were supposed to exist, according to legend, but her
mother had never mentioned the topic. Here was proof. It
had to be.

'Finally,' he said.

The non-sequitur bewildered her. It wasn't
surprising. Men always made her anxious, good looking
ones more so. Here she was standing in front of one that
made her body react in embarrassing ways. She needed to
be suspicious of him, angry at how he'd led her on a wild
goose chase. Instead, she found herself beguiled by eyes
dark enough to qualify as black, a square jawline daubed
with black stubble and long hair the colour of a raven's
wing.

He bowed, never taking his eyes from hers, formal
and perfectly measured.

'Lorcan Dubh.'

She didn't know many fae words but that one she
did. *Dubh* meant black and that defined him perfectly. Not
just the hair and the eyes but the caramel colour of his
skin, which was unusual for the fae. But there was

something else. Darkness hovered around the man, an intent which she didn't trust, and his demeanour spoke of shadow and night.

Protocol demanded she return the bow. Mother had instilled some of the social expectations of the fae into her as a little girl. They'd visited their home once or twice when she was very small. She didn't remember any of it beyond her mother's anxiety and the awkwardness of the meetings, but she'd been drilled within an inch of her life to behave in the correct way. "The fae have standards," Mother told her repeatedly. "They've upheld them for longer than human beings have existed, the least we can do is to honour them."

His prissy formality swept away her attraction, her anger and resentment immediately filled the space. She'd had her fill of fae and the dangers they posed.

'Why the circular trip around the town?' she snapped.

His reaction faltered, enough of a flicker to tell her she'd annoyed him. Good. It was easy to imagine a man with his looks and physique expecting women to fawn over him. Well, she was going to be nothing like that. Her dry throat and beating heart tried to tell her otherwise but she ignored them.

After faltering, the million-megaton smile returned to bathe her in its warmth. 'I was told to expect some resistance, Frida. I hope I can call you by your first name, even though we haven't been formally introduced?'

More bloody fae protocol. She let her heavy sigh answer for her.

He grinned. 'I needed to make certain we weren't followed. You appear to be popular with others of my race.'

She snorted her impatience. If he wanted to talk like he was in a fae court, that was his business. His clothes and behaviour screamed his social status. This man was beyond the two lowly types she'd met earlier. This preening peacock represented power and authority, so situations like this were normal to him. They were engaged in some kind of negotiation and that worried her. An agreement with the fae wasn't just binding, it carried awful penalties for any failure, worse still, incurring a debt. Her mother had warned her of the danger of fae debts.

When she didn't reply his smile faded slightly. He looked around their secluded little grove beneath the copper beech tree, betraying a slight apprehension.

'I suggest we find another location to have our conversation.'

His words increased her misgivings, she had no intention of going anywhere with this stranger. His brilliant smile might insinuate charm but everything else set off warning klaxons in her head.

'No.'

Her heart sounded like an entire percussion section in an orchestra, so loud the stranger couldn't help but hear it. He had to know how scared she was. Her fingertips reminded her of the option they offered, should he try anything, but that was too drastic. She knew that. His status told her he was on official business, and there'd be hell to pay if she blasted some emissary from either the Light or Dark Court. He didn't like her terse response, and those eyes, the colour of darkest chocolate, trapped her, like a stoat with a rabbit.

'You don't trust me. After your experience earlier, I understand why. But there is danger here, Frida. Great danger. For you, in particular.'

Her throat tightened and turned to sand. All she could do was nod. He did the same and glanced about him again.

'You have my word that you will come to no harm in my presence.'

That made her blink. Fae didn't make such promises. It brokered too many debts, too many unacceptable consequences. She found herself staring into those eyes; they told her he'd registered her acknowledgement of what his promise meant. Only now, much too late, she realised she needed to get inside the mind of this man. It would have to be subtle. He'd know what she was doing and resent the intrusion, but she had to.

She wished her skill possessed greater finesse. She needed the texture of a spider's web, but she'd be lassoing him with heavy rope. She hoped he'd understand. She reached out and instantly his eyes turned colder. He didn't speak but watched her carefully. With tentative steps, she felt his resistance but then it dropped, like a curtain. He'd invited her in. Her search was cursory; there were places with barriers but that was to be expected. She knew enough to establish his motives weren't harmful to her. Even in the hall of a large mansion you could discover something of its inhabitant, and the same was true here.

She pulled back and took a deep breath to calm herself. She gave him the slightest of smiles, all she could manage, but he accepted it.

'Has that helped?'

The warmth had returned to his eyes again. She told him it had, at least to some extent. Since she couldn't see beyond his dark aura, she didn't trust him, but she didn't have any choice.

He set off at a brisk pace, forcing her to run to keep up with him, his cloak flapping behind him like a bat. He didn't speak but this wasn't the time for small talk. He led her around the outside of the Minster to the rear of the building and a small car park. Before the war, when fuel was available, the place would have been full of trades people and clerics' vehicles. Now it was empty. They hid in the shadow of the building, between two large buttresses.

He awarded her another of his beaming smiles. 'Thank you, Frida. I'm sure you will have many questions but even this place is dangerous. We can't stay here long. I must not be discovered until the time is right. But I wanted to speak to you in advance of that.'

'Do you know about my family?'

The rest of his message could wait. This man knew her secret. She wondered if he was searching her mind; she couldn't feel anything but her skill in that department was almost zero. Perhaps he'd get a sense of her desperation if he did.

'Yes. Yes, I do.' Another smile, this time intended to reassure. It failed. 'I cannot imagine how you have survived all these years, alone and helpless. You must appreciate some of us wanted to help you after your mother's death. But the war prevented that.'

The sympathy and the mention of her mother was all it took to summon tears, she fought them back. He waited, watching her struggle with her emotions.

'There's so much I don't know,' she breathed.

He nodded. 'I'm sure there is. And I can help. But not now. Not here.'

'Tell me why you're helping me then? And why I'm in danger.'

He peeked around the two stone buttresses and moved close enough to her so that she could smell his scent, an enticing mixture of spice and masculine musk.

His reply was little more than a whisper. 'You don't realise how complex those questions are, Frida. But I will try to explain the basic details.' He took a deep breath. 'You must know your family are hybrids, part human, part fae?'

He watched her reaction, making her feel dreadfully self-conscious. No one had ever defined her background in such a clear and succinct way. She granted him the slightest of nods.

'Good. Your family has lived with that secret for generations. When the fae abandoned this world, your heritage was largely forgotten. The invasion changed that. Suddenly you were a threat, a potential spy. The trouble is, on the other side of the portals, there are fae who see things the same way.'

She knew most of this. Mother had tried to explain it in her final moments.

'But your government is negotiating with both Courts to seek help in finding another world to colonise. The politics are complicated and ever-changing. A significant proportion of the fae resent all this. They opposed the war in the first place, preferring human beings thought the fae were the stuff of legend. Now they know we're real. Even worse, humans are mounting incursions into our realms. Yet no one is stopping it.'

Another quick check beyond their dark corner of the building.

'My father knew your mother, your grandmother too. He has spent years investigating stories connected to your family and he's formed a theory that links you to this expedition. He's negotiating with both Courts for me to join the mission.'

'Why?'

'Primarily to protect you. I can't explain any more now. There are too many unanswered questions, aren't there?'

He sought her reaction, she nodded. He smiled again but it retained the same darkness which hovered around the man.

'Father believes others have formed the same conclusion about your family. He doesn't think it's an accident that you were invited onto the expedition.'

'But ...?'

Frida's mind whirled at what she was hearing, taking her back to a conversation in a dingy little office where Elsa had told her about a trip to another world. How it would be an adventure they could share together, a chance to escape the misery of the past and make a name for herself once they got back. Little of it mattered to her. The important thing was to accompany Elsa, help her achieve her dream; the woman who'd become a second mother. She stared into the man's impossibly dark eyes. They held sympathy.

'Frida, it cannot be a coincidence that you survived the attack on the expedition team and were then attacked by an assassin. I'm sure you've realised what it means?'

She found herself nodding. 'Someone doesn't want me to go.'

He took her hand with such speed it stunned her. He gripped it and looked into her eyes. His resolve was palpable, emanating from him in waves. 'Father thinks it may be more than one person.'

She remembered the dead boy talking about the Order of Freyja. This man might be able to shed more light on this mysterious group, she didn't trust him though. He had no idea of the irony of his next words.

'You cannot trust anyone, Frida. I mean it. No one. I can do little more than warn you, for now. Once you arrive in our realm, my father and I will do what we can to help.'

'Why should I trust you?'

He still held her hand. He chuckled and released it. 'I told you. My father knew your mother and your grandmother well. They were formidable women. I can see the latest member is no different.'

She wanted to believe him, not least because of his smile. She could bathe in the charm he exuded but experience warned her against it. Yet this man's father had known her family. She vaguely remembered her mother hosting fae visitors when she was very young, perhaps he'd been one of them.

From some distance away the distinctive clump of boots on stone slabs warned of approaching soldiers, guards most likely. Her new friend hurriedly reached into a pocket in his trousers and pulled out an envelope with a bright red seal.

'Read this later. Stay safe until I can join you.'

The sound of boots echoed against the Minster walls. Frida ran. A quick glance over her shoulder showed her mysterious messenger sprinting in the opposite direction, cloak flapping. She turned the corner and collided with someone dressed in army fatigues. It was so unexpected, so sudden, she staggered back far enough to take in the sight of Lieutenant Wheeler who gasped for breath as he righted himself from the collision.

'Are you all right, miss?'

Major Olsen was at his side, he dismissed the question with an angry wave. 'What were you doing, Miss Ranson? You seem to be in a hurry.'

His cold eyes zeroed in on hers, searching for answers. She didn't need her skills to sense his hostility.

'Running.'

Olsen maintained his hostile gaze. 'There's a fairy spy in the area. A second one. Strange that you're in the same vicinity. Again.'

'Do you plan to murder this one, too?'

'Sounds like you've allied yourself with the enemy.'

'How can they be the enemy? Our government is asking them for help.'

She watched him grind his jaw and allowed herself a smile. The younger man gently shook his head.

The ginger beard parted to reveal a reptilian smile. 'Now I'm leading the expedition, I have selected my team. You, Miss Ranson, are not on it. I need people on whom I can rely. And I don't trust you. Not in the slightest. My recommendation is that you leave York. I hear they're looking for muscular women on the farms, you'll fit in well there.' He chuckled to himself and strode off.

Lieutenant Wheeler gave her a pained look of sympathy as he scuttled after him. She called out, her voice rising an octave so it sounded weak and hysterical, making the urge to blast the smug bastard even stronger.

'Why did someone as good as Elsa want to marry a murderous bastard like you?'

She held back her tears until the two men turned a corner. With the dam breached, they tumbled down her cheeks. They'd waited patiently since Lorcan's mention of her family and her loneliness.

He'd understood.

Keeping her secret had meant never trusting anyone and remaining alone made that easier. She hadn't been the only orphan in the war, she knew that. Girls her age had little choice but to allow others to take advantage of them – it was the only way to find food and shelter. Her physique, her strength, made her different; they were features men rejected, no one wanted a freak. To have someone call her a hybrid felt strange. It wasn't just the absence of the scorn either. For the first time in her life, she had met someone who already knew her secret and she found it comforting.

Yet, the opportunity to meet those people had been snatched from her. She wasn't going on the expedition. The timing was the worst part. If she'd known earlier, Lorcan's father could have intervened. But it was too late. They'd be waiting for her in their realm, unaware of Olsen's decision.

Her tears stalled, their salty reservoir drained after so much disappointment and rejection. As her thinking cleared, she remembered she'd placed the letter she'd been given into a trouser pocket. She took it out, strolled over to a small park and sat on a bench and stared at it. Two elderly women carrying shopping bags, earnestly discussing the poor quality of meat and its likely sources, walked past but ignored her.

The contents of the letter would probably torment her even more, now she couldn't meet the man who'd written it. The paper was of a high quality, neatly folded and secured with red wax, a stylised symbol of a pair of wings formed the seal.

She gasped and blinked in surprise before pulling up the sleeve of her shirt. She'd forgotten about her scar, it was nothing more than a raised wheal of skin, no bigger than a fingernail. Now she scrutinised it, holding the seal next to it. It matched the symbol perfectly.

She tore open the letter, eager for answers.

My dear Frida,

First of all, I owe you my most profound apologies for failing to reach you after your mother's death. I let her down as well as you. It is a debt which I will repay, of that you can be certain. I have persuaded my son to deliver this letter in the hope he finds you well and proud of your heritage. Be assured you will not be on your own for much longer.

You will be aware of the tensions which exist on either side of the portals. On our side, we fight with one another about the future of our race. Some of my fellow fae believe that we should continue to remain aloof and trade on our own heritage. They are fools. As time passes, my race grows increasingly infertile. It is the penalty of our longevity. Census data shows more than 50% of our population cannot breed. Any mathematician will tell you eventual extinction is inevitable, unless radical solutions are found.

You are an example of such a solution. You are half fae and half human, a hybrid. Your family have shown how this genetic combination brings out the best in both our races. However, some of my people believe this to be a dilution of our bloodline. A ridiculous idea which presupposes there are alternatives, there are none.

I explain this because the Light Court are willing to negotiate with your government to help them colonise another realm. In exchange we plan to encourage more sexual relationships between our races. The Dark Court are less than enthusiastic about this development.

Now for a confession. When I could not reach you, after your mother's death, I took matters into my own hands when the war ended. I approached your government and told them about you.

Please forgive me if my actions caused you problems. I did it with noble intent, not only for you, dear Frida, but for both our races.

However, as Lorcan may have already explained, in taking this action I'm aware I may have placed your life in jeopardy. Your government pledged to protect you, I trust they have been true to their word. They value what you represent. Yet others will see you as a threat.

Your family have always been formidable. They are warriors. You have specific skills which should ensure your survival. Stay true to that heritage. Trust no one until they have proven themselves to your satisfaction. When we meet, I will explain more. To do so via this medium would be foolhardy. Until we meet, Frida, stay safe, trust your instincts, and remember your family's heritage, it will sustain you.

Yours,

Yaalon Dubh

She read and reread the letter, then stared at the final statement in the hope of an explanation. What was this family heritage? Mother had explained their dual ancestry and the need for secrecy, but nothing more.

This man had blown her secret wide open and hinted at a heritage he'd assumed she understood. One her mother, for whatever reason, had chosen to take to the grave.

Chapter 6

'The post-war political challenges, imposed on those of in government, a need for a new way of thinking. The fae had things we wanted, we had things they needed. It meant a swift transition from enemy to awkward ally. Not everyone agreed with this strategy, on either side of the portals, this made things even more difficult.'

'Downing Street and the Fae' by Sir Rupert Hall, OBE.

With her mind in turmoil, her future uncertain and friendless, Agnes provided the distraction Frida needed. With nowhere else to go, the Minster had been her only option. Their mutual loathing of Olsen quickly brought the two women together. Agnes repeatedly swore under her breath as Frida recounted her encounter with the man; two young women against a bigoted misogynist. By the time they had finished their mugs of tea, Agnes' sense of indignation led to decisive action. Frida would stay with her.

Despite her generous invitation, her new friend's perspective on life reflected massive differences. Agnes's sense of entitlement was alien to Frida, the idea that when something went wrong, someone would put it right. Admittedly, on this occasion, that person was Agnes. It didn't take long for more examples of entitlement to turn up.

The "little place" Agnes called home was palatial compared to anything Frida had ever known. Daddy had bought it as somewhere for her to relax after a hard day's work. His words. During the war, the whole family exiled themselves to their home in Kensington, London. It was a hardship, remaining in one place for so many years, but somehow, they had managed. After all, the shops were nearby and the government had instructed the army to form a protective barrier around key parts of the capital, like Kensington. The wealthy needed to be kept safe.

Agnes' description of those years defined another world for Frida, one she now shared. They sat around a dining table, eating a meal of pasta and bolognaise sauce. Agnes loved to cook. It wasn't an exercise in survival, it involved assembling ingredients into a delightful dining experience. In other circumstances, Frida might have condemned it all but she'd never eaten such good food before.

'Layla won't allow Olsen to kick you off the team, you know.'

Agnes delivered the statement with a certainty born of the same sense of entitlement. Frida forked more of the wonderful food into her mouth and mumbled something that sounded like uncertainty.

'I guarantee it. Layla has powerful backers, financial and political.'

It was the second time Agnes had mentioned the forces behind the expedition. It reminded her of how Dubh Senior had shared her secret heritage with the government. She wasn't sure she was happy he'd done that. It went against everything her mother had instilled in her. But her present situation was more precarious than her mother had anticipated. Perhaps powerful allies were important now. Agnes' comment made Frida reconsider the consequences of rescuing Layla from the hotel fire. By inadvertently saving the woman's life, they had forged an alliance. Such political machinations went well beyond

Frida's experiences. She had entered a very different world suddenly and it wasn't one she liked.

Agnes took a sip of some wine she'd opened. Frida had never drunk wine before and wasn't very keen on it, even though it was a good vintage and the right grape to accompany pasta. Whatever that meant.

'I don't know if you've noticed but Layla and I aren't close. In fact, I'd go so far as to say we're rivals. Her knowledge of Vanaheim and the nine realms made her the obvious choice as the expedition's consultant. She had a formidable reputation before the war. In comparison, I'm a lowly PhD student with a fascination for Norse mythology. Daddy got me in front of a few important people in the government so I could present my theory that the population of Asgard might be the fae in a different guise.' She waved a fork airily, indicating her surroundings. 'And suddenly, here I am. Except Layla now believes the theory was hers.'

It reinforced the importance of entitlement again, along with the way money and power played into it. Agnes pushed away her half-eaten bowl of pasta with a sigh, the casual wastage of valuable food shocked Frida enormously.

'I phoned Daddy and told him about Olsen murdering that boy, by the way. Told him I wanted something done, for Olsen to be disciplined or something. I'm not sure anything will happen though. Daddy isn't very interested when it comes to fairy welfare.' She stopped herself and looked up, a little bashful. 'Sorry. I mean, the fae. He's a Neanderthal on that subject. His friends are the same.'

'So why is the government negotiating for the fae's help for this expedition?'

Agnes swirled the wine in its glass and took another sip. 'It's a means to an end. We can't mount the expedition without it appearing like an invasion. That would lead to another war. We can't have that. The world is on its knees. When you look at how climate change is making things worse, we need a quick solution. We need to colonise another world. It's practicalities really.'

Frida tried another smile but it wouldn't form. She placed her own cutlery into her bowl, making sure they were just as straight and neat as her hostess'. She took another sip of the wine and wished she hadn't. Agnes' simple view of the world didn't match the hardship and misery suffered by everyone beyond her flat.

She thought about her letter from Yaalon Dubh and how he'd described something similar happening on their side. Humanity and the fae needed each other and were prepared to bury their differences to achieve their respective goals.

'Still, that's stuff Daddy and his friends will sort out. I'm busy enjoying myself providing the information on our destination, making myself indispensable.'

'Why?'

Agnes gave a girlish giggle, Frida imagined her behaving the same way with her school chums.

'I want in on the expedition. I'm determined to get to Vanaheim.'

'I see,' Frida said and hoped she didn't sound too horrified by the idea. It worked because it scored another giggle as Agnes picked up the bowls and took them into the kitchen.

Frida followed, ready to help in the clearing up, but it appeared there wasn't any need. Mrs Thorpe would clean up in the morning, when she came in to do the laundry and the shopping. Agnes really did live a tough life.

'Aren't you worried? About going to Vanaheim? It'll be dangerous.'

Agnes shrugged. They would be escorted by experienced soldiers and, despite his flaws, Olsen's reputation was formidable in such environments. Everything would be fine. It was obvious she wasn't interested in hearing any other opinion. Agnes had other plans.

'I'm going to get changed. I have a date.'

Agnes' life included romance. Specifically, the freckled-faced Corporal Billy Frears. He was someone for whom Daddy would not approve but that was part of the fun. Agnes called it forbidden fruit and gave Frida a knowing look.

'It's his night off tonight so can I ask you to keep all this to yourself please, Frida?' Another girlish giggle. 'Especially if all goes according to plan and I bring him back here.'

Frida did her best to restrain the mixture of embarrassment and horror she felt. Agnes appeared oblivious, she had one thing on her mind.

'The walls are quite thick in these old buildings and we'll try to be quiet.' Giggle. 'Though I can't promise anything.'

Frida smiled and hurried to the spare bedroom, using the excuse to try on the new clothes Agnes had bought her. She'd been told, in no uncertain terms, that she needed to change out of her soot-covered outfit.

It was a warm night, and her room felt stuffy. She opened the window and stared out onto the street below. Without streetlights, darkness owned the city, and only bobbing torch beams identified the occasional passer-by. She had a bath, the sensation of soaking in really hot water helped her relax. It didn't work completely, her mind wouldn't allow it. The contents of the letter generated too many questions, but the events of the day finally caught up with her. She crawled into bed, resting on a mattress so soft she floated on clouds, to fall asleep almost as soon as her head hit the pillow.

She woke to the sound of grunting noises and Agnes' voice calling out Billy's name. Frida pulled the pillow up around her head. The couple's activities made her think of Lorcan and that made her feel even more uncomfortable.

A cool breeze woke her a second time. She had no idea of the time, but everything was quiet next door thankfully. She smiled, pleased for Agnes. Perhaps her boyfriend might bring her down to earth and get her to face up to reality. She turned onto her side. On the other pillow rested a piece of paper that fluttered in the breeze. She sat up, heart racing, reached over and opened it.

'Apologies for the cloak and dagger stuff. Meet me by Constantine's statue now.'

Frida leapt out of bed and rushed to the open window, one curtain flapping on the outside of the frame. It had to be how her secret messenger had got in, except the climb to her third storey window needed the skills of a monkey. Outside was a wall of solid darkness.

It had to be Lorcan, she decided as she got dressed. Perhaps he'd found out about Olsen taking her off the expedition team. Except it seemed unlikely, equally as unreal as completing such an arduous climb, despite those amazing muscles. The phrase 'cloak and dagger' methods didn't sound like a phrase the fae would use either.

Resting her hand on the door handle, Frida took stock. She could be heading out to meet another assassin, though that seemed unlikely. They could have killed her in her bed. Why summon her outside, where she could defend herself more easily?

On the street, all was quiet and dark, except for the moon. The ghostly outline of the Minster reared up in front of her, along with the statue of the Roman emperor enthroned at its entrance. Her mind prickled its familiar warning, followed by waves of uncertainty and a spike of determination.

'Please don't blast me.'

She turned around, fingers flexing instinctively, ready to fire at whatever waited. There was only darkness.

'I'm not a threat. I promise.'

The voice was above her. She looked up, feeling a slight breeze on her cheeks. 'Show yourself then.'

'Very well.'

She twisted ninety degrees to find a man in front of her. At least the outline of his body against the moonlight behind him. He looked like a ghost. She had to control her urge to blast, gritting her teeth in the process. 'Who are you? What do you want?'

He spoke with an accent. She'd worked for a German couple on their farm years ago, until the local people decided to burn the place down in their need to rid the land of dirty foreigners. This man sounded similar, though his accent was softer.

It took a moment to notice the other significant factor. She had to look up to find his head. Look right up. She was tall but this man was a giant.

'My name is Jonas Klein. I've been sent to help you.'

She wanted to say she didn't need his help, didn't like men breaking into her bedroom in the middle of the night either. Words wouldn't form properly. For a split second she wondered if he was standing on something but a glance down at his feet, such big feet, proved he wasn't. He really was a giant.

'Yes, I'm a giant. At least that's what people say to my face. At other times they call me a freak. People judge by what they see.'

If she'd wanted a large dose of reassurance from this man, that speech provided it. She understood the misery associated with the word freak. She'd lived with it throughout her life but perhaps not to the extent of the character in front of her.

'I'm sorry,' she found herself mumbling.

She could just make out his silhouetted shoulders shrugging.

'I thought it best we spoke privately before I make my entrance.'

It was a strange term to use, making him sound like an actor. Or was he talking about a performance he was to give, by pretending to be someone else.

'I have no idea what you're talking about.'

That must have surprised him because his mind shifted gear. She felt his concern ratchet up into a broader form of anxiety.

'Do you know Freddie Galbraith?'

'Who?'

The other man's unease rose another notch. 'Blonde haired, scar on one cheek, belligerent guy.'

'No. Never met him.'

The big man didn't reply immediately, he moved closer to the statue and sat on its steps, head in hands. Frida stood in front of him, just able to make out the outlines of his face.

'When he didn't report in a couple of months ago, we wondered if something was wrong but we hoped he didn't want to break his cover. Clearly, he didn't make it. Someone got to him before he reached you.'

'When you say *we*, who are you talking about?'

'The government. We received a request to protect you once your family heritage was shared with us.'

Yaalon Dubh had been as good as his word.

'But it's clear someone in government circles is working against us and betrayed Freddie to our enemies.'

'Do you mean Humanity First? Because they might have been behind the attack on our hotel yesterday.'

Though it was too dark to read his expression, his mind did it for her. Firstly, there was his reaction to the terrorist group, something akin to a cold shiver through his brain. Secondly, she could read his indecision, no doubt trying to work out how much she knew, how much to share.

'They're a possibility. Personally, I don't think so. This is bigger. There are those in Parliament who think our negotiations with the fae is wrong, in many ways. They're not against leaking information, even if it costs a life.'

His emotions spiked. This other man had to have been a friend.

'And you're here to do what?'

If he said the words "protect you", she would get angry. He didn't answer straight away, perhaps he sensed the impending danger from her tone of voice. When he did reply, his voice developed a different tone, softer, even wistful.

'May I call you Frida?' She said he could. 'You are truly exceptional. You provide a solution to the fae because you are proof of the benefits that come from the merging of our races. The same is true for human beings. Your special talents might be replicated in others like you, in the future. Imagine how that could help us.'

Frida found herself trying to imagine a race of people with her talents and the problems they caused. It seemed better to stay silent and wait for the man to continue.

'I'm here to make sure nothing happens to you. You are a precious commodity, Frida Ranson. We need to make certain no harm befalls you.'

She turned away from him, stared into the wall of darkness that surrounded them. Yesterday she'd met a representative from the fae with the same intention, now she had his human counterpart. A bloody giant, no less. All for her. A freaky orphan no one had cared about for years. She sensed the man's patience, his sympathy too. Here was someone else who might understand her misery.

'You should know I've been taken off the expedition team by Major Olsen.'

The giant chuckled. She liked the sound.

'That's been dealt with. I'll inform him of his mistake in the morning.'

'He won't like that.'

'No.' His voice hardened, took on a rough edge that suddenly made him sound like a very different man. 'He won't like a lot of what I say, including the government's unhappiness at his decision to murder a fae boy.'

'You heard about that?' It made her wonder just how influential Agnes' father was.

'He's a necessary evil, Frida. We will need his military experience in Vanaheim, he's a useful man in a crisis. But he needs to be kept on a tight leash.'

'Like a Rottweiller.' Frida laughed, Jonas joined her.

She found herself smiling, reassured again. Olsen had been dealt with and this big, friendly giant could be a useful ally. With Layla, she had two. Once in the fae realm, she'd have three. She wasn't on her own any longer. It led to a sigh of relief.

'Get some sleep, Frida, thank you for meeting with me.' He turned to go.

'Wait a minute. Tell me how you got into my room. It's three storeys high, a sheer wall.'

He was little more than a dark shape against a black background. 'That was the easy part. I was more afraid of you waking up and blasting me.'

'Tell me.' She wasn't letting this go.

'I grew up in a circus. I'm strong and years of training have made me exceptionally agile. Goodnight Frida.'

A circus performer – that explained his reference about making an entrance. She watched him vanish into the night, lost in a whirling flood of thought processes fed by what he'd told her. While Elsa had been in charge, everything had been simple. Now there were conflicting factions from the two races and she was caught in the middle. She'd spent her life seeking the shadows and now everyone wanted to thrust her into the spotlight. What was worse, she couldn't find a way to stop it from happening.

Lost in thought, she ambled past the Gothic lines of the Minster where moonlight turned it into a stage set.

Familiar sparks of warning struck her as she sensed something waft past her, ethereal, fluid, ghost-like. She shivered.

Then it was gone.

Chapter 7

*"For a hardened military veteran like myself, balancing
the conflicting interests of politicians, academics and
security, never sat well with me."*

Interview with Major Sven Olsen, QGM

A visit from royalty couldn't have caused greater
excitement or tension. Frida watched the preparations
with amusement. Major Olsen looked stressed. In
comparison Layla glowed as she supervised the event,
jabbing her walking stick on the stone floor to punctuate
her instructions. She had surpassed herself, much to
Agnes' annoyance, by inviting a fae academic to the
Minster. The first official visit by a fae since their retreat
after the war.

The building and its surroundings bristled with
security, overseen by Olsen in red-faced mode, yelling
obscenities at his soldiers when they didn't react fast
enough. His anger hadn't faded in the intervening two
days since Jonas had arrived with the news that the
government wanted Frida back on the expedition team. If
anything, it had got worse.

Frida and Agnes watched Layla stalk the Minster's
crypt, scrutinising last minute details. She'd laid out all
their research on the large table in the centre of the room
so the Very Important Person could admire the collection.
According to Layla, it represented the finest, most
complete collection of Vanaheim source materials,
offering detailed insights into the mysterious world. As she

circled the table, tutting and sighing at books set out slightly askew, Agnes' temper boiled.

'Layla, give it a rest. Everything is fine.'

'Fine?' The older woman looked up, aghast. 'Fine isn't good enough. Professor Ruarí Salann is the leading expert on Vanaheim throughout the fae realm. He's fanatical about detail, obsessively so. I need to prove we are credible if he is to offer his help. I want him to marvel at what I've put together for him.'

'We've put together, don't you mean?' Agnes hissed.

Her implied criticism was waved away. 'Yes, yes. It's a combined effort.'

Agnes simmered silently. Frida took her hand and squeezed it discreetly. It earned her a tense smile of appreciation. It wasn't a natural gesture for Frida but sharing the flat had brought the two of them closer together, insofar as chalk and cheese could ever be entirely compatible.

'I'm going down to the vaults. Our guest will come through the portal imminently. Remember, keep everyone else away from the research. We don't want any mishaps or, worse still, anyone protesting. This is a purely academic event, politics cannot be allowed to invade our pursuit of knowledge.'

Layla stomped through the doorway which led to the staircase which would take her into the bowels of the Minster, where a doorway to another dimension waited.

'Some hope of that,' Frida said as she watched the woman leave.

Olsen was already down there with half a dozen soldiers, he wouldn't be interested in the pursuit of knowledge.

Agnes moved closer to the table and returned the items Layla had just rearranged into their original position. She gave Frida a mischievous grin.

'Are you going to tell me the truth about your big, friendly giant then? Because there's something going on between the two of you.'

Inwardly, Frida groaned. In the last twenty-four hours Agnes's relentless pursuit of the topic had caused impatience to flare on both sides.

'I've told you, there's nothing going on. I don't know why the government want me involved. He hasn't told me.'

'And you haven't asked, of course. I mean, why would you?'

'He just said they wanted me there. I'm not sure he knows the reason. He's just a messenger.'

'Yeah, a big, powerful one that intimidates Olsen. And if he was *just* a messenger, he wouldn't be going on the expedition as well. Come on, Frida, I'm not stupid. I know you're lying.'

'Why don't you ask your father?'

'I have and he's even more evasive than you.'

Agnes stopped moving around the books and stared at Frida with the expression she had come to dread. She had shifted into investigation mode.

'Let me tell you my theory.'

Yeah, definitely investigation mode. Frida groaned silently for the second time.

'Your ability to shoot bolts of lightning from your fingers means you're not entirely human. If you were, there would be others who could do that. It explains why you keep it secret. So, if you're not entirely human, I'm guessing you have some family connections with the fae. There are stories of Norse gods who could do the same thing, Odin for one.' Agnes paused, and the wicked sparkle in her eyes intensified, sensing victory. 'This is the bit that's not so clear. The government have learned about your secret. Or perhaps they already knew. Either way, you're an asset to them now. During the war, you would have been accused of spying but now you're a bridge between the two races. They need you as a symbol of peace and reconciliation.'

Her smile widened, turned into a grin as she read the growing anxiety on her friend's face. Rescue came in the form of excited voices from the cellar staircase. Agnes flicked a glance at Frida.

'This is not finished,' she mouthed.

Professor Ruarí Salann might have got away with pretending to be human. His receding hairline diminished the naturally enlarged forehead of the fae and his almond shaped eyes were rounder than most. They were grey, like steel and just as hard. When he was introduced to Frida, they intimidated her, and she almost backed away from the sheer force of his personality. Thankfully, Agnes was quick to shake the man's hand and impress on him how she'd developed the theory of the Norse connection to the fae. It drew silent and unbridled indignation from Layla. She resorted to manoeuvring her guest toward the table and its exhibition of their research, ensuring he had his back to Agnes.

Olsen remained a short distance away, by the doorway to the vault and its portal, resentful and contemptuous of all the fuss. Nonetheless, he'd insisted on being present, even though the lack of space meant there was only room for the three women, the professor and his unnamed assistant. He'd meet civic and military dignitaries at a reception in his honour later.

The politics and the tension made Frida regret her promise to Layla. Her place in this political pantomime served no purpose except Jonas wanted her to provide feedback later. She was starting to feel like a spy these days and she hated all the deception. Agnes abandoned her, to barge between Layla and the fae professor. Left on her own and forced to listen to academic debate about source materials and triangulation left Frida the target of Olsen's glowering looks.

There was nothing to spy on, she decided, so while no one was looking, she'd escape. She discreetly made her way to the Perspex and wooden staircase that led up to the nave while the others conducted a debate over some ancient and dusty tome. At the top of the staircase, she glanced back a final time to make sure no one had noticed her exit.

Her eyes met the steely gaze of the fae professor. It unnerved her, his scrutiny leaving her feeling naked. She shuddered. He was fae – his psychic skill-set would exceed hers – he could be penetrating her mental defences at that very moment. She realised it might be her own paranoia but it didn't matter, his expression left her feeling violated.

Oblivious to it all, Layla thrust another document in front of him, to evidence whatever argument she needed to prove. Frida briefly considered penetrating the man's mind, but her heavy-handed attempt with Lorcan stopped her. The man would be offended and it would cause an awful political incident. Layla would be furious with her and that would scupper their friendship. Plus, everyone would discover her own psychic skill secret, the other blunt weapon in her arsenal.

Movement in the corner of the crypt caught her eye; something shadowy crossed the doorway to the vault. She hadn't been looking properly, couldn't be certain she'd seen anything so she put it down to her paranoia. Judging by the shaft of sunlight at the main entrance to the Minster, it was still sunny and warm. She'd go for a walk, leave the tension and suspicion behind.

As she turned to go, her mind triggered its warning bristling sensation, her skin tingled. With no one else nearby, everything seemed normal enough yet a nagging sense of wrongness bothered her. Frida took a couple of steps down the staircase.

The air felt different, lighter somehow, as though the politics and the tension really were affecting the air itself. Layla, regaling the professor with an amusing anecdote, placed a hand on her chest and paused for breath. A second later Agnes's head dropped and she pressed fingers against her temples as if massaging a headache. Over by the doorway to the vault, Olsen's usual florid features had lost their colour and his forehead glistened with a sheen of sweat. He leaned against the doorframe and shook his head.

How could the air change? Something might be wrong but charging in shouting a warning wasn't going to help, not until she had something definite to report. Layla finished her story, the professor laughed politely but suddenly leapt forward to catch Layla as she staggered and dropped her cane. He held her around the waist to keep her upright. She offered a weak smile, thanked him, and promptly collapsed at his feet. Agnes hurried toward her, looking terribly pale herself. She collapsed at Layla's side. The professor's assistant was next. The great man looked around in confusion, seeking help from Olsen in the doorway. His normally belligerent expression had turned into bewilderment as he slid down the doorframe to slump into a heap, his head lolling on his chest. The professor turned to Frida but it was too late, like a tree felled in a forest, he fell over and lay unconscious.

Frida found herself standing amidst a carpet of bodies. At least their lack of movement looked like death. No one moved. She couldn't detect any signs of breathing. In seconds the room had changed from a hive of excitement and activity to a mortuary. Panic threatened to overwhelm her. She fought the urge to scream for help, to sound like a helpless female yet that's what she was. Something needed to happen. But what? There was no one left to ask. The guards patrolling the entrance would know. They were trained for events like these. At least, she hoped they were.

As she turned to run for help, movement caught her eye. She stopped.

In the doorway from the vault, stood a woman. At least something which suggested femininity. It wore a diaphanous gown that floated around its slim body, greys and blues shimmered within its fabric like no clothing Frida had ever seen. Its face told her it wasn't human, or fae for that matter. There was no nose, only nostrils hidden behind thin flaps of skin which vibrated slightly, its skin was like parchment, dried, flaking in places. The eyes, larger than normal, found Frida.

Suddenly the air around her wasn't there. She panicked for a second as the need to take in air became all-consuming, she held her breath, tried to calm herself at the same time. The creature took a step closer. It grinned, displaying needle-like teeth the colour of dried cheese.

That was all Frida needed. She raised one hand. Too much and she risked destroying everything in the small room. Beams of energy leapt from her fingertips and struck the creature, flinging it against the far wall like a rag doll. It crumpled into a heap, a smoking hole in the centre of its chest, head lolling forward as if to examine the damage.

Air returned with a whoosh, a gust of wind that almost knocked Frida down the staircase as it sought to compensate for the vacuum in the crypt. A quick check of each of the comatose victims showed they were still breathing. The fae professor was the first to stir, though Frida kept her distance from him, preferring to kneel by Layla and Agnes and rub their wrists. He sat up, woozy and disorientated but even then, his scrutiny of her made her feel vulnerable.

'What happened?' he asked.

Frida pointed at the body of the creature surrounded by the folds of dress which no longer looked like gossamer but more like shredded lace. He shook his head.

'Is it dead?' he asked quietly. He stared at the blackened blast mark which penetrated the creature's chest, then at Frida. 'Did you do that?'

The intensity of his gaze frightened her. Thankfully, Agnes stirred and Frida turned her attention to her friend's recovery. Behind her, Olsen woke, demanding hoarse explanations and croaking for the guards to do their bloody job properly.

Within minutes the crypt heaved with people providing medical support and scowling in their endeavours to show security really did exist. The guards by the portal in the vaults were slowly regaining consciousness but had no memory of what had happened. Olsen's face might have regained its usual ruddy colour but the cause was embarrassment – he'd been beaten by one creature who'd overcome everyone without a shot being fired.

Professor Salann stood over the body with a look of distaste. 'I believe this to be a disir, an air spirit. There are stories of such things but I confess to never having seen one before. They were creatures described in tales we tell our children, I never imagined they actually existed.'

Olsen marched over to him. 'And did this thing accompany you? Because it's a bloody big coincidence we're attacked the moment we open the portal.'

The older man said nothing for a moment but perused Olsen's face with his head on one side as though trying to make sense of him. 'Is that an accusation? Because if it is, you risk endangering the expedition. I will return and inform the two Courts of this serious breach of trust. And security.'

Breathlessness and pale, Layla staggered over to the two men, leaning heavily on her cane. The seriousness of the moment was etched into the lines on her face. 'He's not saying that Professor. Are you, Major? Tell him you're not. Before this incident blows up in our faces.'

Olsen's red cheeks almost turned purple as his anger seethed just below the surface. He slowly exhaled and straightened his shoulders. 'I need to establish how that creature arrived here. There is no accusation.'

Professor Salann's steely eyes narrowed. 'In my culture, such misunderstandings are immediately followed by an apology. It is a measure of a man that he can accept his fault, overcome his pride to make good his relationship at his own cost.'

The two men glared, and even Layla waited, nervously watching the Major's reaction.

'I apologise for any misunderstanding, it was not my intention to cause offence.'

It earned him a curt nod of the head.

'Thank you, Major. I must assume that thing followed us before your men closed the portal. I assume they did close it?'

It was obvious they hadn't. Or if they had, not immediately. Olsen's blood pressure rose still further, he looked like he was about to explode.

The professor smiled and pointed at Frida. 'This young woman's prompt action in destroying this creature saved our lives.' He bowed his head at her, lower than he'd done with the Major. 'I'm intrigued how you managed it. You aren't carrying a weapon.'

The heads of every person in the room turned in Frida's direction and their scrutiny rapidly turned into suspicion. Frida knew those looks well and they always led to events which ended badly. It had been a risk betraying her secret in front of Agnes, one which had paid off for once. This was different. Layla might not react too badly but the fae professor would report back to his superiors what she was, what she could do.

83

Worse still, Olsen would find out. He'd call her a spy, a traitor and, despite what the government said, refused to allow her on the expedition. At the very least, he'd never trust her, not even slightly.

These thoughts sped through Frida's mind to justify her instincts. She ran.

Olsen's hoarse barking followed her through the nave as he called for his soldiers to stop her. They were too slow to react. She sprinted into the blinding sunshine. All she could see were dark outlines of buildings at the edge of her vision, not the towering hulk of Jonas Klein. She smacked into him, semi-concussed by rock-like muscles. He enveloped her in his arms to keep her upright but she pummelled his chest in her desperate need to escape.

Her vision cleared enough to see read his bewildered expression.

'What's happened?'

The answer came from the bellowed commands inside the Minster, calling her name. The big man scooped Frida up with one arm, swung her round so she clung to him piggy-back style. He set off at a loping sprint around the side of the Gothic building, with a speed and ease which astonished her. In less than a minute they were amongst narrow alleyways. They stopped in front of a derelict building surrounded by scaffolding. With one powerful leap, Jonas grabbed a metal bar and hauled the two of them up onto a dusty wooden platform. He squatted so she could climb off his back. He wasn't out of breath and hadn't worked up a sweat. On the other hand, Frida's legs felt like jelly. He led her through a window frame into a room containing a mattress, a chair and basic cooking utensils. She recognised some of his clothes on the chair, this had to be where he lived.

Jonas remained at the window, peering out over other derelict buildings to the Minster. The sounds of consternation and angry army officers could be heard. Frida joined him, still slightly awed by his strength and agility but mainly by his readiness to hide her.

'I've given away my secret.'

In fits and starts she told him what had happened. He listened and chuckled at her description of everyone's faces as they drew their conclusions about her involvement in the creature's demise. He reached down and took her hands, as though expecting to find evidence of her explosive actions.

'They're going to imprison me. That's what Olsen wants. He'll hate me even more now.'

Jonas stroked one of her hands gently, she found it comforting. He knelt down so he could look into her face. Another gesture of reassurance, of friendship.

'It was going to happen eventually.' His smile widened. 'On the expedition there are going to be times when your talent will be necessary. It might save lives, like it has today. I think you've overlooked that part.'

He was right. He sat down on the dirty floorboards and patted the space next to him. The noises from the Minster faded. Here, alone with this giant of a man, she felt safe. She joined him on the floor and returned his smile.

'Thank you,' she said. It was no more than a whisper, partly in case anyone heard them but also because her awkwardness meant saying anything was difficult.

For the whole of her life, she'd kept herself apart from others, running away the moment anyone began to suspect she might be different. The need for secrecy was her mother's mantra. Before her death, family life had been isolated and lonely, living in a small cottage, miles from anywhere. She'd been allowed to go to school, but on the condition she didn't make friends and kept herself to herself.

She looked up into the big man's smiling face, aware she'd lost herself in her memories.

'At least you managed to keep your secret for a long time. When you're my size, there's no point. Everyone can see I'm not normal.'

He chuckled and she joined in. That was the crux of it. She could no longer pretend to be normal. But with that realisation came a sense of relief. She didn't have to pretend any longer. She returned Jonas's smile and it felt nice.

His own smile dimmed. 'Another attack is bad news. It suggests the threat we face increases. After your archer friend, and whoever blew up the hotel, our enemy is using creatures even the fae don't understand, or even believe existed. It's like if we sent the Loch Ness Monster to attack the fae, isn't it? They're no more informed about these things than we are.'

They stared at the open window. Outside they could hear the activities of York citizens, going about their daily routine, oblivious of it all. Jonas shook his head.

'Makes you wonder what they'll send next.'

Chapter 8

'We are not so different from the human race. If our history of social division, manifested in the endless wars between the Light and Dark Courts, shows us anything, it is the benefit of working together to achieve common goals.'

'Two Races, One Goal: A Polemic by Professor Yaalon Dubh

The noise of two dozen nervous and belligerent soldiers echoed around the vaulted spaces of York Minster, robbing it of its majesty and religious decorum. Frida eyed them suspiciously. One of them, a man with enough beard to hide a dozen nesting birds, glared at her as he held court over his comrades busily checking their backpacks.

'Still say it's wrong. We shouldn't be talking to the fucking fairies, never mind travelling to their world. Can't trust the bastards, that's what I say.'

He shot Frida a look of intense contempt, one those around him couldn't miss. They mumbled their collective agreement, enough to give the man the courage to voice his opinions loud enough to echo in the Minster's nave.

'They could turn on us the moment we get there. I reckon it's a trap. They couldn't defeat us on this side of those bloody portals so they plan to finish the job on their side. And all because the government listens to lying bastards who pretend to be human beings.'

Frida's pulse rate soared and her fingertips throbbed. She'd withstood this barrage of abuse for two days now, and she'd had enough. After the suspicion and veiled threats she'd received from Olsen, it made sense he'd turn his soldiers against her. Somebody needed to be taught a lesson. A cool hand rested on her wrist.

Agnes smiled at her. 'Ignore him. Animal likes winding people up, don't let him.'

'Animal?' The name matched the man perfectly, it wasn't just his bear-like size and hair but his belligerence too.

'Billy says most of the unit think he's an idiot but they're too scared to say it. Some hang around him like a school bully, it gives them status because they're pathetic losers.'

She hooked her arm through Frida's and headed for the crypt as though they were out for a Sunday afternoon stroll.

'Billy says they're all scared, deep down. They've spent ten years fighting the fairies and now, here we are, travelling to their world like tourists. He says it's new and soldiers don't cope with stuff beyond their training and experience.'

They reached the staircase. The large table in the crypt had gone, along with the rest of Agnes and Layla's paraphernalia, it made the room look three times bigger. Agnes hesitated and took a breath, as though she was about to walk back into a vacuum. With grim determination on her face, she strode down the staircase with deliberate steps. Frida admired her fortitude.

'You like Billy, don't you?'

Agnes gave her usual girlish giggle and blushed. 'He's not like any of my boyfriends in London. They were so preoccupied with themselves, you know the type, vain and arrogant. Money meant everything. Billy is so different, he's kind and caring. And in bed, well...!' Her eyes flashed with mischief and she giggled even more.

Frida managed a smile but the conversation had entered embarrassing territory. Agnes' stare only made it worse.

'Can I ask you a question, Frida? A personal one?' There wasn't a pause for an answer. 'Are you gay? It's all right if you are, I had a friend at school who turned out to be a lesbian so I completely understand if you are.'

Frida had hoped Agnes might have been different. In the last few days, while they'd shared the flat, their friendship had led to a lot of laughter. There'd never been any fun in life until she'd met Agnes, trying to stay alive each day didn't generate many laughs. She'd never let anyone get that close to her before either, she'd even grown accustomed to her friend seeing her in underwear. But, as usual, Agnes had fallen for the stereotype. As a large and muscular woman, she had to be gay.

'No, I'm not.' She kept walking toward the vaults, where preparations for the journey through the portal were completed.

Agnes rushed after her, took her arm, pulled her back. 'I'm sorry, I didn't mean to offend you. It's just that you don't talk about men. Or anything to do with sex. It just made me wonder. That's all.' She peered into Frida's face, searching for acceptance. 'Are we OK? I hope so. Us women need to stick together!'

Her mischievous twinkle returned and it made Frida smile. 'Yeah. We're OK.'

Lieutenant Wheeler burst through the doorway, looking stressed and flushed. 'We're ready to go. I'm going to fetch the unit so if you ladies would like to be one of the first to step through the portal?'

He sped off and Agnes clapped her hands in excitement and strode purposefully down the staircase into the Minster's vault, Frida followed with greater levels of trepidation. Admittedly she was going to see Lorcan Dubh again – that was exciting – but she was also entering a world she knew more about than most of the others. Fae culture wouldn't be an easy place to navigate, there were far too many rules for one thing. But Jonas' warning remained with her, whoever was trying to wreck this mission had chosen to use creatures neither race understood. It was unlikely those attempts would stall now. On home ground, they would probably increase.

Agnes gasped at the sight of the effervescent curtain of energy as it tumbled from the keystone in the stone archway. Even though it was positioned at the farthest end of the vault, it lit up the room with a warm orange glow.

'It's like Buck's Fizz!'

Frida had no idea what that was but nodded anyway.

The sight of the portal took her back to one of her earliest memories, in the ruins of a historic building, deep below the ground where she'd met her first members of the fae. Portal energy formed different colours, depending on the local geology, she found out later. This time the shimmering curtain was a pale green, the same colour as her mother's blouse. The coincidence helped distract her from the pain of his mother's iron-like grip on her hand. She waited, aware of her mother's tension, sensing the need to remain silent. Finally, two stern women stepped through the portal, only to admonish her mother. It shocked the young Frida, she'd never heard anyone speak to her mother that way. Her mother bowed her head, there was no other reaction. That was it. The memory had no more to offer. Except the lasting perception that the fae were an unfriendly and uncompromising lot.

Agnes hurried toward the portal as Layla and Major Olsen disappeared through its glittering waterfall of energy. She watched with an awed hand over her mouth, like a child seeing an act of magic. In a way, that's what it was. A wonderful, awe-inspiring means to travel to another dimension by taking less than a dozen steps.

Agnes turned. 'I suppose you're familiar with these things?'

'I wouldn't say familiar.'

Her answer was irrelevant, Agnes had already taken a step toward the portal and, at the last minute, reached out a nervous hand to her friend. Together they walked through. The sensations were new. She'd seen portals but never travelled through them, the fae had come to them. The impression she'd gained was that she and her mother weren't welcome on the other side.

The tumbling tachyons made her skin tingle, her entire body prickled just as it did when warmth returned to cold skin. Perhaps it was her innate manipulation of energy coursing through her veins, which amplified the sensations, but the buzz made her light-hearted for the first time in her life. She understood what the word *thrill* meant now.

And then it was over. They were out the other side, in a large cave, its wide entrance framing a picture of a park filled with flowers and trees. The image sprang to life as they left the cave, one that differed in so many ways from the world they'd left. The blue sky and bright sunlight were the same but the similarities ended there. People strolled in the park in couples and small groups, a scene of casual relaxation. Their arrival caused some commotion and concern but nothing like the panic Frida had anticipated. The authorities must have warned the local population what to expect. So different to what had happened when the fae arrived in her world a decade earlier.

From amidst a larger group of well-dressed and imperious fae, stepped Professor Salann. He smiled his welcome and introduced Olsen and Layla to the dignitaries surrounding him. Agnes instantly abandoned Frida so as not to miss out on the academic get-to-know-you session. Salann nodded briefly in Frida's direction but otherwise paid her no attention, for which she was grateful. She smiled to herself as some of the professor's friends circled Olsen to make polite chit-chat, he looked the most uncomfortable she'd ever seen him.

She jumped when someone behind her spoke her name.

Lorcan Dubh had dispensed with the cloak in favour of shirt and trousers, in a shade of purple so deep it was almost black. His long black hair had been oiled into a slick ponytail. The style emphasized the curve and sharpness of his cheek bones which, in turn, drew attention to the limpid chocolate pools of his eyes. Frida's heart skipped a beat. Agnes would have had no doubt about her sexual orientation if she'd witnessed her

92

reaction, she hoped the man at her side hadn't picked up on it. It was doubtful, given the fae psychic ability. Her mother had told her it was the height of bad manners to access another's mind without permission, she hoped that was still true.

'Welcome, Frida.' He performed the necessary formal bow. 'It's good to see you again. I hear you rescued our esteemed professor from a disir, of all things. My father is going to want to hear all about that. He's waiting for us now.'

He had quickly dispensed with the usual Fae social protocols, Frida was glad of that. He extended an arm to point at a stylish coach with tasselled curtains in its windows. A young man in a smart grey uniform sat at the front, holding the reins of two white horses.

'What about the others? They'll wonder where I've gone.'

They were already walking to the coach.

'Don't worry. Nothing around here happens without everyone knowing about it.'

Which explained nothing but Frida was prepared to go along with the invitation. The coach had just enough room for two people sitting close together. That was reason enough for the trip, but Yaalon Dubh had answers, at least she hoped he did. Yet more motivation.

Their journey was short. It took them through narrow avenues of willow and silver birch which dappled the sunlight and offered shade without denying warmth. Cottages lined the route with gardens filled with an artist's palette of colour, their perfume wafted through the open windows on a gentle breeze. She was in paradise and it made her smile, her nervousness evaporated. Even so, she was aware of the man sat next to her, watching her reactions to the scenery.

'It's a very different place, isn't it?'

He smelled of spice, she could feel the warmth radiating from his body. But his question reminded her how far they'd travelled without saying a word, as though he'd known how she'd react. She looked at him, to be confronted with his million megaton smile again. She grinned back instinctively.

He chuckled, a sexy, deep-throated sound. 'I was so shocked when I arrived in your world. Horrified is perhaps a better word. Not just because of the damage from the war but the strange weather, the floods. It's like the planet has given up and in its death throes.' He stopped, the smile vanishing. 'I hope you don't mind me making such an observation?'

She didn't object. How could she when she was hypnotised by this man's smile?

They entered through double gates, onto a drive which took them up to a house double the size of anything she'd seen so far. Well-maintained gardens surrounded the single-storey building, a stream ran parallel to the drive, it gurgled over small rocks, to splash into pools proliferated by water lilies. In the doorway stood an elderly man, leaning on a silver walking cane. He beamed his welcome with the same bright smile and dazzling brown eyes as his son.

The two men led Frida to a lawned area where a table held glasses and a large pitcher of sparkling clear liquid, along with a varied selection of meats, bread rolls and fruit. They waited for her to sit down before joining her. Her mother's voice chimed in her head, she mustn't slouch, to nibble at food and not eat like a starving animal and, above all, to be respectful. Conversation was informal but followed traditional lines: her journey, her reactions to this new world and her host's willingness to provide for her whatever she might need. All the fae protocols hard-wired into their brains and their culture. Frida hated it. She wanted answers and all this polite exchange served no purpose at all.

'Thank you for your letter, Yaalon.'

He'd insisted on her calling him by his first name, a sign of enormous trust and respect in fae society. He smiled and nodded. He'd spotted her readiness to move on to the real topic at hand. He took her hand and squeezed it. She knew this wasn't normal behaviour for this race, and the shock on his son's face confirmed it.

'I cannot apologise enough for not being able to reach you, after your mother departed. I made a promise and failed to keep it. For this reason, I am in your debt.'

He held her eye so she understood the importance of what he'd just said. She bowed her head slightly to acknowledge her understanding of this momentous gesture.

'Thank you. I am grateful and honoured. Being here, with you and Lorcan, makes me feel like I am amongst friends for the first time. I have been so lonely.'

She didn't know where the words came from or why she'd spoken them. They'd appeared out of her mouth without being aware of their escape. The same was true for the tears that formed in her eyes now. She felt stupid. Lorcan handed her a handkerchief, beaming his smile as always. His father wore it too, except his had a distinct tinge of sadness. While she dabbed her eyes and tried to recover, the older man maintained a steady flow of explanations.

He told her how he'd known three generations of her family, even visited her grandmother on one occasion, when the human world held fewer threats. His affection for her family was obvious, particularly her grandmother. He talked about how he'd failed to thwart the fae's intentions to invade, how it had cost him his position at the university. He'd reclaimed it later, when his predictions came true and his wisdom recognised.

'But I'm worried history may be repeating itself already. Powerful factions are working to prevent any further collaboration between our races. The war has made both sides distrustful. Some in our society plan to use this suspicion to further their own ends. My communication with your own government, Frida, suggests the same is happening there. We must be careful. Both in what we say but also who we can trust. It is why I have arranged for Lorcan to accompany you on this expedition. He will act as liaison.'

He turned to his son and said something in their own language. The young man stood up, bowed to Frida and entered the house, his father watched him before turning and leaning closer to the girl.

'My son and I have had a strained relationship. Its resolution has been recent and fraught, he's undertaking this task with some degree of reluctance. In our society, there is dishonour associated with acknowledging a father's debt, but Lorcan has accepted it. I tell you this privately so you can understand why he may not always be so cheerful and cooperative. He is prone to certain dark moods. Throughout his youth, until quite recently, he lived a different life. I confess I didn't understand him, I let him down. It drove him away. He became a mercenary soldier, he fought in battles filled with unimaginable horror, experiences which remain with him to this day. He is well-equipped to ensure your safety.'

Frida bristled and the old man chuckled.

'Not that you need protecting! I learned that lesson very painfully, thanks to your grandmother! But sometimes you need another person to watch your back. That will be Lorcan's role.'

His smile matched the warmth of the sunshine and she basked in the kind-heartedness it evoked. She liked this old man, his charm, good manners and affection. It sparked some idle speculation, how things would have been different if he'd successfully rescued her after her mother's death. The answer was simple. Life would have been much, much better.

She started to say as much, again without knowing she was going to do it, when his expression changed. She thought she'd offended him somehow as a frown formed on his face, etching the existing lines deeper into his forehead. It took a moment to realise he was looking over her shoulder. She turned as he stood up, fumbling for his cane. He said something in their language which she didn't understand.

Three figures strode up the drive toward them. Women in gowns which swirled without the aid of any breeze, made from material which caused colours to merge as the fabric billowed. Frida recognised them, her heart leapt into her mouth, these were more creatures like the one in the crypt. Professor Salann had called them disir.

The old man looked at Frida, panic on his face now.

'Vatnavættir!'

Frida raised her hands, felt the reassurance of her fingertips pulsing with energy. She was not going to let these creatures harm the old man, even though she had no idea how that was possible when they were in open air.

In a synchronised movement, the three creatures raised their arms. The nearby stream leapt into the air to form a wall twice her height, blocking the creatures as Frida prepared to blast them. For the briefest of moments it hovered, water flowed upwards, to fall back on itself before repeating the process. The wall broke suddenly, startling her with its force. It roared toward them with the speed of a galloping horse and the devastation of a tsunami. It struck, knocking Frida backward, flattening her on the ground. Water enveloped her with such speed she had no time to recover. It buffeted her in every direction until up and down lost all meaning. Holding what little breath remained in her lungs, she tried to claw her way out of the maelstrom, colliding with objects caught up in the flood.

Her lungs burned in their attempt to find more air as she fought against the force of water pummelling her body like a boxer. She was a piece of flotsam, nothing more. Consciousness ebbed away as her need to breathe turned from panic to benign resignation. Through the swirling water and darkness hovering at the edge of her vision, she caught sight of the outlines of the three creatures standing over her drowning body. Her lungs finally surrendered to the water, its spiralling currents overwhelmed her, robbed her of all sensation. Suddenly it was gone and she slumped onto hard ground, to gulp in air like a floundering fish. Disorientated, dazed, she struggled to her feet, aware of the noise of someone's grunted efforts.

Lorcan fought her three assailants, wielding a sword with the same speed and fluidity as the water bludgeoning him from every direction. As each wave rose to overwhelm him, he avoided its attack with the agility and grace of a dancer.

He'd already injured one of the creatures. Liquid that might have been blood but could have been anything flowed from a deep shoulder wound that left one arm useless and limited the ability to manipulate water. As her brain started working again, she marvelled at Lorcan's skill as a swordsman. His blade was little more than a blur as he feinted in one direction, then drove forward so swiftly it surprised the second victim as he sliced open an arm. Instantly, the frenzied flow of water swirling around him diminished.

Frida raised her hands to blast the uninjured vatnavættir. Except nothing happened beyond a low fizzing noise. The water, she realised with a curse, had grounded her energy. She still felt weak but, as it always did, anger gave her strength. She picked up one of the wooden garden chairs and ran toward the billowing figure, its attention focused on Lorcan. One of the others spotted her intention and drove water at Frida but lacked the power to pose a threat. With all her strength, she smacked the chair into the uninjured creature's head, knocking it senseless to the floor. With the chair still in her hand she rammed its wooden legs into the creature's heaving chest, impaling it.

The other two vatnavættir emitted an ear-splitting screech at the sight of their dead sister. The distraction was all Lorcan needed, with two swipes of his blade, their heads tumbled onto the soaking wet ground and the waters stilled.

With a low groan, Lorcan ran toward the sprawled body of his father, crumpled like a piece of driftwood. He knelt sobbing as he cleared the old man's face of mud and grass. Frida stood some distance away, unsure what to say or do, deciding it was best to let the man grieve. Except she wanted answers and now she'd been denied them. Guilt rose up but she dashed it aside, she'd waited so long to discover the truth. Anger took its place. She glared at the bodies of the three vatnavættir. Her fury didn't stop there, it extended to whoever had sent these creatures to stop her from finding out the truth about her family.

When he stood up, Lorcan looked nothing like the man she'd first met. With his broad shoulders slumped, his eyes vacant, he looked defeated. For a man normally filled with energy, none of it remained. Once again, Frida reasoned, she'd brought assassins to someone else's door.

'I'm sorry. This is my fault.'

He searched her face as though seeking why she'd said such a thing. She hadn't known she was going to say it until the words left her lips but she meant it. Death followed her, like the darkest shadow.

'No, it's not. Father knew he was a target. We'd talked about it.' He glanced at the body, tears tumbled down his cheeks but he carelessly wiped them away, took a deep breath and straightened up. 'There had been threats, Frida. Nothing specific. He'd been asking too many questions and demanding answers which unsettled certain people. Our society is tearing itself apart. This conflict goes beyond the conventional wars between the Light and Dark Courts. It strikes at the heart of what is to become of our race.'

100

'Your father called those things, vatnavættir.'

The mention drew the man's attention to the bodies. His face was filled with revulsion. 'They have always been the stuff of mythology. Creatures from children's stories.'

Just like fairy tales, Frida thought. Here they were staring at things even the fae didn't think could exist.

'And yet they're very real. Like the disir that attacked us in York.'

That made Lorcan look at her, something dark crossed his face but it vanished too quickly for her to work out what it was.

'Father predicted something like this. A few weeks ago, he came back from work and said he'd discovered something.'

'What was it?'

Lorcan gave a sad shake of his head. 'He wouldn't say. He wanted proof before making any accusations, otherwise he'd show his hand too early. He said the truth was so shocking no one would accept it.'

He let out another heavy sigh and shivered. Though the sun was warm, her soaking wet clothes made Frida tremble. Lorcan invited her into the house to get dry. The place was as she imagined it, typical of any academic. Shelves crammed with books that had multiplied into stacks and covered every flat surface. He flung a towel at her, an action that broke social etiquette and betrayed the scale of his grief. Her clothes might be saturated but she'd put up with the discomfort. They had more important matters to deal with.

Lorcan grabbed a blanket from an armchair by a fireplace. She followed him back outside as he knelt to place it over his father's body. He remained there, lost in thought. Over on the lawn, trapped against a large rock, were papers. Frida picked them up. They were soggy; the uppermost sheets fell apart in her hands and the handwritten notes on the rest were illegible.

Lorcan joined her, the dark aura she'd seen in York surrounding him.

'I'm sorry. Father sent me to fetch his notes on your family ... If I'd returned sooner ...' His grief, rolling off him in a black cloud, threatened to overwhelm her. 'He wanted it to be a presentation. Years of his research. He was so excited.'

She stared at the dripping pages, all the information she needed and it was now just so much papier mâché. They turned back to stare at the body. She'd liked the old man straight away, she'd felt a connection which went deeper than she'd expected, someone who could understand her and who she was. Now she remained none the wiser. Her one source, lost forever.

'I should have been better prepared.'

Lorcan spoke the words as more of a plea than a regret, as though he wanted a second chance to change things. He kept clenching and unclenching his fists.

'I don't know what else you could have done, Lorcan. Who would have expected an attack like that? And the way you fought those things.'

He shook his head. 'We'd only just started speaking again. He convinced me we had a battle we could fight together. That's why I came to find you.'

'Why didn't you get on?'

A long pause; she'd said it softly and wondered if he'd even heard her. He shook his head with sadness that meant his shoulders drooped even further, tears tumbled down his cheeks.

'He wasn't much of a father when I was young, lost in his books most of the time. When Mother died, he shut himself off. I was a kid turning into a man. He didn't like my friends, the things I did. Who I was. I went crazy for a while. I left home, joined the army. Became a mercenary. But eventually the blood, the savagery, the horror, it gets to you. I came home and found him engaged in a different kind of battle.'

It explained his dark aura to some extent, she'd seen it in others who'd witnessed so much brutality and bloodshed. The trouble was, all too frequently, that darkness could overwhelm them, turn them into different people. All it needed was a trigger.

He looked at her and the ghost of his smile reached his lips for a brief moment.

'We need to get you back to your people.'

Chapter 9

*'We had Humanity First; the fae had The Order of Freyja.
Both organisations wrought bloodshed and mayhem in
their attempts to reshape our world.'*
'Downing Street and the Fae' by Sir Rupert Hall, OBE.

Another horse-drawn coach with uniformed driver, the fae
equivalent of a taxi, arrived and took Frida back to the
hotel where the rest of the team were billeted. She
ignored the scenery this time. Her mind churned. She
relived the attack, the sensation of being so close to
drowning suddenly felt real and frightening. The sight of
Lorcan's grief remained vivid. His energy, his smile, robbed
by the loss of his father. Worst of all, her anger simmered
with the knowledge she was no closer to discovering her
family's secrets.

The expedition team's hotel was a large, timber-
framed building, like something out of the Middle Ages,
though inside there was greater luxury than anything she'd
found at home. Layla met her and immediately wanted to
know where she'd been. She explained, her story
gathering a bigger audience which included Olsen and
Agnes by the time she'd finished.

'Do you think you or the old man were the target of
the attack?'

Agnes displayed her usual curiosity, none of her
empathy, as she fired questions Frida really didn't want to
answer. Being back amongst human beings didn't feel
right; she couldn't relax or be herself, always pretending to
be someone else. Her brief time with Yaalon Dubh had felt

so different, so relaxing. Like home. Perhaps she was more fae than she realised.

She laid on the bed in the room she was to share with Agnes and stared at the ceiling, imagining what might have been in the notes Yaalon had made for her. It left her with an even greater sense of frustration.

The evening meal changed little. She finished her food quickly and hurried outside, into the balmy night air. Jonas found her and offered what comfort he could. He sat on the floor next to her chair so they were both at eye level; it was typical of the sensitive nature he displayed toward her these days.

'I spent the afternoon reconnoitring the city. We're in the fae capital, Ainmire. It's little more than a large town, compared to what we'd call a city. It's built around its university, and the whole place is given over to all things academic. Your friend was a professor there, wasn't he?'

She wandered how he knew, since she hadn't told anyone about the Dubhs.

'I get the impression there's a great deal of academic rivalry, not surprising as it's such a prestigious institution. But something isn't right here. There's so much tension, but I can't find the cause. It's like people are afraid but trying hard to pretend they're not.'

'How do you know all this, Jonas?'

His smile was full of mischief. 'I might be big but you'd be surprised how easily I can blend into my environment. It's part of being a spy.'

He hadn't called himself that before, though he'd implied it the night they'd met. His scrutiny sounded a lot more extensive than sitting on park benches pretending to read newspapers. Frida hadn't come across many spies before, as far as she knew.

'What are they afraid of? Us?'

'No. I travelled the length and breadth of this town. People whisper a lot. They look furtive when they talk. That's never a good sign.'

'The war will have changed them, like it did us. I think the whole of their society is in conflict. They have new priorities and see different ways to achieve them.'

'Is that what your friend told you?'

The casual way he asked told her she'd said too much.

'Just thinking aloud.'

He nodded and smiled at her. 'You didn't say why you were with these people. They'd whisked you away before I came through the portal. They were waiting for you then?'

He might have been giving her his big, friendly giant routine but his expression was anything but gentle. The advice she'd had from Lorcan and his father sounded alarm bells in Frida's head. She couldn't trust anyone. By his own admission, he was a government spy. That meant he might be an ally but only for as long as they were on the same side. In her brief stay with Lorcan and his father their welcome had made her question her loyalties. She realised Jonas was waiting for an answer.

'The professor was a family friend, apparently. He'd known my grandmother briefly and wanted to introduce himself.'

According to her mother, the best lies were those which contained some truth.

'I see. And the muscular man who met you in the park?'

'His son.'

'I'm surprised you weren't worried, going somewhere on your own, in a foreign place, with a man you didn't know.'

'I can look after myself, Jonas.' Her reply sounded harsher than she'd intended but his questions were starting to irritate her. 'Despite all the attacks, I'm still here.'

He chuckled and patted her hand fondly. She drew it away but he didn't notice.

'I know. I'm sorry. Only I don't know what my bosses would do if anything happened to you, especially now we're on fae soil. We can't be certain of their motives, remember.'

'You seem to have forgotten something, Jonas.' He frowned, tipped his head to one side. 'I'm part fae. I have connections on this side of the portal too.'

Jonas nodded and smiled again. 'Yeah. I had forgotten. Thanks for reminding me.'

He stood up, still smiling. 'Better get some sleep. Big day tomorrow. We set out for a new world. One big step for mankind and all that.'

She didn't understand the reference but casually wished him good night. After all his kindness in the last few days, she didn't like to think of Jonas as being suspicious, or worse. He, and Lorcan for that matter, kept telling her not to trust anyone. It led to her feeling perpetually paranoid and she hated it.

Sometime survival meant being deceitful. There was no avoiding the reality, she was in the middle of a conflict where allies and enemies all looked alike. Jonas' comment about not trusting the fae had angered her, more than it should. It looked like the fae side of Frida Ranson was making itself known, and she liked it better than the human one.

Her bedroom was empty – no doubt Agnes was having fun with Billy – and the last thing she wanted was another interrogation. After a hot bath, Frida crawled into bed and, despite everything, sleep found her immediately.

Something jolted Frida out of a dream where something dark and insidious tried to suffocate her. She heaved in a huge lungful of air before realising she was awake and breathing normally. On the opposite side of the room Agnes slept soundly; Frida envied her. Dreams had turned a lot more vivid lately, full of unseen threats, often so real she couldn't tell if she was awake or asleep. Tonight, there'd been one more ingredient, little more than a whisper, her dreams containing a voice she strained to hear.

When she heard a soft thump downstairs, she had to check if she was still dreaming. She got up, trod silently out of her room and onto the landing, vivid memories of another night in a different hotel uppermost in her mind. At least this time she was on the first floor, easier to reach the ground floor if things went badly. She'd already reached the conclusion they would – that was fast becoming normal these days.

Another soft thud.

She extended her senses into the darkness below. Instantly she picked up the urgency, the determination, the cruel intent. This time she didn't hesitate in taking action. She dashed back into her room, pulled on clothes and woke Agnes who tiredly told her to go back to sleep. She yanked her sheets off the bed and ran out the room. Downstairs, in the darkness, she sensed movement, whispered commands. The mind giving them was not human, even she could tell that.

'We're being attacked!' she yelled at the top of her voice and repeated it as she took two steps at a time. At the bottom of the staircase, she collided with a figure, dressed in black from head to foot.

The force of the collision knocked her assailant into the opposite wall. She lashed out with a foot and hit something that caused her victim to double up and groan. Turning her head in time to see a pair of wild eyes rushing toward her, she raised a hand and emitted a bright bolt of energy. It felled her would-be attacker and, in its brief burst of illumination, showed more of them heading in her direction. More blasts soon had the corridor littered with bodies and the pungent smell of seared flesh.

From upstairs she heard Olsen bark commands, then members of the unit appeared, in varying stages of undress. She flicked a light switch, nothing happened.

The ground floor of the hotel had narrow corridors that made it more like a maze. In the dark, it only added to her confusion. Olsen pushed past her, gun in hand. He registered the collection of bodies but ignored them, just as he did Frida. He sprinted toward the main entrance, his unit roaring their fury behind him. Except that wasn't where the attackers had come from. The assailants Frida had felled came from another direction.

Layla, now at her side and panic in his whispered voice, took her hand and held it. 'What's happening?'

'Come with me.'

Agnes' frightened voice floated through the darkness. 'Don't leave me behind!'

Both women screamed as gunshots from the hotel reception echoed along the narrow corridors. Olsen's barked commands and panicked shouts and grunts of hand-to-hand combat quickly followed.

'It sounds like they're trying to get in the front entrance,' Layla whispered.

Desperate to avoid the fighting, the three women set off in the opposite direction. They arrived in the hotel kitchen, empty now but with a door to the outside which had been forced open. An explosion made Layla and Agnes scream a second time.

'We need to get out of here!' Agnes called as she ran to the door.

'Wait!' Frida called out. 'We don't know what's out there!'

Agnes froze, stark shafts of moonlight illuminating her fear. Layla joined her, took her hand and told her Frida wouldn't let anyone hurt them. Quietly, carefully, too frightened to breathe, they crept toward the door. A huge, distinctive shape appeared in front of them, silhouetted by the moonlight.

'Jonas?' Frida gasped.

Up close she could see he had blood on his face.

'Is it just the three of you?' he replied and glanced over his shoulder into the darkness. 'I think it's safe now. A few ran past me, but I assume you got them, Frida?'

She perused his face to find answers to the urgent questions forming in her head. How had he known about the attack before she'd shouted her warning? He had to have been outside already. Why? The sound of battle shunted the questions to one side. As Jonas shepherded Layla and Agnes into the night, she accessed his mind, assuming he wouldn't sense what she was doing. Except she couldn't; it was too closed down, just a sense of anxiety and determination that was visible on his face anyway. That only raised more questions.

Uncertain what to do next, she followed Jonas and the two women into a cobbled courtyard. Stacked against its walls were crates, boxes and a couple of barrels, and beyond the courtyard she could just make out a garden. That was where Jonas led them next, a space full of vegetables, bushes and fruit trees, provisions for the hotel's kitchen. A path led round a corner of the hotel, presumably to the main street and the front of the building where the conflict continued.

'We need to get you to safety,' Jonas hissed at Frida. 'This is a full-scale attack. They mean business.'

While Agnes and Layla looked at each other in panic, Frida's unanswered questions reasserted themselves.

'How do you know all this, Jonas?'

'I told you what I've been doing since I arrived. All this happened faster than I'd anticipated. The failed attempt on your life made them speed up their plans.'

'Who is this 'they' you're talking about?'

Jonas glanced into the darkness, then up into the sky, it prompted a frown. 'The Order of Freyja, of course.'

His reaction drew Frida's attention to the night sky at the same moment as her skin sizzled with its usual early warning signal.

A whooshing noise reached them, followed by the sound of something flapping, like a large tent in a high wind. Flame erupted out of the darkness, a long column of fiery fury, striking the hotel roof. Memories of the war instantly told Frida what waited above her. She'd seen dragons strafe whole streets and leave them as blackened bits of carbon, the people in them no more than ash. She joined Agnes and Layla in their screams and the need to run as far as possible into the night.

Chapter 10

'Vaettir: a mythical race of creatures beloved of so many children's bedtime stories.'

'Extract from a Fae dictionary'

Flames leapt into the night as the entire building exploded, illuminating the underside of the creature responsible for its havoc. It corkscrewed as it turned to wreak more fiery destruction, twisting its long and sinuous body like a huge snake rather than a dragon. It looked nothing like the monsters Frida had seen during the war; they were large and cumbersome with wings wide enough to blot out the sun.

It hardly mattered. Its capacity for destruction was the same. A thin streak of flame, no wider than its body but with white-hot intensity, blasted the roof and charred its ancient wooden beams in seconds. Out of the kitchen door, through which the four had escaped only moments before, flames belched as something inside exploded.

Jonas and the three women cowered in the darkness, partly hidden by a string of apple trees. For Frida it wasn't just the destructive horror, it was the shock of witnessing it in the fae realm. Someone had sanctioned this attack; they didn't care about the fae who lived and worked in the hotel either. The same question kept repeating itself in her head, who could do such an awful thing?

Gunfire rattled over the noise of a building rapidly giving itself up to obliteration.

'They need my help,' Frida called out.

The need to expel her anger forced her out of hiding. She needed to find the fight and join in, and the sneaky bastards in black made perfect targets to satisfy her need for vengeance.

From out of the darkness Jonas was suddenly at her side. He grabbed her wrist and glared at her. 'You need to stay here.'

She blinked. He held her eyes with the steely resolve of someone who was not going to give way easily, and his command only angered her further. She was about to snatch her hand away but stopped herself as she glared back at him. His anxiety billowed over her with enough force to convince her he wasn't being protective. He didn't see her as a woman who couldn't look after herself. He was worried about something else.

Frida took a deep breath. He spotted it and smiled, reminding her that Jonas Klein was a kind and sensitive man. Their relationship had deepened in the past week, their abnormalities giving them a common bond, and he'd quickly become a friend. Except now, his mysterious behaviour challenged that connection and suspicion eroded her trust. His knowledge of the attack might be the result of being a good spy but it could also be a careless mistake by someone working for her enemy. That possibility prompted another question. What if Jonas had been involved in the bombing of the hotel in York? That was impossible, she told herself. Jonas hadn't arrived in York at that point. Except he might have been hiding. Yaalon Dubh's warning was making her paranoid.

'Why?'

He maintained his unflinching gaze. 'They're here for you, Frida. This is a distraction. They want to capture you. They failed earlier, and they won't allow that to happen again.'

Layla and Agnes, close enough to hear the warning, shrank against an apple tree and peered into the blackness surrounding them.

'It makes sense,' Agnes hissed and instantly cowered against the tree trunk as though she expected something to launch at her out of the velvet night.

Jonas released Frida's wrist, as though the other woman's agreement offered enough conviction. His gaze still didn't waver. 'They destroyed the hotel deliberately, forcing you into the open.' He pointed up into the sky, where the dragon flapped its sinewy wings into the night. 'It makes us vulnerable.'

Everything he said made sense. It left her feeling silly and impulsive. She glanced at the other two women, who nodded panicked agreement. The realisation shocked her. These people, whoever they were, chose to destroy buildings and kill their own race in order to capture or kill her. Yaalon's sodden notes might have explained the reason, which prompted the possibility she'd been the target of the attack. Lorcan and his father had believed differently but everything happening now was too much of a coincidence.

'All right,' Frida said. 'But I refuse to do nothing while the rest of the expedition are getting slaughtered. I'm going to find a position where I can act as a sniper. You two stay hidden where you are.'

Agnes and Layla nodded energetically. Jonas' agreement came after a moment's thought, and he gave her a terse nod of the head as they set off. They'd taken only a few steps when Frida's skin tingled and her brain fizzed. She stopped, dead. Jonas, instantly alert, reached for the impressive looking knife he kept in his belt.

'There's something out here.' she whispered.

'Can you sense where?'

'It's …' Once again, she wished her abilities were sharper, better honed. 'It's moving. Fast.'

Frida snapped her head toward the courtyard from where they'd escaped the hotel, the one place still illuminated by the flames. Nothing. Something on the edge of her consciousness approached from the alleyway to the road. Her attention shifted to the orchard. Nothing. Realisation hit her, hard.

'It's not moving fast. There are several of them. At least three.'

Jonas positioned himself with his back pressed against Frida's. 'Remember, it's you they want. I'm not important. Don't let them get you.'

She wanted to tell him that he did matter, that she wouldn't abandon him. Screams from Agnes and Layla shifted her attention back to the orchard. She started to move but Jonas grabbed her arm.

'Don't. They're drawing you into the darkness. You can't see to fight.'

'But—' Her plea abruptly halted as Jonas gasped and stared at his feet.

The ground had come alive. With only the hotel fire to illuminate them, it looked like the earth writhed around his feet. Seconds later and a tickling around her ankles made Frida look at her own feet. Whatever squirmed around them, now reached up her legs. She tried to kick it away.

'What's happening?' she called out.

Jonas, yanking at the stuff with both hands now, cursed. 'It's the grass. Or tree roots. But it moves so fast. And it's so strong.'

Faster than he could tear the strands of plant-life away, tendrils wound around his legs. With a grunt of surprise, they snagged his wrist as well, trapping him as he leaned over to free himself.

'Frida! Help!'

Layla's voice was tight with panic. A quick glance showed both women strapped to the trunk of the apple tree by its branches. Lengths of vine snaked around the throats of both women as Layla's cry for help ended in choking noises. Agnes looked like she had been mummified by elasticated foliage. With another loud grunt her attention shifted back to Jonas. Unable to maintain his stooped position, he tumbled to the ground. The instant his body hit the earth, it burst into life around him, covering him in twitching, twisting vegetation that rapidly developed the thickness and strength of rope.

The distraction cost Frida her own freedom. More of the rampant foliage climbed up her legs, tying them together. It had all happened so quickly, the shock so great, any attempt to prevent the inevitable had evaded her. Until now.

With fingers splayed, she blasted the earth around her feet, charring the foliage and sending divots of grass flying. Out of the fresh earth sprang lengths of greenery she recognised only from her months of pulling weeds out of farm soil. She'd been told then how the network of some species of weed could stretch across an entire field. More and more of the thickening rope wrapped itself around her. Panic made her break out in a cold sweat at the thought of being strangled by bloody plants. The urgent need to find a way of saving herself evaded her and that made her panic even more. Agnes and Layla were completely hidden now, and Jonas had vanished into a mound of undergrowth which shifted only very slightly as he tried to fight the inevitable.

'I don't know where you are, you bastards! But let's see if this finds you!'

Despite her rising panic, Frida tried to focus her mind on the presences she'd sensed earlier. Splaying her fingers as wide as they would go, to achieve the broadest beam of energy she could emit, she released her fury with a roar toward the alleyway and its dark recesses. The indiscriminate destruction made her gasp as her beam of energy struck everything it touched, flinging objects into the air where fire could obliterate it.

A deafening howl rose over the noise of the explosion. Among the objects falling back to earth, a body flopped onto the grass like a dead fish. It quivered for a second before lying still, arms and legs sprawled in unnatural positions.

A howl rose a couple of octaves to become a scream, a sound of grief rather than horror or fear. The foliage wrapped itself around her body with urgency now, it reached her neck and stretched to trap her arms. It left her no choice but to flail her arms wildly, emitting blasts of energy in any direction. As she twisted back and forth Frida noticed Jonas' mound had stopped moving. She called out to him just as his knife's blade repeatedly stabbed holes in the blanket of foliage stretched over him.

His huge hand reached out and ripped the hole open even further. Relief coursed through her body, fuelling her confidence.

'I've killed one of you. Stop now, otherwise I'll do it again.'

The tendrils wrapped around her neck tightened with frightening speed. The intention was clear. Fury like she'd never known before filled her body. It raged inside her, desperate for release. She gave into it by flinging her arms out toward the hotel courtyard where she'd sensed another presence.

It was too late. Strangled by thin strands of foliage which stretched and tightened, darkness encroached on her vision. She gasped for air that wasn't there. The world around her shrank, and all she could do was to focus on the need to breathe. The last of her strength ebbed, and the only thing keeping her upright were the strands of foliage which wound around her. They'd succeeded. She'd lost. Her head swam.

Suddenly, she could breathe again. The botanical coils wrapped around her relaxed.

As her vision returned, the destruction she'd created in what had once been the hotel courtyard lay before her. The fire offered enough of a glow to light up another broken body, stretched over an upturned barrel.

Jonas was at her side, hacking away at the dying strands that shrivelled at her feet. That was not the case for Agnes and Layla. Some of the foliage had even started to display small flowers. Frida reached out with her senses.

'There's another one of these things somewhere.'

Jonas sprinted over to the two women, to hack with his knife, only for his work to be replaced by twice as many strands. Frida joined him, desperate to save her friends from a death she'd imagined for herself only seconds before. The urgency, the fear and the need for her anger to find a target raged within her. Their assailant was close. Its terror provided the tell-tale location. This thing was not just scared but filled with regret. Its grief at losing its comrades was almost palpable, the overwhelming sense of loss was broader than that. Her limited capacity to read another mind didn't matter here; it was impossible to miss the assortment of negative emotions this creature projected. Whatever it was, it was in crisis.

She felt ridiculous talking to a tree in the orchard, but she was sure the third presence was somewhere close by.

'Don't hurt my friends anymore. Please. I know you're frightened. I can sense it. I'm sorry your friends are dead too. I didn't want to do that, but I had no choice. I'm sensing something similar with you. I don't think you are a killer. Let my friends live and I promise not to harm you.'

Jonas' attempt to rip and tear away the foliage around the two women suddenly made him gasp. He yanked away small branches and the hole remained, growing until Layla's face could be seen.

'It's working,' he said and kept stripping away the endless number of branches.

'Thank you!' Frida said to the darkness, trying hard to maintain some warmth in her words. She wanted to cry at the prospect of them all surviving the attack.

'Do you guarantee my safety?'

The voice in her head startled her. It had been many years since she'd communicated telepathically, once a source of fun with her mother.

'Yes.'

Frida remembered how this form of interaction went beyond mere words. It carried emotions with it. Her mental affirmation would convey her intentions far more convincingly. Seconds later the foliage surrounding the two men wilted and shrivelled.

Thank you, Frida said in her head. She conveyed a high degree of gratitude but attached a sense of relief and recognition of her assailant's courage. 'Why don't you show yourself? I feel rather foolish talking to a tree.'

A creature stepped out from behind a tree a short distance away. It was female but a significantly younger version of the others who had attacked Frida. Another billowing gossamer gown confirmed the similarity but its facial features were different. Skin resembled the bark of a silver birch tree, bone white and paper thin, dry and flaky in places. Its skull lacked hair apart from wisps of green fuzz. There was no nose, it was like the disir, flaps of cartilage moved slightly as it breathed. But it was the eyes that drew Frida's attention. They were wider than a human's, less sclera and with a bright green iris. Even then, that wasn't what mattered. They held enormous sadness.

As Jonas freed the two women and laid them on the ground, rubbing their wrists to increase blood flow, Frida made certain she gave the creature all of her attention. These things had consistently attacked her but now she had one willing to trust her. She had to build that trust to find out more about her enemy's intentions.

'What are you?' Frida asked.

'Skogvættir.'

'Like those who manipulate water and air, you do the same with plants.'

The creature leaned its head to one side, as though considering the thought. 'We are part of nature.'

Frida nodded. 'Who sent you?'

Fear surged, escalating to epic proportions within seconds, and the skogvættir's eyes searched the darkness. Frida beamed another reassuring smile and telepathically broadcast the need to trust her.

'I won't let anyone hurt you. In fact, if you answer my question, you can leave.'

The young skogvættir eyed her suspiciously before tipping its head to one side again. Despite what it had done, she felt sorry for it. She sensed its surprise at her promise, and it offered some hope.

'I don't think you wanted to attack us, did you?'

There was the mental equivalent of a shake of the head and a wave of regret. 'We had no choice.'

The answer was honest, the wave of regret and grief impossible to ignore as it crashed over Frida, leaving her shaken. It removed the last vestiges of distrust and dislike for the young skogvættir. In its place grew an awareness that they were both young and being manipulated by others. Frida found herself communicating that idea, reinforcing the message with the anger and resentment she felt about her own situation.

'Tell me who is making us suffer like this, because I am going to stop them.'

The force of her declaration surprised her. It grew out of Yaalon Dubh's death and the rawness it brought. Along with it came an appreciation of the helplessness this female experienced. Frida knew all about that. She'd spent her life unable to avoid the insults and the scorn. Even now she had no choice but to tolerate Olsen's bullying because she was powerless to stop it. Almost unintentionally, she projected those feelings and it had the effect she wanted; the skogvættir's fear eased and curiosity took its place.

'But I need your help. Please.'

Frida allowed the gentle probing of her mind, proving her promise was genuine. It gave her chance to check on the progress of Agnes and Layla, who were now sat up and watching the exchange in confusion. They were going to be a problem if they couldn't appreciate the kind of bond she was forging with this creature. The skogvættir's mind cleared to provide her answer, and Frida smiled her reassurance again.

'The man. The important man. The Order.'

The skogvættir's mind might have cleared but its ability to understand the night's events was something else. She got a sense of the awe and fear for The Order and the man who led it; he represented something terrible, shocking.

'The Order of Freyja?'

Another telepathic head nod followed by a lot of trepidation.

'They want to capture me?'

And a third.

'Why?'

The skogvættir wasn't clear about that. Frida represented danger. It took a moment of careful questioning to find out if she posed a threat as an

123

individual or if she was part of something bigger. Yaalon Dubh's assessment was that the fae distrusted the human race, perhaps they saw her as its representative for some reason. The answer was definitive. The Order believed she posed a threat to everyone.

'Everyone?' Frida couldn't understand how that was possible.

'They fear what you will become.'

The skogvættir's eyes peered over her shoulder as the others moved closer, wary of it still. She explained everything to them.

'How could you pose such a threat to everyone?' Layla asked, her voice hoarse and little more than a whisper. Agnes eyed the creature with undisguised hostility.

'Where are they?' Jonas asked.

Frida repeated the question in her head. 'Where is The Order?'

The answer came as a finger pointed into the night, beyond the burning hotel. Gunfire had ceased. Whoever was behind the attack knew it had failed.

'Will you take us there?'

The poor skogvættir looked petrified at the possibility.

'Only to show us where they are, so I can stop them. Once you've done that, you'd be free to go. Like I promised.'

That brought objections from the others but Frida waved them away. The young skogvættir's mind filled with the same level of grief and loss as before. Tears welled up and tumbled down the white flesh on its face.

'I have nowhere to go. My sisters and I ...'

She couldn't continue as overwhelming sorrow almost incapacitated her. With fractured and ragged thoughts, the skogvættir could only communicate its hatred of The Man and his Order, for his wickedness especially. What form it took wasn't clear but Frida gained an impression these creatures were slaves, subjugated into being assassins. The skogvættir's mind collapsed into a muddle of grief for the loss of her sisters and fear of The Order's retribution. Their telepathic link opened a channel of communication which operated on a deeply emotional level to convey the misery of the skogvættir's life. When they finished Frida hugged the female, she stiffened in surprise initially before realising the purpose of the gesture. It helped calm her, and her appreciation wafted through her mind like a warm breeze.

'I will show you.'

The skogvættir offered a wan smile as she transmitted an image. A large and intimidating building filled with dark rooms and all kinds of horrors. Frida recognised its outline. Jonas had pointed it out to her when they arrived.

'The university?'

The word meant nothing to the female but something Lorcan had said suddenly drifted up from the recesses of her memory. He'd talked about how his father believed something was happening there, placing doubt on who had been the target when she and Yaalon had been attacked.

The others watched with increasing belligerence.

'Why were you hugging that thing, Frida? It tried to kill us,' Agnes snapped.

Layla remained silent but her scepticism was evident in her frown.

Frida explained, doing her best to capture some of the emotional impact she'd felt. The Order of Freyja had to be an evil organisation if it treated people so badly, notwithstanding their wanton destruction of the hotel and the murders they'd committed. By the time she'd finished, the need for punishment drove urgency into her voice. These people, whoever they were, needed to be stopped.

'We're going to visit the university,' she said, before the others could say anything.

Agnes and Layla shared sceptical looks, reminding her that Major Olsen would be furious. That was the icing on the cake for Frida. The thought of irritating that bastard was an unexpected bonus.

'I'm coming with you,' Jonas said.

He matched her determination; he wasn't negotiating, he was going with her. Frida shrugged, took the skogvættir's hand and marched off toward the remains of the hotel.

Chapter 11

*'Ainmire is the capital of the fae realm. Its status above all
the other cities lies in its status as the home of the realm's
most prestigious university.'*

'Gazetteer of the Fae Realm'

Layla had been right about one thing, Olsen turned
apoplectic.

It was later, a good half an hour or so after his
tirade and dire warnings, when Frida experienced the first
stages of regret. As they approached the university's huge
monolithic structure, the young skogvættir grew
increasingly frightened and unpredictable. It needed
constant reassurance to stop her running away, not a skill
Frida thought she possessed. Her name was Scholr. At
least that was how Frida chose to pronounce it, after
realising she wasn't clearing her throat.

Jonas was no use either. He steadfastly maintained
they were making a big mistake, sounding too much like
Olsen, though his reservations lacked the expletives. They
were strangers in a strange land, enemies until recently,
amidst locals who couldn't be relied upon. Olsen had gone
further, claiming the fae would relish the chance to kill
humans, after torturing them most likely. Jonas, like Olsen,
didn't trust the skogvættir either. She'd tried to kill them
and, as the only survivor, would do and say anything to
avoid the same fate.

Frida had done her best to convey the horrors in
the girl's mind, the undefined wickedness committed by

the Order but she'd failed. Words couldn't capture the emotional trauma of sharing another woman's vulnerabilities. According to Jonas, their shared experiences meant Frida wasn't being objective. It made her gullible and risked capture. As for Frida, these were the reactions of people without the ability to connect with another mind, to experience suffering beyond the use of mere words. They were also the responses of men. Frida had experienced similar kinds of vulnerability and fear, but Olsen and Jonas would never grasp what that was like. Convincing them was doomed to failure.

Sharing those feelings with the young woman was one thing, dealing with the behaviour they triggered proved difficult. She relieved some of the girl's skittishness by promising they were only going to reconnoitre the university, find out precisely where the Order was based. They'd report them to the relevant authorities, let them deal with things. There wouldn't be any danger, they were just going to have a look. The closer they got, the more the skogvættir's anxiety and her readiness to flee increased.

In desperation, Frida resorted to distraction, enquiring about things she saw on the route and remarking on the beauty of certain places. The city reminded her of pictures in history books of her own world. Each street was little more than a cart track with delightful cottages on either side, their gardens filled with flowers producing heady scents in the night air. It was the opposite of everything she'd ever known, growing up in a world at war with nature. Here they lived in harmony with it and that felt right. She'd experienced such comfort and relaxation in Yaalon Dubh's garden, it had felt like home. It provoked a pang of sadness. She could have grown up in this world, if the war hadn't intervened.

The only anachronism in this idyll was the university building. It looked like a giant had dropped a huge stone cube into the centre of the city. Where spidery lines of pink and purple hinted at the arrival of the dawn, it dominated the skyline. The building made a statement which contradicted everything else about this world. It gave the fae capital its status with deliberate intimidation.

As she strode along a wider boulevard which led directly to their destination, her uncertainty triggered a memory of a similar occasion as a child. She recalled a training session, their last, her mother would die two months later. She'd mastered the manipulation of her energy, impressing her mother with her speed in acquiring the range of techniques. They'd moved into exploring ways in which the manipulation could be adapted and methods to vary its use. After all, as her mother always maintained, she was more than just someone who could blast things from her fingertips.

As was common for the training session, they'd moved to a meadow just outside their village, secluded enough to hide their activities from prying eyes. They stood in front of a stone slab, a remnant of previous training sessions, and on it was an egg.

'That's your breakfast.'

Frida looked at her mother in confusion. The egg didn't need to be raw, she was told. For the eight-year-old girl, the solution evaded her. No matter how much she tried to reduce the intensity of energy she released from the fingertips, the result would be the same, the egg would explode. Hunger drove her to be more creative. The answer lay not in cooking the egg but to apply energy to heat the stone slab. The incident led her to think about how she could use energy to do more than blast things. It took most of the morning for Frida to sustain the small but consistent amount of energy required to heat the remnants of the stone slab. By that time one egg wasn't enough, but thankfully her mother had brought bacon too. Breakfast had never tasted so good.

The lesson taught her how subtlety, never a quality Frida displayed, could sometimes offer better solutions.

The memory acted as a bitter reminder of the loneliness that was to follow. As a little girl, her mother's skills were a form of magic while she was a blunt weapon, lacking in finesse and limited in capability.

The memory left her feeling bitter and resentful but it went further, sapping her fragile self-confidence. She remembered how her mother would accuse her of being headstrong, others would level the same criticism later. Jonas too. As it so often had in the past, the criticism provoked her into carrying out her plan, for no other reason than to prove everyone wrong. She wanted vengeance against whoever had killed Yaalon Dubh. She held the Order responsible for the hotel bombing which meant they'd killed Elsa too. How could the others not see what was so obvious?

As they approached the university, one issue nagged at her resolve, eroding it with every step. She hadn't considered the danger. She had Jonas and her limited abilities to keep her safe. She looked over at the big man at her side, his face set in a mask of determination. Even though he'd told her she was making a mistake and failed to think things through, he hadn't hesitated in joining her. He hadn't used the word 'protection' – he knew her well enough to avoid the consequences – but his motive was clear enough. He glanced at her. She smiled her appreciation and he smiled back, shook his head and sighed. It made her feel a little better, until they arrived at the base of the stone cube. By that point the skogvættir girl wasn't the only frightened one.

The first rays of dawn found black-garbed guards patrolling the well-kept grounds. Frida recognised them instantly, confirming they were in the right place. She'd encountered some of their comrades in the hotel. Scholr instantly flung herself against a wall to merge with the shadows, only the sclera of her terror-filled eyes visible.

'Hyroa!' she hissed.

'This is the right place,' Frida whispered to Jonas, to prove she'd been correct and to convince herself her instincts were spot on. The big man nodded.

'It doesn't prove anything,' he said. 'If you want anyone to believe what you've been told, you need evidence.'

Frida had reached the same conclusion; reconnoitring the place wasn't enough. She turned to the skogvættir.

'We're going to look inside. You can leave if you want. That was my promise.'

It earned a sad smile. 'I have nowhere to go. I will show you the way.'

A cellar doorway, hidden by a large flowering shrub, offered a way in she was told. It would be unlocked, an entry point for the guards at the change of shift. They waited until the patrol turned a corner and sprinted across a lawn to the door. Sure enough, it opened easily.

They found themselves in a narrow corridor, lit by amber-coloured crystals built into small alcoves in the wall. It led to a spiral staircase, its stone sides smooth with the passage of time and bodies, from there, on to another corridor. They ran, Frida doing her best to keep her senses open for attack but her anxiety levels, ratcheting up with every twist and turn, made that difficult. Scholr led the way, with a fierce determination which hadn't existed in the streets and didn't help Frida's anxiety levels either.

They arrived in a darker, narrow corridor, filled with the pungent smells of filthy bodies, stale air and raw sewage.

'Where have you brought us?' Jonas grabbed the skogvættir and lifted her painfully thin form off the ground, her bare feet dangled beneath the frayed edges of her dress. He'd bunched the fabric into his fist, almost throttling her. She looked down at him, terrified.

Frida placed a calming hand on the big man's bicep. 'Let her explain.'

He lowered the girl to the ground.

She didn't take her eyes off him as she spoke. 'Please help me. Please. My brothers and sisters are prisoners. I can free them.' She pointed along the corridor to a bunch of ancient-looking keys hanging from a hook on the wall.

'Why would a university have prison cells?' Frida asked.

'It wasn't always as you see it now,' Scholr babbled. 'Long ago this was a castle, a palace of a king. Above this level things are different, for some people.'

'We have to free them.'

Frida expected Jonas to argue with her. Instead he simply nodded. She saw the same revulsion which he would have seen on her face. It wasn't just from the acrid smell either. Her senses warned her worse awaited them. They couldn't ignore Scholr's pleas.

With the keys located, the female skogvættir scurried along the corridor, unlocking each door and flinging it open. More of the supposedly mythical disir emerged from the cells. A pathetic and ragged collection compared to the ones Frida had encountered before. These were prisoners who'd been subjected to years of neglect, forced to live in their own mess, in a world of darkness and solitude. Most of them were female, though so emaciated it was hard to tell. Nearly all of them were ancient too. A couple of old men, wizened, bald, and stooped with arthritis, staggered out of one cell, clutching the door with skeletal hands. The group looked astonished to be free as they met in the corridor, shaking heads in disbelief before hugging each other like long-lost friends. They made no attempt to escape. The young skogvættir spoke with hushed urgency in her guttural language. As one, they all turned to Frida and Jonas, blank faced and lost.

Scholr led the way back to the staircase, her frail and decrepit entourage staggering along behind her. If they were going to escape, they'd need a lot of luck. As they clambered up the stairs, a younger figure with pale skin and hair the colour of green grass remained behind. Scholr smiled at him. They shared an urgent conversation which ended with them turning to Frida, their pleas written across their faces.

'Naschr wants to free his lindwyrm too,' she said.

'His what?' Frida asked.

The girl and boy exchanged a look, and the boy gave a single nod.

'It attacked you tonight, set fire to the building.'

'The dragon?' Jonas snapped.

The girl shook her head and wrung her hands. Though it was obvious the boy couldn't speak their language, he saw the girl's reaction and Jonas' anger. Tears formed in his eyes. Scholr squeezed his hand, eager to provide explanations on his behalf.

'Not a dragon. Lindwyrm. Please. Like all of us, Naschr had no choice. Please. You do not understand what we ...'

'Where is it?' Frida asked quietly.

'This way,' the girl said, brightening up instantly.

They followed the boy to the end of the dark corridor and a final door which he threw open. It drew a deep-throated rumbling that made the hairs on the back of Frida's neck stand up. The boy hurried into the darkened room, making noises that might have been calming reassurances. The girl prevented them from entering with a look of caution, so they waited at the door.

Rusty cogs turned, grinding out their complaint, as the roof opened, allowing pink shafts of dawn to illuminate the creature that watched the boy's progress. It waited, hunched in a space that was too small for such a beast, knowing what was about to happen, shifting its attention from the roof to the boy and back again. With the roof retracted, the boy hurried over to the animal. It lowered its snake-like head, emitted a deep purr, and offered him the same muzzle that had spat fire at them an hour earlier. The boy stroked it, speaking in the same affectionate voice and then stepped back.

The lindwyrm raised its long neck so its head drew level with the ceiling, sniffed the air, looked down at the boy and snorted before launching itself into the early morning sky. He hurried back to them, tear stains on his white flaking skin, and bowed in front of Frida and Jonas.

Scholr grinned as though she'd accomplished everything she needed. 'Now I will show you where to find the Order.'

They hurried back the way they'd come, up the staircase again but along different corridors that widened out with each corner and junction they navigated. The boy stayed with them, rather than attempting to join the others. It was obvious he had feelings for the girl. Other things weren't so apparent, such as why the university imprisoned creatures and mistreated them so badly; it contradicted the idyllic image of the world beyond its walls. Frida reprimanded herself. These weren't creatures, they were people. A race which the fae believed to be nothing more than myths and yet were locked away like dangerous prisoners. Yaalon's comment to his son, that people wouldn't believe what was happening in the university, started to make sense now. At least on a superficial level. It still wasn't clear what the Order of Freyja wanted or why they behaved in such despicable ways.

Another set of stairs brought them out onto a wide, carpeted corridor – they'd left the original parts of the castle and were in the university now. On the walls, Frida could make out dusty portraits of fae academics, including Yaalon Dubh, smiling back at her. The artist had captured the mischief in his eyes and the warmth of the smile he'd passed on to his son. She stopped and stared at it, suddenly tearful. The girl stood by her side and said nothing for a moment, her need to find the right words taking time.

135

'I'm sorry. My vatnavættir sisters had no choice. They torture us. We must obey.'

Jonas reminded them they needed to keep moving, or they risked being discovered. The two skogvættir immediately took the lead, staying close to the walls and the shadows they provided. The corridor led to a circular hallway with a grand staircase leading upwards, where a large stained-glass window allowed shafts of early morning sunlight to create rainbows of colour on the silver bannisters. Two more of the black-garbed security guards, Scholr called them hyroa, marched down the steps, chatting quietly. The four hid beneath the staircase as black boots stomped past their faces to continue their journey along a corridor toward the main entrance.

With the guards gone, they crossed over the hallway to a pair of large, ornately decorated doors. The boy paused and suddenly looked fearful. The girl translated for him.

'Naschr comes here for orders. He connects to animal minds. Like Lindwyrm. Powerful weapon. First order, to destroy homes. Next order, your hotel. Perhaps you can find what you need here?'

Frida smiled at the lad, though Jonas' face was a grim mask. She thanked them.

From the hallway the sound of voices startled them. The two hyroa were returning.

The boy opened the double doors quickly and they hurried into a bare passageway that led to another pair of doors. A transom window provided the only light, suggesting the courtyard had to be on the other side.

The boy threw open the doors, letting in the pink light of dawn. The courtyard was a garden, complete with water fountain, flowering shrubs and a colonnade on the opposite side. In the centre of the courtyard stood two dozen armed hyroa with stern and fierce expressions. In front of them, the grinning face of Professor Ruari Salann.

'Isn't this ironic? So many attempts to capture you and then you walk in and give yourself up.'

Chapter 12

'Vanaheim's mystery arises from the surprising lack of information which exists compared to the other Norse realms. The Prose Edda, the compilation of works from the 13th century writer, Snorri Sturluson, defines the other eight realms in detail. Of Vanaheim, it says nothing.'

'The Viking Realms' by Dr Layla Quinn.

The aging professor's cold eyes swivelled to take in the boy.

'Well done, Naschr.'

The kid shrunk under the man's gaze which shifted back to focus on Frida, emanating smugness. While his expression angered her, it also confirmed everything Jonas and Olsen had said; she had been headstrong. More hyroa arrived to surround the pair, cutting off any chance of escape. It didn't stop Frida from wanting to blast the smug bastard in front of her but she'd caused enough trouble for herself and Jonas. She allowed her wrists to be bound behind her back with thick rope, in the belief an opportunity would present itself at some point. The whole time, Salann wore the same sneering expression which she'd encountered in other men. His arrogance made him desperate to boast about his guile. With luck, he'd provide some of the answers she wanted, and a quick glance at Jonas told her he was of a similar mind.

One more thing confused her. Scholr's contempt and confusion showed she hadn't been part of the betrayal, her eyes never leaving the boy who refused to look in her direction. His mind hadn't been particularly shielded, so she should have picked up on his intentions. Why hadn't she? Even now, something didn't make sense about him. He looked contrite but his mind harboured an underlying current that hinted at determination. There wasn't time to discern anything more than that, since the professor had started his lecture.

'I knew if I provoked you enough, your foolishness would lead to your capture. I confess I didn't think you'd give yourself up like this. I was surprised when I heard you were on your way.'

'You are The Order of Freyja? I saved your life when you visited York. I stopped you from being suffocated.'

He chuckled softly.

'That was all a charade, Miss Ranson. An event I staged to discourage your authorities from going ahead with your foolish expedition.'

'But you were suffocating too. I saw you.'

'No, what you saw, was an exceptionally good performance. I impressed myself, I must confess. I had ingested a chemical which retained oxygen in my bloodstream to ensure I didn't lose consciousness and would survive long after the others had died.'

'You were prepared to let people die? To stop the expedition. Did you bomb the hotel in York too?'

'Yes, our first attempt to persuade your government to abandon the Vanaheim expedition.'

Her hatred for the man who'd murdered Elsa and dozens of soldiers threatened to overwhelm her. She calmed herself.

'Your Order is nothing more than a group of murderers.'

He curled his lip, and fixed Frida with the same look he'd used when they'd met in the crypt, except this time it didn't intimidate her.

'I have the privilege of being the current leader of The Order of Freyja. We were formed when this was a castle and served a different purpose. Over many generations, we have been steadfast in our duty. I am deeply honoured to be the man to thwart your benefactor's attempt to escape.' He smoothed what little hair remained on his head in a preening gesture, this man truly was in love with himself.

Frida shook her head in disbelief. 'I have no idea what you're talking about. What benefactor? What escape?'

He blinked and frowned, paused, mid-preen before snorting disdainfully. 'Don't insult my intelligence by playing the innocent, Miss Ranson.'

At last, it sounded like she might get some explanations.

'I have no idea what you're talking about.'

Salann looked at Jonas who shrugged.

'She's right. Sounds like you know more than we do.'

The professor's arrogance slipped slightly as he considered what Jonas had said.

'Are you suggesting you are unfamiliar with Njord?'

Frida and Jonas shared a look and shrugged simultaneously. Salann glanced around at his assembled

140

guards as though uncertain how to react. When he turned his attention back on them, the smugness had returned.

'It hardly matters. Someone manipulated you and brought you here for the same reason, but they have failed. You are now in my custody.' He gestured at the hyroa to escort the pair away.

Who was Njord? The name rang a bell in Frida's head but she couldn't remember why. This man had answers and she wasn't going to waste the opportunity.

'Wait. How can you be certain we're not being manipulated now? You said yourself you were surprised I walked in here, without an army. This could be a set-up.'

He halted the guards, puzzled again. All of his complacency had vanished, so had the grin. He was out of his depth and only now starting to realise it.

'Who is Njord? What is your Order trying to do?'

Salann pushed back his shoulders and raised his chin, some of his pride resurfacing.

'We prevent the greatest threat, to all nine realms, from escaping his prison. It is what we have always done. You, Miss Ranson, offer him a means to escape. To my knowledge, you are the last. Your death ensures he will always remain trapped.'

Suddenly the answers she wanted didn't sound so appealing. She could feel Jonas watching her, the two skogvættir too. Salann read their concern and his smugness returned.

'I don't understand,' Frida replied, the tone of her voice rising as genuine anxiety swept away every other emotion. Her fingers were already burning through her bonds; one good wrench and she'd be free.

'Frida?' said Jonas, his voice tinged with a nervous edge.

As she turned to him, the air around her wavered like a heat haze. The ground shuddered. Everyone stumbled. Some of the hyroa even fell to the ground, unleashing their crossbow bolts in the process. One of their number fell to the floor dead, a bolt lodged between shoulder blades. At the same time, water in the fountain developed a mind of its own, hurling itself in a solid column of water to topple a line of the hyroa like bowling pins. They writhed in its swirling currents, desperately trying to breathe.

Even before they'd got to their feet the ground rumbled once again, this time shaking with such force the garden itself looked like a wave breaking on a beach, rising up to fall at the farthest end of the courtyard, directly below the colonnade's columns. The structure collapsed into a mass of masonry and dust, crushing the men and women lined up beneath it.

Frida struggled to her feet and found the guards that had been behind her and Jonas were now dead. In their places were the people they'd released from the cells. The two old men leaned heavily against the doorframe, as though it was the only thing keeping them upright. Their bodies slumped as a wide chasm opened up where the colonnade had been and several of the hyroa tumbled into it, screaming.

Salannn staggered toward Naschr, eyes bulging.

'What have you done?'

The young man stood upright, smiled but said nothing. Before Jonas or Frida could react, the professor drew out a knife from his belt and sliced open Naschr's throat. Scholr rushed to the boy and kneeled, manoeuvring his head onto her lap, while babbling something in her language. Fat tears dripped onto his face.

Salann screamed at the surviving hyroa to loose their bolts at the decrepit figures manipulating their surroundings. Frida, furious at the boy's murder, drove all her strength into breaking the ropes around her wrist. They snapped without any difficulty. She blasted three hyroa aiming their crossbows at the old men, but it didn't matter. Simultaneously they clutched their chests, groaned and collapsed, dead by the time they hit the ground. The earthquake halted.

Frida spotted two more of the black-garbed figures aim at her. Her bolt of energy blasted them so far backward they landed in the gaping chasm in the courtyard. One of the old women had picked up Salann's knife. She hurriedly hacked at Jonas' bonds, succeeding in freeing him only to be killed by a bolt in the neck.

Bewildered, Salann stood amidst the chaos, surrounded by a dozen of his hyroa. A roar echoed around the courtyard, prompting all of them to look up into the salmon-pink sky. A black, sinuous shape swept over them. With its second pass, the animal's long neck craned downwards. It spotted the young skogvættir's corpse and emitted a deafening howl. Scholr screamed something in her language at the beast, pointing at Salann in the process.

The message couldn't have been clearer. The young woman gathered Frida and Jonas and drove them into the cavernous doorway, followed by her siblings. Salann bellowed for the guards to fire at the lindwyrm, but it was too late. Deadly columns of fire strafed the courtyard, incinerating everything, including the hyroa. It turned with amazing agility for another pass, swaying its head from side to side, catching parts of the university building.

Frida, Jonas, Scholr and her siblings watched from the relative safety of the doorway as the courtyard filled with flames, smoke and screams of agony. With no reason to stop, the lindwyrm kept up its attack long after it was possible to see anything but fire and smoke. There were no more crossbow bolts to prevent it from expressing its fury at the death of the boy. The intense heat forced all of them deeper into the building, Scholr hugging Frida. The message she conveyed radiated yet more grief and it drew tears in Frida's eyes.

'You need to get away quickly. Others will be here very soon.'

'What about you and your brothers and sisters?'

The girl's smile was tragic in its irony. 'Thank you for setting us free. You must go. We have no future. We will continue the fight.'

As they spoke, a loud explosion rocked the building, glass shattered and smoke billowed toward them.

As Scholr turned to go, Frida took her hand. 'Why don't you have a future?'

The same sad smile. 'Long ago we were taken from our home. I was very young. We cannot go back there.'

'You're from Vanaheim, aren't you?' Frida asked.

The young skogvættir nodded. 'My sisters tell me it was not a happy place. There is great danger there. The things that wicked man said are true.' She held Frida's eyes for a moment. 'For Naschr's sake, please do not go.' She reached up and kissed Frida on the cheek. 'You must leave. More hyroa are on their way.'

She hurried back to her family who stood in a line in the doorway, ragged, crooked and determined. Beyond it, fiery vengeance rained down on the building as fire took hold. Jonas and Frida sprinted into the hallway, a dozen hyroa rushed toward them from all directions. With a shriek of fury, Frida blasted them before they could fire their crossbows. Outside on the street dense smoke and flames burst out of the university's windows to billow into the morning air.

They ran as the sky's palette of dawn pinks deepened with the addition of fiery oranges and reds. Finally, out of breath and in desperate need to stop, Frida halted at a street corner and held a hitching rail, its smooth surface polished by thousands of horses' reins. Her legs felt weak, her brain empty of all thought. She couldn't run any farther, not until she'd dealt with the one thing which dominated her thinking.

According to Salann, she was a danger. A threat to this world and her own. In fact, all nine realms if what Agnes had explained was true. The conversation she'd had with her friend in the Minster's crypt triggered the significance of the name Salann had mentioned.

Njord.

He'd led a war against the Asgardian gods and lost. According to the Order, his escape from imprisonment involved her somehow. A Norse demi-god.

'I don't understand, Jonas. How has everything has got so complicated?'

The big man placed a hand on her shoulder, a gesture of support accompanied by a smile which didn't reach his eyes. The professor's declaration had shaken him too; she'd seen it in his face, as well as in the horror-filled expressions of Scholr's family. He didn't reply straight away, forcing her to provide her own reassurance.

'He must have been insane. I've heard academics can lose their grasp on reality.'

He turned his attention away, to peer in all directions as though he expected them to be caught at any moment. Frida could tell he didn't believe that answer but he was reluctant to say what he really thought. Like Jonas, she knew The Order was bigger than one crazy professor, it had a history for one thing and a ruthlessness born of desperation.

Because of her people were dying. Had already died. All because she offered this Norse megalomaniac the means to escape the world they were about to visit. How that would happen remained a mystery. And why her?

Frida stared into the boiling colours in the sky. Destruction caused by a desperate need to stop her from committing some terrible crime.

'What are you going to tell the others?'

That forced him to look at her. There was no point lying, the result of their investigation into the Order of Freyja could be seen in the flames leaping into the sky.

'We'll report what Salann told us. We don't know if it's true. He could be mad, he could be lying, we don't know.'

'But it wasn't only Salann. Scholr said the same thing.'

'I don't know, Frida, I really don't. This has got out of hand so quickly. We need to stop and think. Perhaps go back home, report this to the government. See if there is evidence to prove what we heard this morning?'

'What will happen to me?'

His pause was a second too long. 'Nothing. Why should it?'

'Didn't you hear what he said? Someone arranged for me to be on this expedition, to get me to Vanaheim. I assume they're the ones working for this Njord character. They've got me this far. I doubt they're going to give up now.'

She shouldn't have done it. It broke all the rules, but Frida needed to find out what Jonas was really thinking. With her limited skills, she couldn't penetrate his mental barriers. He'd been trained to withstand her attempts, his thoughts were locked away behind heavy doors. He couldn't hide the panic though, that was too big a beast to conceal. She had to use another lever to pry his mind open.

'After all, you could be that person, as far as I know. Your mental barriers tell me you've got something to hide.'

His eyes found hers and burned with an anger that flared and then vanished.

'Is that what you think, Frida?'

'I don't know. You have all this information about the Order, the people in this city, and you tell me you're working for the government, but how do I know that's true?'

'Would Olsen have allowed me to insist on your inclusion otherwise?'

'Exactly! You insisted I came along after he'd refused.'

He didn't take his eyes off her for a long moment. When he did, he strode along the street until arriving at a small park. She followed, hesitant and uncertain. He plonked himself down onto a wooden bench and stared at the ground. Frida did the same. If he was the person trying to get her to Vanaheim, he might try anything in his desperation. She sat beside him, fingers ready to defend herself. His silence ended with words directed at the ground in front of him.

'What I'm going to tell you is a classified secret. I would be grateful if you kept it to yourself.'

He looked into her face until she nodded, and then returned to staring at the ground.

'I volunteered for this mission. It was my way of honouring the memory of Freddie Galbraith. He was ordered to find and protect you. When he didn't report in, it was obvious the government was compromised. No one should have known about Freddie or you. His death and the bombing of the hotel showed how high the stakes were for everyone. At that point, the government thought it was Humanity First. They didn't know anything about the Order of Freyja until Agnes mentioned them to her father. He and his government buddies quickly realised how complex this mission had become.'

Jonas took a deep breath. Frida sensed some of the relief he felt now came from unburdening himself but grief and guilt flowed from him in equal measure.

'What had started out as a simple reconnoitring mission to colonise another world had turned into something darker, more political and certainly dangerous.

That's why the government came to me. I had a background which no one else shared.'

He looked up into Frida's face to watch her reaction. She gave none.

'Freddie was my best friend. I wanted to find the people responsible for his death so I could kill them. But the other factor is the classified secret.'

His scrutiny deepened but remained impassive.

'I was a member of Humanity First. I joined when I was young, naïve, desperate. Freddie caught me. He rescued me in a way. The authorities gave me a choice. I could go to prison for twenty years or find out what had happened to Freddie and keep you safe.'

As he searched her face for a reaction, she could sense his need for validation, though he made no effort to hide it. She could guess why.

'Imagine how Olsen and his soldiers would react if they knew my secret.'

Frida swallowed hard as she processed his confession. It didn't exclude him from her suspicions, in a way it made him even more of a candidate. If he still worked for Humanity First, he wouldn't want the expedition to go ahead. She countered that against everything he'd done for her since they'd met. His common sense, his courage and belief in her made for a stronger argument in his defence. He reached over and tentatively took her hand – she didn't snatch it away – his guilt and grief made sense now.

'I'm trying to keep you alive, Frida. It was Freddie's mission and I'm doing it in his memory. While we were in York, I discovered the Humanity First cell. They knew about you. It's why I killed them. Well, and for Freddie too.

149

But now? I have no idea what we should do. I think that's Olsen's decision.'

Frida groaned. She dreaded what that meant.

Chapter 13

"You think you know fear. As a soldier you encounter it in many ways. I was not prepared for what awaited us in Vanaheim. None of us were."

Interview with Lieutenant Tristan Wheeler, CGC.

Olsen's reception resembled the smouldering embers of the hotel. His unit were no different; they surrounded him, bloody, battered and angry. He didn't wait to hear their report.

'I've lost three men this morning. Good men too. The fairies had promised we'd be given diplomatic immunity while we were in their world. Goes to show how much we can fucking trust them, doesn't it?' He glared at her. Not Jonas. At her. His attention shifted to Agnes for a second before switching back. 'I understand this attack was intended to flush out and capture you, Miss Ranson. These fairies think you're some sort of threat.'

Agnes blushed and stared at her feet.

'Is that true?'

'Yes.' The answer wasn't as defiant as Frida had wanted. Her voice shook.

'Three men dead. Yet you hugged one of the fucking bastards that attacked us, treated her like a friend. Is that true?'

'Yes, but ...' The hatred from the mass of soldiers washed over Frida like a tsunami. She spotted the bearded face of Animal lean across to a couple of men nearby and

151

whisper something. She recognised their responses; she'd witnessed other men make the same promise. She was never going to get through to these people. They wouldn't understand the difference between the fae and slaves used by the Order of Freyja. There was no distinction because they weren't human. It was that simple.

Jonas moved to complain but a raised hand and thunderous look silenced him.

'Right from the start I questioned your loyalty. You were always the one found with fairy spies, and you escaped the hotel bombing unhurt. But when I report all this, when I throw you off my fucking team, what happens? Olsen's gaze swung back to Jonas. 'I'm told in no uncertain terms to take you back. You're important. Which only leads me to think our government is so corrupt and full of fairy lovers like you, Miss Ranson.'

His face was bright red now and his eyes bulged, while his team regarded Frida with the same loathing. Olsen stood up, and those seated on the ground instantly moved aside to allow him to walk toward her. He gritted his teeth.

'You might not have delivered the killing blows to those three men but I hold you responsible, Miss Ranson. The fairies say you're a threat to them, they want you dead. I can't say I blame then. There's only one thing I regret. Do you know what that is?'

She wasn't going to dignify his theatrics with a reply.

'That they didn't ask me to hand you over before they attacked. I wouldn't have hesitated. I'd have dressed you up in a fucking silk bow if they'd wanted that.'

He knew what he was doing. The image provoked contemptuous agreement and mumbled comments. Frida could guess what they were saying, having heard it throughout her life.

'Listen to me carefully. I'm sending the bodies of my men back through the portal this morning. You are going with them. I'm in charge of this expedition, not some prancing politician. What I say goes.'

Cheers and jeers echoed around the derelict remains of the hotel as the soldiers got to their feet. Layla looked frightened; Agnes didn't shift her attention from the ground. Even Jonas looked uncertain but moved a little closer to her side. Olsen didn't move, just stared directly at her, unblinking, as crazed as the madman they'd left to be roasted at the university. Frida flexed her fingers, ready for trouble. The events at the university now appeared to be small and insignificant. That changed seconds later.

'Olsen! Olsen!'

Faces turned to the anxious call from a figure on horseback. Lorcan Dubh's horse skidded to a halt on the gravel yard beside the hotel, he leapt off the animal and sprinted into the melee of soldiers, scattering them with his urgency. If he was aware of the tension, he didn't show it.

'We need to get all of you out of here. Fast.'

He looked at the startled faces and their lack of reaction.

'This city is full of very angry people who want to make your team suffer for burning down part of the university.'

'What?' Major Olsen bellowed. It took him no more than a second to turn his attention back to Frida. 'What did you fucking do, you stupid bitch?'

Lorcan's voice rang out, everyone turned to look at him, despite Olsen's fury. 'Listen to me, Major. Allocating blame is pointless. The fae hate humans, to them you are all the same. They're mobilising the entire city to capture you. You need to escape. Fast.'

With Olsen's face like granite and not moving from Frida's face, the urgency in Lorcan's voice drew everyone's attention.

'The fae need your help if we are to survive as a race. The same is true for humanity. We need each other. But the war has sewn so much distrust we cannot forgive the other side when mistakes are made.' He looked across at Frida, his sincerity and determination almost palpable. 'This city is filled with corruption. The Order of Freyja has infiltrated the executive positions in this city and murdered people, including my father. They've convinced enough of our citizens that you are the evil ones here, not them. She is not their only enemy.' He jerked a thumb at Frida. 'You all are and they will kill you, without hesitation.'

Panicked murmurs spread throughout the team. Some of the soldiers declared how they lacked a defensible position, others that they were trapped and outnumbered. Lorcan held up his hand for quiet just as Olsen opened his mouth. His murderous look hinted at a willingness to stand and fight, but it wasn't shared by all his unit.

This time Lorcan's voice held hope, the sound of someone who knew what he was talking about.

'If we are quick, we can escape before they gather the numbers to pose enough of a threat. These are normal people we're talking about, not soldiers. They won't have many weapons, not at first. If we give them an hour, they will.'

Lieutenant Wheeler pushed to the front of the crowd of soldiers. 'Where do we go? Back to the portal in the park to get us home?'

'No. They're massing there now. They assume that's what you'll do. They think this is a hit-and-run attack.'

'Where then?' Olsen growled.

Lorcan pulled a notebook out of the back pocket of his trousers. 'My father spent years investigating The Order of Freyja. It's why they murdered him. I found this notebook in his things. We need to get to the university. It's built on the foundations of a castle. It was once a guard post. A fortification on top of the portal to Vanaheim.'

Loud gasps almost drowned Olsen's reply.

'You're suggesting we—'

'You have no choice. Fight a battle here, and you will lose. Everyone will die. And let me be clear, it won't just be death. They will desecrate your bodies. Your families will never have any closure knowing what was done to your corpses.'

That drew wide-eyed looks of horror from everyone.

'Or you can join me in getting to that portal before they realise what we're doing. The plan was to go to Vanaheim. We're still doing that, just a lot faster than planned.'

Olsen scowled at the suggestion but a quick scan of his unit was enough. He was a military strategist, and his people were vulnerable and outnumbered. Escape was the only option and with the portal to Earth blocked, they had no other choice. He gave the order to move and a two-minute window in which to get ready. The unit sprang into action, only Animal pausing for a moment to mouth something at Frida. She didn't need to be a lip reader to know what it was. Agnes remained a short distance away, clearly frightened, ignored by Layla and Jonas as they hurried over to Frida. Lorcan joined them, serious and resolute now.

'My father's notebook has enough information to help locate the portal. After that, it's over to you. I hope you're ready because the dangers we face are going to make this threat look like a warm-up act.'

Nearby, Agnes gasped and placed a hand to her mouth. 'But you said...'

'I know what I said. All of it was true. It is the lesser of two evils. Now I need to speak to Frida privately, if you'll excuse me?'

The others moved away and joined the gathering assembly. Lorcan's smile made Frida want to cry. She might have appeared unconcerned by Olsen's abuse but beneath the surface she was ready to scream at the universe for its injustice. Lorcan rattled off his words like a machine gun spat bullets.

'I was searching through my father's work when news reached me of the university fire. I don't know what you've found out from your visit there, but I assume the fire means things didn't go well. Whatever happens, let me assure you of one thing. It is my duty to honour my father's debt, and I will do everything in my power to keep you safe. And if it gives me a chance to kill the bastards who murdered him, that is a bonus. Are we clear?'

All Frida could do was nod as they hurried to join the rest of the expedition.

They hitched Lorcan's horse to a light four-wheeled trap they found in the hotel's garden. Layla and Agnes climbed on board, Frida sat next to Lorcan on the driving seat, and everyone else ran. It was still early, so few people were on the streets of Ainmire. They looked perplexed at the sight of human soldiers jogging through their city, unaware of any link to the smoke which spiralled into the early morning sky.

Layla sat behind Frida, a reassuring hand on her shoulder, a comforting tone to her voice. 'I don't understand how such a respected academic could do such things.' She lapsed into silence, shaking her head repeatedly and frowning.

Frida stared up at the column of grey smoke which filled the sky in front of them. Olsen's words looped in her head despite her efforts to shut them out, and for one good reason – he was right. Her ignorance might be a defence, but it hardly mattered when so many people had died. It made no sense why her mother hadn't talked about her heritage, unless her silence meant she'd been kept in the dark too. Questions remained unanswered. Who were the others who could have freed Njord? Why was she the only one left? How was this escape supposed to work and did she have any control over it?

Travelling to Vanaheim increased the chance of her turning into some kind of weapon of mass destruction. Her ignorance left her trapped, unable to escape whatever waited for her on the other side of the portal. The thought scared her beyond any fear she'd ever felt before.

Lorcan's urgent voice penetrated her thoughts.

'Frida? I might need you to clear a path for us.'

He slowed the horse down. In front of them, a barrier stretched across the road, hastily cobbled together from an old cart and tree branches. A dozen stern looking men stood in front of it holding garden implements.

One muscular specimen with a scar down his face, running through a white-orbed eye, shouldered an axe. He curled his lip, spat on the floor, and spoke in a growl. 'You can wait here till the authorities arrive, Lorcan. We have questions.'

'Gaal, you know who's behind this and you know I'm not going to let them kill anyone else. You heard what they did to my father?'

The other man sighed heavily. 'Aye. But they said he'd been causing trouble.'

Lorcan's body language shifted as his shoulders stiffened. He remained on the driving seat of the trap but looked ready to leap from it and throw himself at the man.

'Causing trouble is asking innocent questions, is it Gaal? Because, when we fought together at the Battle of Falias, I remember you asking difficult questions of our field commanders all the time.'

A shake of the head followed a lusty snort at the memory. It was the sidelong look at the other men, still glaring at Lorcan and his passengers, that had the greater effect on the one-eyed man.

'Yeah. Well. Sorry Lorcan. But them's the rules.'

Clearly unsatisfied by the lack of acrimony, another man stepped forward, shouldering Gaal out of the way. He was as thin as the pitchfork he held. He grimaced, revealing a mouth full of rotten teeth.

'We want that bitch arrested.' He jabbed the pitchfork in Frida's direction before bringing it back to its upright position again. 'She burned down the fucking university. She needs to pay.'

'I didn't burn it!' Frida yelled at the man. 'It was a lindwyrm the Order of Freyja kept caged. It was their own fault!'

Lorcan placed a calming hand on her arm, exerted enough pressure to get her to sit down at his side again. She obliged, grudgingly. From behind them she heard Olsen barking orders to get moving, and the men in front of them bristled at the threat. The pitchfork holder took another step forward, his aggression causing the horse to nicker anxiously.

'I told ya. Give us that bitch or suffer for it.'

'Oh, I'll make you suffer!' Frida screamed. She raised her hands and incandescent energy rippled through the air and struck the cart, blasting it into kindling. The horse reared up, tipping the trap, sending Agnes and Layla tumbling off their seats and onto the floor of the vehicle. Lorcan shook the reins and the panicked horse raced through the smoke of the burning cart and branches. Men flung themselves to either side of the street, shaking fists and cursing once out of the way of the horse and cart. Only Pitchfork chose to try and stop the soldiers jogging after the trap. A bullet from Olsen's gun felled the man, blasting apart his face.

No one on the trap spoke. Lorcan concentrated on calming the spooked horse. Agnes and Layla struggled back onto their seat as they sped through the main streets of the city.

Its commercial and community centre was busier, people hurrying to work – the Ainmire equivalent of rush hour. Everything juddered to a halt as they witnessed a silver-headed girl, green eyes blazing, at the front of a trap, with two dozen human soldiers jogging behind her. Several of the bystanders took out communication devices. Others harried the procession, creating a running scuffle with the protestors which inevitably slowed them down. The expedition's line extended, and desperate soldiers fired shots into the air to disperse their attackers, but their goal was a simple one. Delay them.

Lorcan rounded a tight corner, hurling Agnes and Layla into the side of the trap. The university towered in front of them, its monolithic walls rearing up into a smoke-filled sky. From their perspective, a pillar of rock formed the corner of the building, ascending from a steep escarpment jutting out of the surrounding earth. Its original role as a castle was obvious; it made an excellent fortress. The university had been constructed on top, squashing the castle.

In the grey-blue distance where smoke looked like a winter fog, they heard the mob before they saw it.

Tristan Wheeler, red-faced and breathless, ran alongside the trap. 'There's a large gang approaching behind us, we're …'

He caught sight of what was coming toward them from the opposite direction and stopped. The look on his face said it all. They were trapped.

Chapter 14

"In war the need to think on your feet can be the difference between life and death, victory and defeat. It means reviewing a decision you were prepared to die by one minute ago and then changing it to another which offers survival."

Interview with Major Sven Olsen, QGM

Lorcan leapt off the trap and scrambled up the incline toward the ancient castle wall where Hawthorne bushes hid a narrow wooden door. The rest of the expedition team didn't need his beckoning hand to follow him; the approaching mobs of angry fae offered all the motivation they needed.

The team poured into a wide trench, the dried remains of a one-time moat, as two groups converged to form one mass of furious fairies. The expedition team huddled around each other, guns aimed at the approaching menace, trapped and aware their weapons wouldn't be enough. Lorcan rattled the ancient door. He stood back to give Frida some room.

'It's probably not been opened in centuries but don't blow it apart, we need it as a blockade.'

With everyone breathing down her neck, Frida focused her attention on the ancient and rusted lock and tried to shut everything else out. Managing the release of energy was never easy in stressful situations, fear or anger tended to increase its intensity, rather than reduce it. She closed her eyes and focused on a steady and constant release of energy, telling herself it was no different to cooking that bloody egg for breakfast. Even then, her urgency ran the risk of heating the metal too quickly and melting the lock inside the door. She took a breath and calmed her breathing, picturing her energy seeping into the aged lock mechanism, and shut out the impatient pleas behind her.

Penetration of the metal suddenly eased, turning pliable as her energy moved through it like soft cheese. She withdrew her fingers and yanked the handle. It came away in her hand and with it chunks of the lock mechanism. She pushed at the door, wincing as it scraped against a stone-flagged floor. Forcing her way inside, the sour tang of damp decay hit her nostrils. The others rammed her against the door in their desperation to get away from the screaming horde behind them. Lorcan called out instructions to follow, the tangled mass of frightened people hurried past her, through another doorway into an even darker corridor. Frida waited for the last of the team, Olsen, shooting at the nearest of the fae onslaught as they entered the old moat. Together they pushed the door closed, jamming it in place in the hope of creating a few seconds of delay. They ran to the far end of the room and stood in a doorway which offered a viewpoint but very limited protection.

'Can you bring the room down? Without killing us?' Olsen snapped.

Frida had no idea but she didn't care. She pointed her fingers at the stone ceiling. Cracks stretched like a spider's web across its surface, suggesting weaknesses in its geological structure. Hammering on the outside door told her those valuable few seconds were all she had.

Frida released all the energy she possessed – holding it back had been almost impossible – the relief was instant. Her incandescent energy lit up the room. Its arcing traceries of white light sought out the fractures and penetrated them, triggering a rapid sequence of loud cracks and billowing dust, then silence. A hand grabbed her arm, Olsen's face loomed out the swirling muck, mouthed something, pulled her backwards. The ceiling collapsed, along with part of the wall and doorway where they'd stood seconds before. Olsen and Frida ran as their world fell around them.

The floor shook and shifted; they stumbled, grabbing the skin-scraping walls of the narrow corridor. The dust, the dark and the deafness forced them to rely on touch as they forced their way forward, all sense of direction lost. The corridor led downwards, that was all they knew. Just as Frida began to wonder what had happened to the rest of the expedition team, a light appeared up ahead.

They arrived in a huge cavern, the height of a cathedral, its space even more daunting. Shafts of light from gaps in its roof turned it into a stage set. Even so, that wasn't what caught Frida's attention. A stone archway dominated the space.

The Vanaheim portal.

By the time she and Olsen had arrived in the centre of the cavern Frida's ears popped and she could hear again. She stared in amazement at the huge portal, so much bigger than any she'd seen before. Yaalon Dubh had been right in his analysis of the building's original purpose, this had been a major thoroughfare at one time. His son was already on his knees at the base of one side of the archway, repositioning the first of two ignition crystals to

163

open the doorway. He called out directions for Agnes, knelt at the other archway, to position the second crystal in the correct way to create a suitable circuit. The expedition team waited and watched, their animated discussions echoing around the cavern.

Beyond the archway, shafts of light illuminated the portal, wraith-like wisps of smoke wafted in trapped air currents. Tristan and Jonas clambered over a pile of fallen rocks, examining objects and showing them to each other. Registering the arrival of Olsen and Frida, they beckoned them over. Jonas' anxious voice pointed to the chasm above.

'We're below the courtyard,' he said. 'This rift was created by the two landvættir.'

'The what?'

Jonas ignored Olsen's irritable tone, keeping his attention on the large hole. He spoke to Tristan rather than the man's commanding officer.

'The attacks we've encountered were carried out by a race that could manipulate natural elements: air, water, earth, flora and fauna. They obeyed Professor Salann. He kept them as his slaves. This is the work of two old men.'

'Two old men did this?' Olsen said as he stared up into the wide crevice that looked like a giant had split it open with an axe.

'Most of the hyroa fell down there.' Jonas pointed to broken bodies amidst the rubble from the courtyard. 'Some of them may have survived.'

The young lieutenant cleared his throat, pointed upwards. 'This is a natural fissure, which probably made it easier to force the ground apart. I think the survivors clambered down the tree roots. They're strong enough to support a man's weight.'

Olsen's eyes followed a route from the bottom of the fissure to the stone archway. 'Those bastards came down here and used the portal.'

Tristan sighed. 'Yes, sir, looks like it. There are recent footprints in the dust. Jonas told me about the leader of this order. We think he might have escaped too.'

Jonas reached out to Frida, placing a friendly hand on her arm. It was meant to comfort her but it was going to take a lot more than that. She could feel Olsen watching her.

'The dragon didn't kill him?'

Jonas answered for her. 'Everything was on fire, and there was so much smoke we couldn't see anything.'

Olsen remained silent for a moment as he took in the scene. His lieutenant watched, his eyes nervously flicking to Jonas.

Olsen clambered over the rocks to pick up the broken remains of a crossbow. 'Your old men created an escape route. I'm not convinced they were on your side. This hole gave the survivors protection and a means of escape from that bloody dragon.'

He stomped off down the rock scree before either Jonas or Frida could provide an answer. Tristan followed behind, shaking his head.

Jonas remained with Frida, fist clenched in fury. 'That man's prejudice stops him from seeing what is obvious to everyone else. He blames the fae for everything.'

As the man in question arrived in front of the portal, a group of soldiers moved to intersect him, led by Animal.

He pointed at Frida, his scowl almost hidden amidst his forest of facial hair. 'Major, you said we wouldn't bring her with us. You said she's trouble. Yet here she is.' The man's deep bass tone echoed in the cavern, drawing everyone's attention.

Olsen stood his ground, looking up into Animal's hairy face, his own empty of expression. 'What would you have done, corporal? Left her for the bloody fairies, no doubt!'

'Aye! We didn't destroy their precious university, she did.'

Jonas grabbed Frida's arm and held it in a firm grip.

Olsen said nothing for a moment but looked around the cavern, taking in everyone who'd turned silent now. He wiped his face, brushed dust off his uniform as though it had no right being there. If he was trying to look relaxed and unconcerned by the tense situation, it was convincing.

'You surprise me, corporal. You've served with me for how long now?'

Animal's frowned deepened. 'Five years, sir. Six this October.'

Olsen nodded as though they were discussing the likelihood of rain. 'In that time, corporal, have you ever known me leave any of my people behind?'

'She's not one of us. She's part fairy for a start. I say leave her here.'

The moment those final words left his mouth, he dropped his eyes to the floor. His friends discreetly shook their heads as Olsen stared directly at the other man, his focus unswerving.

'Are you giving the orders now, corporal?'

'No, sir.' The aggressive tone had vanished. 'I just think ...'

'Do you, corporal?'

Animal's face showed his consternation at the loss of direction again. 'Do I what, sir?'

'Do you think?'

The big man opened his mouth but no words escaped.

Olsen raised his voice and looked around the cavern again. 'Some of you may be under a misunderstanding, so let me explain something nice and clearly so we don't have any more repeats of situations like this.' He took a deep breath, more for dramatic emphasis than anything. 'This expedition has a mixture of military and civilian personnel. We have historians and engineers as well as soldiers. I lead it. So that there is no doubt about that fact, I'll repeat it. I lead this expedition. You should understand, for this reason, military law applies and I am judge and jury. The civilians on this team need to be kept safe. At no point will we abandon anyone, no matter the cause. We will abandon no one.'

He looked around the group, at the eyes drawn to the ground or the ceiling. A few watched each other for their reactions, found none. Awkwardness dominated.

'I'm aware of what I said earlier. All of you with military experience understand how situations can change rapidly, and when that happens, we review our decisions, we change them accordingly. Our escape was an example of that. We had no choice. In fact, thanks to his swift action, our fae liaison over there probably saved our lives.' Olsen nodded his head in Lorcan's direction; the surprise on his face was comic.

'But we all need to understand something.' He took another deep breath and raised his voice still further. 'We were given orders to explore an entirely unknown location. If it is successful, we may find a new home for our people. When I agreed to lead this expedition, my superiors were eager to point out we are also creating history. Our actions will be recorded and, for years to come, analysed by other people. I will not allow those records to include any action where men and women under my command take matters into their own hands. Military law applies in such situations and can, in extreme circumstances, lead to execution. I will not hesitate in sanctioning punishment for any attempts at mutiny. Have I made myself clear?'

Animal and those around him grudgingly grumbled their agreement but Olsen was having none of it.

'I said, have I made myself clear?'

'Yes, sir!'

The two words resounded throughout the cavern as soldiers snapped to attention. Olsen nodded once, spun on his heel and walked over to talk to Lorcan. The expressions of sullen resentment on Animal and his pals told Frida the matter wasn't over. She knew their type from the farms where she'd worked as a teenage girl, where her gender made her vulnerable. They would bide their time. They would wait until she was alone or at night where no one could see. They would try to make it look like an accident. Olsen might consider the matter over. Frida didn't.

Agnes, eager to make amends, went to great pains to point out that soldiers like Billy weren't like Animal. She smiled, joked about Billy's talents until Frida strode over to join Lorcan without saying a word. He pointed at the base of the archway where Olsen was already examining the crystal and its copper plated vessel.

'There's residual energy there. It proves it was opened a short time ago.'

'How long? Olsen asked.

'No more than a couple of hours. They will likely stage their attack when we go through. We're going to need to be ready for anything.' He turned his attention to Frida. 'You're going to be his target.'

She nodded. A big part of her hoped Lorcan was right. She felt responsible for Scholr and Naschr. Salann's escape gave her a second attempt at the vengeance they deserved. He smiled at her. He thought the same way, he'd be doing the same for his father.

Lorcan aligned the final crystal on its copper-plated platform and the portal came to life. Its beauty caused the hardest of soldiers to coo and gasp. A jade green waterfall tumbled from its keystone to ground itself in the rock at their feet. It fizzed and sparkled, a semi-translucent curtain of pure energy. If there had ever been an argument that the fae performed magic, this was it.

Frida stood at the entrance, Lorcan at her side, knives held ready. Olsen agreed for them to go first, to meet Salann's attack, while he and his soldiers offered back-up. They turned to each other, grim-faced, until

Lorcan gave her a quizzical frown and pointed to the shimmering curtain.

'Your eyes are the same colour.'

She shrugged off its irrelevance. Vengeance was all that mattered to her and it waited on the other side of the portal. They stepped through the event horizon.

Frida hadn't experienced many portals but this experience was nothing like she'd ever known. Her skin prickled with such intensity it made her yelp in surprise. The sensations expanded, penetrating muscle and sinew so that her entire body reacted to the energy. Her pulse rate rocketed, her breathing sped up as the stimulation demanded her attention. She'd never been so aware of her body. Every part of it, from her toes squeezed together in her boots to the tingling in her scalp. It was the same buzz she felt when she released all her energy at once, only amplified beyond measure.

Overstimulated and roiling with energy, a long forgotten memory, fuzzy with time, bubbled up from the recesses of her mind.

She and her mother sat opposite each other in front of a warm fire; her mother held her outstretched arm. She remembered the pain, so sudden and powerful. It caused her to look up at her mother in bewilderment, not understanding why she could be happy at her daughter's discomfort. The pain vanished, to be replaced by sensations that ran through every vein and artery in her body, thrumming in its intensity. Then it was over. Her mother's smile widened as she reached out to hug her, to tell her what a brave girl she'd been. There had been sweets as her reward.

Amidst the swirling energies of the portal, those same sensations coursed through her again. Except stronger now, an electrical surge that sped through every cell of her body, exhilarating and frightening her in equal measure. The portal's green light wobbled. She had no other way to describe it. Colour vanished for a second, rippling away as if blown on a strong wind, only to return and consume her, robbing her of her breath.

Utterly unprepared, she staggered through the portal, her brain addled. Dizzy and unable to concentrate, she scrabbled for purchase, praying Salann wasn't waiting. As soldiers stormed forward, throwing themselves to the ground, ready to provide cover for their comrades, Lorcan dragged Frida to one side. His strength and urgency thrust her against his muscular body. Even that pleasure couldn't penetrate her disorientation.

'Are you all right, Frida? What happened?'

She blinked and stared at his face, summoning up his name from the masses of cotton wool that filled her brain. He stared into her eyes, frowning. He had nice eyes, she decided.

Jonas's anxious face swept into view. 'What happened? Did the portal malfunction?' he asked.

'I don't think so,' Lorcan replied. 'Did you see what happened?'

The big man nodded, not taking his eyes off Frida as she gazed into the middle distance. Lorcan still held her, searching her face for answers.

'Something happened to her. It was as if she absorbed the portal's energy. Then it exploded out of her again.'

'Frida? Are you all right?' Jonas asked, shaking his head repeatedly.

Like the flick of a switch, normality returned and with it, self-consciousness. On instinct, she pushed Lorcan away, embarrassment consuming her and enflaming her face.

'I'm fine! I'm fine!'

In the absence of an attack, she'd quickly become the focus for everyone. She guessed what they were thinking. It had started. Whatever waited for her in this realm, it had introduced itself. Olsen barked commands to his unit, admonished them for behaving like gossiping schoolgirls. It drew a chuckle from a few of them as Lofty, a lanky young man with arms and legs like twigs, sashayed in front of them, blowing Animal kisses in the process.

Frida was grateful for the distraction.

Lorcan lowered his voice but remained embarrassingly close to her. 'Are you sure you're all right?'

She told him to stop worrying. He smiled at her, his usual blazing flash of eyes and toothpaste advert display of perfect teeth. His scepticism was easy to read. Not surprising, she couldn't expect him to believe her words when she didn't.

She made a point of looking at their surroundings, as if everything was normal. They were in another large cave but light flooded in from a gaping entrance only a short distance away. There was heat too. A humid, overpowering heat that filled her lungs, making her hot on the inside as well as outside. They were baking in an oven.

Everyone staggered to the cave entrance, sagging and sweating, even Lofty lost his youthful enthusiasm. Together they stared out at the landscape laid out below them. They were high up on a mountain, the jungle beneath them spreading out as far as they could see.

'What a shithole!' someone complained and it drew murmurs of agreement.

The overwhelming colour palette of this realm prompted another voice to add their assessment.

'The place is the colour of diarrhoea.'

It ended any further attempts at description. If this was to be the new Garden of Eden, they'd come too late. It was clearly dying.

'Major, you need to see this.' Billy's voice, full of apprehension, couldn't hide the trembling of his voice.

The group dispersed as Olsen strode toward the young man at the edge of the cave, he pointed to a small nook shielded from the relentless heat of the orange disk in the sky. Huddled in its recesses were three skeletons, bleached bones with arms and hands held up in gestures of self-protection.

Chapter 15

'The expedition team's actions in Ainmire led to soured relations between the fae and Humanity for some time. Intense diplomatic activity rescued the situation but only after all of the team's intelligence had been shared much later.'

Minutes from inter-agency government meeting

A pathway led down from the cave entrance, clinging to the sheer cliff face by defying science and gravity. It didn't look man-made but no one could explain how it could connect directly with the cave. The scientists and engineers in the team debated how it might have been created but couldn't agree on a theory. The regular soldiers stared at them in bewilderment. Animal and his crew formed a tight knot and kept their distance from the others. The looks directed at Frida left her all too aware of what would be going through their minds. Her weird behaviour after travelling through the portal had been one more reason to distrust her.

The pathway might have been unnaturally convenient but it was also narrow, dangerously so. Wide enough for just one person, its crumbling edge offered a faster route to the ground below. The vertigo suffered by Layla and one or two others had them travelling sideways like crabs, so they could keep their backs to the wall behind them. Even the likes of Olsen stayed firmly focused on the stony ground, having insisted on leading the way. Unsurprisingly, he'd insisted on Frida bringing up the rear. It was a decision which brought sighs of relief from many of the team. Lorcan and Jonas, ever faithful, chose to stay with her, but their constant scrutiny was enough to show they weren't immune to the anxiety everyone felt. The first time she lost her footing on the path, both men over-reacted. She offered up a grim smile and rubbed her ankle.

The two men exchanged looks that said they didn't believe her.

Lorcan placed a friendly hand on her shoulder and gave her his usual charming smile. 'Listen Frida, I didn't have time to read all of my father's research but he was worried for you. He thought there were connections between your family and this realm.'

Frida blinked. Salann had said something similar though Lorcan hadn't been there to hear it. Two opinions from very different men didn't make her feel any better. In fact she waited for him to continue with even greater trepidation.

'This situation with Salann is a part of that. I think he had Father killed because he was planning to share his research with you. He would have seen that as collaboration with the enemy. The irony is that even Father recorded his doubts about you coming here.'

'Why?'

Lorcan shook his head, his exasperation just as visible as hers. 'That's what I couldn't find out. I'm not sure Father even knew. He wrote about Vanaheim being a place of exile. When an obscure branch of the fae race rebelled, it led to a war, and they lost. Father thought your family were part of that losing side.'

'Are you saying my ancestors are from this world?'

'This place has been cut off from any other realm for millennia. How would they reach Earth?' Jonas asked.

'I don't know,' Lorcan replied. 'I'm not sure anyone does. But it doesn't mean it didn't happen. It can't be a coincidence Salann and his lunatic order have connected you to this place too.'

From a short distance along the pathway came sounds of consternation, and the three hurried to join the rest of the expedition. It wasn't easy to see the cause of the trouble; all they could hear were raised voices offering theories and differing conclusions. It was only as the three drew level they saw the cause of the debate.

Blast marks on the rocky cliff face created a wide smear of carbon, the result of intense heat striking the side of the wall. One of the scientists ran a curious finger across the blackened surface. The verdict? It was recent.

'A dragon?' Frida asked as she looked up into the copper-hued sky.

'Remember what Scholr said?' Jonas replied. 'It might be the remnant of an attack by another lindwyrm. If Salann and his hyroa came this way, that was their welcome.'

'There are no bodies,' Lorcan said, searching the sky now as well.

Frida peered over the edge of the path and wished she hadn't. The victims might have fallen over the edge. Except at least one body would likely still be on the path, if the attack had been successful. It looked like it hadn't; Salann and his guards must have survived. Lorcan's expression said he was happy about that. He wasn't going to be robbed of his vengeance either.

Within minutes of starting their descent, sweat-soaked clothes clung to bodies, rubbing and chaffing the tenderest of parts. Breathing dragged in hot air which made it worse. Thirsts raged, though no one was brave enough to stop for a drink on the narrow pathway. They trudged on, slowly, watchful for loose gravel and patches where erosion narrowed the rocky trail.

Gradually the jungle canopy drew closer, with it the remote possibility the oppressive heat might diminish. The colour of its leaves suggested otherwise. It looked like everything was slowly dying, a sickening colour of dried vomit stained all the foliage. Once broad leaves had started to shrivel and curl, and even the insect life looked exhausted and ready to drop.

'Do you think it's autumn here?' Frida asked. She really hoped it was because all the other explanations did not bode well.

A large brown shape burst out from the jungle canopy, wings flapping rapidly to cut short Lorcan's reply. It stopped in midair to turn and face its enemy. The lindwyrm was in even worse condition than the one from the university. Its skin lacked any shine, and patches of something that looked like mould covered its snake-like body, leading to tatty wings of dried leather filled with holes. Flames from its jaws roasted the cliff, and the team threw themselves onto the stony ground. As the lyndworm inhaled, pausing its attack briefly, tormented screams echoed off the cliff-face. One of team, too slow in reacting to the attack, turned into a flaming comet as they fell into the thick foliage below. Shots cracked in the super-heated air. The lindwyrm shrieked and dove back into the jungle, only to reappear, strafing the cliff wall a second time.

More gun shots, more shrieks, and the animal backed off a little way, ready to rush them. Laid out on the ground as she was, Frida raised one arm and released a bolt of energy. It struck the lindwyrm, blasting one wing and curtailing its shrieks of pain abruptly. It spiralled silently into the jungle below.

Cautiously, everyone got to their feet, dusted off the detritus clinging to their sweaty bodies and peered into the sky to see if any more monstrosities were part of the welcoming committee.

Lorcan, quick on his feet as usual, held out a hand to Frida as she stood up.

'That's unusual,' he said. 'Do you think it's significant?'

She could only shake her head in bewilderment. He was talking about the jade green hue of her energy bolts. Ever since she'd been able to summon energy, the colour had been consistent. White. Incandescent white. Although the blinding brilliance was the same, the colour was different. The same as the portal. And the colour of her eyes.

Olsen's bellowed commands for everyone to hurry off the path and into the jungle, before any more the bastard creatures turned up to roast them alive. They all obliged, nervous about what else waited for them in this hell of a world. Despite their urgency, Lorcan, Jonas and even a few others, watched Frida with new fascination.

She pretended to examine the ground beneath her feet so she could find answers which remained in short supply. She felt different, some signs were obvious. Her heartbeat and breath kept time with an unknown rhythm, a pulse deep insider her. One so subtle she hadn't noticed it until releasing her energy, but it was there. She paused, her attention drawn by a throbbing sensation in her right arm, the one she'd used to blast the lindwyrm.

The fine scar on the underside of her wrist, which matched the seal on Yaalon Dubh's letter, looked different. The puckered tissue had grown slightly, and something under the skin pulsed with the same greenish hue as her energy bolts. Carefully, almost fearfully, she pressed a finger on the scar and recognised the steady beat. Her finger, pressed against the scar, triggered a vague memory. A time when she'd done the very same thing. A determined effort brought more of the fragmented memory together.

Frida closed her eyes to focus all her attention on the memory, draining it of every detail. They sat at a table, on it a bowl of warm water and a clean cloth. There was her mother's reassuring smile and her gentle voice telling her daughter to keep looking in her eyes all the time. Eyes the same colour as hers. It would all be over quickly. Sharp pain made her jerk her arm, but her mother's grip held it firm. She didn't want to see what was being done to her but she had to know why she was being treated this way.

She gasped as the event played through her mind, dredged from the depths of her brain where it had laid dormant for so long. Blood trickled off her wrist to fall onto her mother's apron. The wound was small, no bigger than a fingernail but it felt deep. It hurt. With care and precision, her mother sewed the wound together like darning a sock. There was a similar wound on her mother's wrist. She remembered looking into her mother's face, wondering how she'd hurt herself in the very same place.

The only conclusion she could draw, her mother had taken something out of her wrist and implanted in her daughter's.

Frida opened her eyes and hurried as carefully as she could on the narrow path to rejoin the team. Her mind raced. Whatever pulsed in her wrist was the result of her mother's actions yet she'd never explained her reasons. For the first time, the possibility she dreaded took on a greater certainty. Salann and Yaalon Dubh might be right; there was some connection between this world and her family, one that had never been shared with her.

Something niggled at the back of her mind, a passing comment made by Salann when she'd been more intent on escape and sensing why Naschr had betrayed them. He'd mentioned she was the last person Njord could use. That had to mean there had been others like her who'd faced similar threats from the Order and died as a result. It could explain the secrecy and why her mother had been so obsessive about it. She hadn't been hiding her fae ancestry but something bigger, something more dangerous.

She reached the others just as the path led them under the jungle canopy, where the heat and humidity increased to sap any remaining strength. The air was heavy, dragging on shoulders, making every step an effort. Even the fittest of their number flopped onto boulders and fallen tree trunks. Sweat-slick clothes stuck to bodies as if glued there.

Their time out gave them a chance to examine their new surroundings, a truly alien world of flora where chlorophyll had no role to play. Dark oranges bled into dull browns, forever reminding them of the proximity of death. Broad leaves halted any movement of air, trapping the heat and the smell of rot.

'Who's going to want to live in this shithole?' Animal grumbled.

It got an exhausted mumble of agreement; anything more was out of the question. Olsen, the only one not to have collapsed onto whatever was available, called out in a voice which did its best to sound animated.

'We keep going. Let's see if we can find a way out of this jungle. Somewhere we can make camp for the night.'

After an hour-long trek they made camp on the edge of the jungle, on an open landscape that offered limited safety from an attack by Salann and his hyroa. They'd stopped on what might once have been a meadow, except the grass had died and turned into dried mud. Weird little hillocks dotted the whole area that led toward a forest of trees which must have died centuries ago. Their bleached trunks and boughs looked like ancient skeletal bones, frozen in a rictus of agonised death. No one cared. They were out of the jungle and night was sweeping in on purple wings to reduce the heat to something bearable. A light breeze even offered to cool them as it ruffled sodden hair. There was no point in lighting a fire, so everyone ate from the dried rations they'd brought with them and washed them down with lukewarm water from their flasks. All that mattered was sleep.

Despite killing the lindwyrm, Frida remained an outcast from most of the unit, they whispered to each other as they gave her suspicious looks. Layla made a point of staying close to her, as did Lorcan and Jonas, forming their own sleepy satellite a short distance from the others. Agnes had wasted no time cuddling up to Billy, much to the amusement of the other soldiers, but she didn't appear to care.

Moonlight brought a chill which woke Frida. At least that was her first thought as she shivered. It took a second or two to realise the sensation prickling across her skin was a warning of danger. From a short distance away,

181

amidst the main group of sleepers, a guard's voice rang out across the silver landscape.

'Snakes! Snakes!'

Frida bolted upright, her attention focused on the guard scanning his gun over the ground. No sooner had he called out than something yanked him to the floor, his gun going off as he screamed.

Something dry slithered over Frida's legs. She drew her knees up to her chin with a squeak and peered into the semi-darkness. The snake comparison worked at first, the length and squirming appearance rang true. Her first thought was there were lots of the creatures, the earth appeared to move. Her opinion changed as one of the things scraped across her skin. Its fibrous texture was rough, slightly warm, nothing like a snake.

The others struggled from the depths of exhausted sleep, uncertain and anxious. Layla screamed as a wriggling column reared up in front of her, waved from side to side for a brief moment, then wrapped itself around the startled woman, pinning her arms to the side of her body.

She called out for help, but the others faced the same fate. It reminded Frida of the apple trees at the hotel though this was happening on a larger scale. Frida searched the moonlit landscape to find the skogvættir responsible. What she saw was the entire unit fighting their individual battles with things that looked like snakes but weren't.

One of the rope-like creatures attacked her from behind, its leathery texture moving with an elasticated ability to snap and tighten around her before she could blast it. The more she fought and wriggled, the tighter it got as it bound her arms to her sides. Another length snapped around her ankles, stopping her from getting to her feet. Screams filled the night air, some stifled too suddenly to mean anything good. The body of an unconscious female soldier slithered past, her head swathed in fibres snaking into her mouth.

From the direction of the jungle, lights bobbed toward them. There had to be a dozen of them. Despite her frantic need to escape, she recognised them straight away. Salann and his hyroa. Frida's warning signs went into overdrive, her skin tingling like it was on fire.

One dark figure drew closer, carrying a fiery torch. The serpentine creatures shrank away from the light to give her visitor a clear path.

'Finally.'

Salann looked very much the worse for wear since their last meeting. His clothes were badly torn, dried blood caked his shirt from deep trenches gouged across his chest and upper arms. One eye was swollen and one ear had been ripped off, along with part of his scalp. Despite all that, he still maintained his smug grin.

'I decided the dodder forest could do the work for us, rather than attack you directly. They're a particularly unpleasant form of local flora, parasitic trees which ensnare their victims with their roots. They drag their prey below ground where they are slowly consumed, I'm talking years. You might have noticed the hillocks? They are the trees' larder. It's a slow and unpleasant death.'

Salann stepped out of the way of another struggling form as it slid past, ignoring its stifled screams. A quick glance to either side showed Frida that even Jonas and Lorcan were fighting their individual battles and appeared to be losing.

'It's ironic. I've spent my life ensuring your family stayed away from this realm. When news reached me that factions of my own race were cooperating with your mother, I had to take action. The Dark Court were making their final preparations for the invasion of your world, so I didn't have much time.'

His smile broadened, and she couldn't take her eyes off his face as he boasted of his actions, despite the choking sounds all around her. Salann's torch halted the tree roots from doing anything more to her, they appeared satisfied to keep her a prisoner for now.

'It involved escaping my world, without being detected, as well as avoiding contact with human beings in your realm.' He chuckled, a sound devoid of anything other than malice. 'It wasn't easy to find your mother, we had to torture her allies to obtain her location. Thankfully she didn't know who I was. It meant I could kill her without her attacking me. I should have found out if she had any offspring, that was my greatest mistake. I risked discovery and the imminent invasion meant I needed to return home urgently. Still, here we are.'

Frida stared at the scarred and jubilant man standing over her, the man who had murdered her mother. Her drowning hadn't been an accident after all.

'My mission is complete. You are about to die a long and unpleasant death thanks to this world's malevolent flora. Truly ironic, wouldn't you say?'

His words became no more than background noise. As she'd done at the university, with the ropes that bound her, she increased her body's temperature. Desperate to avoid the heat, the dodder's roots relaxed their grip, those which pinned her arms and legs together shrivelled. Her efforts were little more than an instinctive reaction, a survival technique lodged in the back of her mind.

One emotion dominated Frida's mind now. Rage.

It infused every cell in her body. Her mind composed a montage of memories, each one provoking greater fury. She recalled with startling clarity the moment she learned of her mother's death, the funeral and then the sequence of orphanages who failed to deal with a silent and secretive little girl. The rubble of a life of loneliness where children who despised her strange appearance hurled cruel insults. Where adolescence meant fleeing attacks from those who viewed her lack of communication as vulnerability. Her rage drew together the half-repressed shards of her life into a mosaic of lonely isolation, born from an obsessive need to keep who she was a secret. It meant never trusting anyone, never sharing her self-doubt and always being on her own.

In front of her stood the man who had killed the only person to love her. The mixture of rage and loss consumed Frida, scorched everything in its wake, nothing and no one mattered any longer. She was on her own and yet her mother's murderer had gone unpunished, and here he was gloating about his foul crime. As her bare arms broke loose of the dodder roots, Frida's skin glowed, a jade-green radiance which illuminated the darkness. She idly examined one arm, sparkling like the energy from the portal. It wasn't important.

Only one thing mattered to Frida.

In front of her was the man guilty of murdering her mother, of so many crimes. Scholr and Naschr. Yaalon Dubh. All dead because of him.

185

All her life led to this moment. She would have her vengeance.

She smiled.

Salann stepped back, robbed of his smug complacency. She got to her feet, shrugging off the last of the dried dodder roots, watching the man gibber something to those behind him. The hyroa stared, transfixed by the glowing figure in front of them. A few dropped their torches as they tried to escape. It was too late.

Vented rage found a voice in a primal roar that filled the night.

Frida exploded.

Chapter 16

"I was familiar with Post Traumatic Stress Disorder and the varied ways it could manifest in an individual's behaviour. Knowing this, I realised there was never a time you could trust someone with the condition. There was no guarantee they would behave in a rational way when under duress."

Interview with Lieutenant Tristan Wheeler, CGC

Pink and purple threads of dawn wove patterns across the sky as dawn discovered a smouldering landscape. Lazy wisps of smoke, the last survivors of the night's events, allowed an early morning breeze to carry them away to oblivion. Individuals, sometimes pairs, stumbled in dazed confusion through the ash to stare at the scene of devastation. Olsen and Tristan moved amongst them, checking for injuries, searching for the missing. Others scrabbled through the lengths of tangled fibrous tissue to find comrades, some unconscious, others exhausted from their efforts to fight the writhing enemy. Occasionally their conversations led them to point at the charred remains of trees, which had stood in their tortured shapes the evening before and now were no more than blackened stumps. The place looked and smelled like a battlefield.

A short distance away, thankfully separate from the rest of the expedition team, Jonas, Lorcan and Layla's attention centred on the unconscious figure laid in front of them. Lorcan had covered her with his shirt, most of her clothes were blackened and burned, though she was otherwise unhurt. Occasionally she'd twitch, otherwise there was little evidence of life, even her pulse was sluggish.

'What are we going to do?' Layla asked.

She stroked Frida's hand gently and with affection, repeatedly pleading for her to wake up, that she couldn't die. Jonas sighed and shook his head, looked at Lorcan with the knowledge he didn't have any answers to the question either. The two men had overcome their mutual suspicion of each other during the night, as they'd waited for another attack from the realm's malevolent flora and fauna. As they discovered they represented sides with shared goals, they'd taken to comparing experiences and found more common ground than they'd realised.

'We can't go back,' said Lorcan, the anxiety evident in his hoarse tone. 'The citizens of Ainmire won't make us welcome, even if we tell them about Salann and his crimes. We destroyed their university. We need to find another way out of this hellish dimension.'

'So long as Olsen agrees,' Jonas said quietly.

Both men looked up to where the man in question strode toward them, his red face devoid of any emotion.

Lorcan grunted. 'You'll need to persuade him then.'

'Me? Why me?'

Layla lowered her voice as Olsen and Tristan got closer. 'Because he listens to you, Jonas. He doesn't trust Lorcan because he's fae and I'm an academic and a woman so I don't qualify on two counts. Take him somewhere and have a private discussion.'

The big man flexed his impossibly broad shoulders and sighed. 'I need to speak with you, Major,' Jonas called out as he marched over to meet the two men. 'Privately, please?'

Tristan looked uncertain as Jonas joined them, and he waited for his commanding officer to nod his agreement before leaving them to their discussions. He strolled, as casually as he could, toward the body of the girl and the two guarding her.

'Will she live?' he asked, his voice lowered.

Layla jumped up and, glared at the young lieutenant before scurrying away in floods of tears. Tristan turned to Lorcan.

'I didn't mean to sound heartless. I just thought...'

Lorcan shook his head and sighed. 'Layla owes quite a debt and she's worried she won't be able to pay it back.'

'Because Frida saved her life.'

Lorcan nodded. The girl that separated them on the ground twitched and gasped but then quietened again.

'She saved all of us last night,' Tristan said quietly.

Lorcan nodded as he glanced over to where Olsen and Jonas engaged in an animated conversation that required more gestures than loud words.

'Does your commanding officer think that way?' Lorcan asked.

The man in front of him, in his filthy, sweat-stained and torn uniform snorted his amusement. 'He's never encountered anything like this before, Lorcan. None of us have. Fighting the fairies' – he blushed and it received a warm chuckle – 'meant having to redefine war in double quick time. I don't think we ever found the answers. And now we're fighting something else we don't understand in a world that's alien to us in every way.'

They met each other's gaze for a second time and shook their heads with the resignation only a soldier could understand. It generated a smile which spoke of a mutual understanding, common ground.

'Who'd be a soldier, eh?'

It triggered snorts of mild amusement and extended hands.

'But we are soldiers, aren't we?' Tristan said. 'Trying to stay alive. And if we're going to succeed, we need to fight together.'

'The sign of a brave man.'

'Or a stupid one. To be honest, I don't care. We can't go on like this, not trusting each other. You've got experience we need. And a wise head. You made the right call back in Ainmire. The old man would have got us all killed.'

'In my army days I was always the one with better ideas than my commanding officer. You can imagine how popular I was.'

'I've tried to be more diplomatic, I'm not sure it makes any difference. Trouble is he's a proud man, Lorcan. He's out of his depth but he can't admit it. Half of his unit are waiting for any indecision on his part to take action.'

'Such as?'

They both glanced over to the main camp where Animal and a few others sat in a circle of dark, angry faces, occasionally looking over at them.

Tristan cleared his throat before lowering his voice still further. 'You know the type and what they're capable of. They've lost respect for Olsen. They've moved beyond insubordination to mutiny and Animal's track record is filled with acts of mindless violence. We'll need to watch him especially, Lorcan.'

'I'll kill him, Tristan. If he tries anything. I need you to know that.'

Tristan nodded, his blue eyes flashing in his soot-covered face. 'I don't have a problem with that solution.'

Despite their bleak situation, Lorcan chuckled and released his smile. 'It's good to have an ally. Since becoming a civilian, I've missed the kind of friendship you form in battle. And whatever we're in now.'

His words received a subtle nod of the head. Groans from the young woman at their feet drew their attention. Her eyes flickered, she twitched, and suddenly her eyes opened wide, filled with panic.

Lorcan dropped to his knees instantly, with a calm voice and carefully painted smile in place. 'Frida, you're safe. You don't need to be scared. You're safe.'

She sat up with surprising speed, surveyed the world around her, then stared at the two men. Lorcan reached over to take her hand but she snatched it away.

He smiled and kept his voice steady. 'You're safe, Frida. You've been asleep. You're OK now. I just need you to relax.'

She leapt to her feet, Lorcan's shirt falling to the ground. She peered at Tristan, shook her head and frowned, before scanning the landscape again.

Lorcan reached into her backpack, held it up a tee shirt. 'Why don't you put on some fresh clothes, Frida? You'll feel better then.'

He sounded like he was talking to a child but his forced serenity worked. She looked down at her tattered and blackened tee shirt, peeled it off in one unselfconscious movement and took the offered top Lorcan handed to her and put it on. She perused his face as though trying to remember where she'd seen it before. She twitched again and jerked a head in the direction of the razed forest.

'Did I do this?'

'You saved our lives, Frida,' Tristan said, while trying to maintain the same reassuring smile. Even so, he couldn't hide the tremor in his voice.

She paid no attention but took a few unsteady steps to where a pair of boots and charred remains of legs were encircled by blackened dodder roots. She stared hard at the grisly remnants and smiled. There was no humour in the expression but a grim acceptance. Lorcan joined her.

'Do you want to talk about what happened? You don't have to, if you're not ready.'

She skittered away like a frightened bird, arms flapping as if to take flight. Cautiously he reached out toward her and placed a hand on her shoulder. She watched him, attention flitting from his hand to his eyes.

He squeezed her shoulder. 'You had us all worried, when you passed out.'

Her eyes widened as she peered over his shoulder. Lorcan didn't need to know what she'd seen. The camp was behind him and the rest of the team would have seen her. Her head snapped in the opposite direction, spotting Olsen marching towards them.

'Why don't we—?'

Frida fled with astonishing speed. She hurtled past a bewildered Olsen, through the blasted wilderness she'd created.

'Frida! Wait!'

Lorcan and Tristan exchanged glances and set off after her.

For a woman who'd recently woken from several hours of unconsciousness, she ran with the speed and grace of a frightened deer. Within minutes they'd passed through the remnants of the dodder forest. Even the trees which hadn't been burned were dead, as though their root systems were connected, and death for one meant death to all.

Frida's headlong flight eventually slowed to a steady jog. Her pursuers maintained a cautious distance so as not to alarm her but she appeared oblivious. From time to time, she'd stop for a moment, look around her, then continue her journey. After a while, it was obvious she had a destination, but in a landscape which stretched to the horizon, neither man could work out what it was. Having lost all sense of time, beyond the steady rising of the day's heat as the sun climbed into the sky, they came to a halt. Breathless and sweaty, they approached the girl, holding up their hands. She glanced over her shoulder but otherwise paid no attention to their arrival.

They stood in a wide and flat expanse of sickly grassland. Frida peered into the distance, shielding her eyes from the glare of the sun. As Lorcan approached her and started to ask if she was all right, she took off across the meadow of mustard-coloured grass. Her destination turned out to be a small copse of trees growing around a shallow depression. As she drew closer, she slowed to a walk, and the two men caught up with her again, while keeping a discreet distance.

'Frida? Are you all right?'

The girl turned, looking startled, as though she was surprised to see anyone. 'Stay away. I need to do this on my own.'

They obeyed with awkward smiles as she took hesitant steps toward the saucer shaped depression, darkened by the surrounding trees. It appeared completely empty, though Frida's wariness suggested otherwise.

'Frida, what are you doing?' Tristan called out before sharing an anxious glance with Lorcan.

She crept toward the copse, body tensed and ready, tipping her head from one side to another as though listening to something.

Tristan moved closer to Lorcan. 'You don't think she's having some kind of psychotic breakdown, do you? I've known soldiers with PTSD behave like this. I'm not saying that's what it is but I'm worried that someone with her ... firepower ... could cause real problems if nothing was done about it.'

They watched her approach the dell carefully.

'I don't think it's that, Tristan. Frida has psychic abilities. I think someone is talking to her.'

The younger man's reaction said he preferred his own theory. They watched her enter the shady dell. She wandered around it, her focus on something the two men couldn't see.

'That professor said there was someone in this world who wanted her here.' Tristan's whisper turned hoarse. 'What if he's the one talking to her? Telling her to do things. Bad things.'

'Njord, you mean?'

'We don't know, do we? All we know is she's dangerous. And unhinged.'

Lorcan shook his head and exhaled loudly. 'No, I can't believe that. Frida has a history here. My father's research suggested her family has a connection with this place. I don't think she's a danger to us.'

'You sure that's not because you care about her?'

'No. No, we're just friends. That's all.'

Frida's attention flitted from one section of the dell to another. She'd bend down to gaze at something, then move on, occasionally turn around to watch something happening at the point where she'd entered. She repeated the process four times before finally standing up and walking out of the dell toward. She seemed like herself.

'Are you all right, Frida?'

She smiled at Lorcan, it looked natural enough on the surface but he knew her well enough to see the distraction behind it. Tristan was at his side, his hand close to the gun at his hip. The girl didn't seem to notice.

'I think so. I had to find out if it was true.'

'If what was true?'

Her frown reappeared for a second but faded, she didn't answer straight away.

'You're going to think I'm crazy.'

Their hollow smiles tried to suggest the idea never occurred to them.

Frida shook her head and sighed. 'I'm sorry. Nothing makes sense. I'm trying to understand what they're telling me, but it's not easy.'

'They?' Tristan's voice rose with trepidation.

Frida tipped her head to one side, frowned again. 'The rest of the expedition team are on their way. I need to stay ahead of them, to avoid trouble.'

'How do you know that?' Tristan asked, his hand never straying from his gun.

'They showed me.'

Lorcan strolled toward the dell. Frida followed him. 'Why don't you show me what you found in here?'

She agreed readily, a lightness in her acceptance that suggested relief. The shadow of the trees in the little dell offered cool shade from the oppressive morning heat.

'It's nice here,' Lorcan said, eager to keep things relaxed.

Tristan waited outside, clearly too hesitant to join them. His reference to battle fatigue made sense in a way; Frida had spent most of her life fighting for survival. She'd only known isolation since her mother's death, and his father had repeatedly voiced his concerns for Frida's mental health. His solution was to provide friendship, a role to be fulfilled by Lorcan. This was the moment to test that theory. Lorcan moved closer, smiling as he reached out a hand to take hers. It was incredibly hot.

'Frida, tell me what you see. Perhaps I can help. My father's research might be useful. Sometimes it helps just to share your thoughts with a friend.'

She nodded. The tilt of the head told him something was happening in her head, either she was thinking or, more likely, using her psychic ability. Tristan's concerns that it might be Njord returned but he pushed them aside. She didn't look anxious or disturbed, just confused. She pointed at the farthest side of the dell, where the ground reared up to support the trees hovering around its edge.

'Can you see them?'

She pointed to minute crystals sparkling in the soil. He knelt and touched one, some of the soil falling away to reveal more of it embedded in the ground. It shone with a greenish tinge. He stood up and looked at her, bewildered.

'They're the same colour as your eyes. And the portal.'

She tilted her head and smiled, this time with greater sincerity. He'd said the right thing. She exhaled loudly, and surprised him by throwing her arms around him and giggling like a kid.

'They're not like us. I'm not sure what they are. They call themselves Nephrite. They don't communicate with words either. I just get these feelings. No, sensations.'

'And are these crystals connected in some way?'

'Not connected. That is the Nephrite.'

'You're communicating with those crystals?'

'It sounds stupid I know. It's why I had to find out for myself. They were trying to communicate with me while I was unconscious. It took a long time for me to realise what they were doing. They get irritated with me because I'm slow. And stupid.'

She released him, suddenly embarrassed, and glanced over her shoulder to where Tristan hovered. He took the gesture to mean it was safe to join them. Frida snapped her head to the entrance to the dell, as though something was moving past her.

'What are you seeing, Frida?'

The sudden joy in her expression at knowing he understood, vanished. 'You'll think I'm crazy.'

'No, I won't. I promise. Father believed you have a connection with this place. I think you're proving him right. Tell me what you see.'

She nodded with greater confidence. 'They told me to come to this location.'

'The crystals?'

'They created a picture in my head so I knew how to find it. I think they're trying to tell me a story.'

She took a deep breath, her gaze fixed on whatever invisible action was taking place in front of her. 'I thought I was hallucinating at first. It's like seeing ghosts. Images float in this place, they come and go. It took a while to work out there's a sequence to them. Because the images are the same green colour, that's how I knew it was the Nephrite creating them.'

Tristan's face was a picture of concern triggered by the mention of hallucinations. Lorcan ignored him. 'Tell me about the sequence. You think there's a story?'

'It starts with an elderly woman sitting in a chair by a window over here.' She pointed at the empty location. 'There was a house here, a long time ago. There are floor tiles beneath the soil in that corner.' She jerked a thumb at the other side of the dell. 'The woman is sewing. There's a little girl playing on the floor, just there,' she said, gesturing to the centre of the space.

Frida turned to the entrance. 'A woman enters, she's quite young. She hugs them both. All three women share the same facial features. I think they're a family: grandmother, mother and daughter. The mother is frightened, though. She's wearing riding clothes. Through the door, the sun is shining, I can just see her horse. It's covered in sweat, she's been riding it hard.'

'You can see all this now?'

Frida nodded, her eyes following the events as they unfolded. 'I can't hear what they're saying, but the mother is unhappy, crying as she lifts up the little girl and kisses her.'

Frida's face creased with sadness as she watched the scene play out again. 'The two women argue. The mother tries to persuade the other woman to come with her as she keeps pointing to the outside world. Grandmother refuses. She's anxious as she holds the hand of the little girl. It's obvious that whatever the mother is going to do is dangerous. I think that's why the grandmother doesn't want to go with her. The mother kisses them both and leaves.'

Frida turned her attention back to the entrance of the dell, watching what Lorcan couldn't see and wished that he could.

'The woman rides away. The grandmother and little girl cry as they wave goodbye.'

Tears filled Frida's eyes as she stared over the meadow they'd crossed earlier, presumably watching the mother disappear into the distance. She turned back to Lorcan, tears in her eyes, her hesitance and shaky breathing telling him worse was to come. 'The story's ending is horrible, but I had to keep watching because it didn't make sense at first. I had to get the sequence right. I hadn't noticed the grandmother and child wore different clothes. That meant time had elapsed.' Frida pointed to the darkest part of the dell as tears continued to tumble down her cheeks. 'Their bodies are over there. It's horrible, what was done to them.'

She searched Lorcan's face. He took hold of her hand again and squeezed it. Words had no meaning, he knew that from losing his father.

She sobbed as she stared into his eyes. 'Whoever killed them was horrible. Evil. I think it's the same person that scared Salann. It's hard to tell, the Nephrite can't explain everything. But this story is important, even I understand that now. The woman who rides away is important.'

'You're making sense of what's happening to you, that's a good start.'

He knew what she was going to ask before she said it.

'You do believe me, don't you? You don't think I'm going mad, do you?'

A quick glance at Tristan showed it was a good thing she hadn't asked him. Lorcan hugged her hard, surprised when she didn't resist his embrace.

'You're not crazy, Frida. Everything you've said supports what Father believed. He thought Njord was a real threat. But if the Nephrite are trying to help you, that has to be a good thing, doesn't it? It means you're not on your own. They're helping you. So am I. Always will.'

He kissed her cheek softly. He felt so sorry for her, and the poor girl needed to know she had at least one friend. He withdrew from the hug and smiled a little awkwardly, though she didn't seem to notice. Her energy had returned.

'Good, that helps. Because the Nephrite have given me another location and I need to get there before the others arrive. They're going to try to stop me.'

Chapter 17

'The Aesir ruled Asgard; the Vanir represented an alternative society but not one the belligerent Aesir could ever tolerate. Their civil war was brief and brutal.'

Norse Mythology: Viking Reflections by Amanda Redford

The castle in the valley looked like something out of a fairy tale.

It reminded Frida of the books she demanded her mother read to her each night before she agreed to go to sleep. She might have been staring down a gentle slope to the river valley in an alien realm now, but the memory took her back to her childhood and the knowledge her mother hadn't died accidentally.

Leaving the dell, she'd happily chatted with Lorcan and Tristan as they set off for their new destination. They hadn't asked where she was taking them, proving they trusted her. As the sun rose in the sky and the heat turned oppressive, they pressed on to the destination in Frida's head. She sensed their anxiety – it was inevitable and natural – but the two men had relaxed slightly. For two soldiers, their conversation was always going to lead to a sharing of experiences but even then their stories brought laughter. At least at the start. Gradually, their tales led to an analysis of military methodology in either realm which was when Frida's mind wandered.

She blamed the Nephrite. She couldn't call her mind her own any longer; it was a dumping ground for their information. She understood little of it but their knowledge demanded space. Her brain struggled to cope. Dormant memories surfaced while her synapses assessed their worth. Her reaction to the castle was one example. It led to revisiting events previously submerged in an untapped reservoir of grief and pain.

She blamed Salann too. His death should have brought satisfaction, but he'd robbed her of more than her mother. He'd denied her a normal life. He was the cause of the decade of misery and loneliness, and now those memories were leaking from the dam she'd built. Each one threatened to increase the rage churning inside her, unsated by her destruction of the dodder forest.

She'd been eight years old, alone in the world and with a secret she couldn't share with anyone, when she'd built a wall behind which she could shut away her misery. Those appointed to care for the strange little girl shared their concerns at her lack of tears and the absence of any emotion. Soon their worries turned into accusations. Why didn't she cry? Didn't she love her mother? Was she a selfish and spoiled child? Their conclusions? She was. No amount of counselling or attempts to find her a new family worked. The little girl was like a dead thing, silent, empty and who treated warmth with distrust and animosity.

Frida found herself staring at the castle again. Sweat trickled down her temples and her hands hurt from bunching them into white knuckled fists. It didn't make sense why watching the castle would make her so angry. She dismissed it, a consequence of her addled mind as the Nephrite continued to send her more irrelevant information.

The castle reminded her of the way her mother expanded on the fairy tales; the young Frida loved to hear about the real world of the fae, fascinated by the differences between the realms. Until, in the midst of the war, when the word fairy became a curse, those stories haunted her. She wondered if their mysterious fae visitors were an advance guard of the offensive, forcing her mother to give up vital information. As she grew older, it proved convenient to believe they had, helping her hate the invaders like everyone else. The lie didn't sustain her; it was a child's fantasy. As adolescence turned into womanhood, and her unique abilities made her into even more of a freak, she had to confront the reality of being a racial hybrid.

As Frida stared at the castle, she heard a woman crying. Looking around, she realised it was her. Tears tumbled down her cheeks, drying almost instantly in the late afternoon heat. She turned her attention back to the castle. Somehow she needed to get those memories back behind the dam before all the leaks triggered a serious breach.

'Frida? Are you all right?'

It was Lorcan. Insistent, irritating her like a buzzing fly.

'Frida? Can you hear me? Frida?'

Lorcan again. He laid next to her on the sickly coloured grass, one hand on hers, beaming his usual smile that always made her feel good. Her irritation faded, He'd been kind and understanding, he'd even kissed her. She'd been so preoccupied with what she'd seen in the dell, their fleeting moment had passed her by. He was the one thing in her miserable world she could rely on.

Before she could respond her senses sounded their usual warning tingle.

Something dark and cold entered her mind. She could feel its tendrils snaking through her synapses, tasting her thoughts, sniffing at her memories. It startled her enough to make her jump, except she couldn't. Pressure exerted itself on her, tried to imprison her. She fought against it, freeing her hands as sparks of green energy arced between her fingertips.

Lorcan leapt backward, hands raised in surrender, fear scrabbling across his face. 'It's OK, Frida. No one is trying to hurt you. I thought you were having some kind of seizure.'

Even after lowering her hands, arcing energy skipped from one finger to another. Both Lorcan and Tristan, the latter visibly trembling, couldn't take their eyes off it.

'Sorry,' she said, and meant it.

'We were worried about you,' Lorcan replied, his usual smile a pretence now. 'You hadn't moved for hours, so we didn't know if something was wrong. Then you started to spasm …'

'I'm fine.'

'Good. Good.' A quick glance at the other man. 'It's getting dark and we thought it best to spend the night here. Make our way down to the castle in the morning.'

Ribbons of orange, red and pink littered the sky like the remnants of a birthday party. It made no sense to Frida. The walk hadn't taken that long, she remembered lying in the afternoon sun, how it dried her tears. How had time moved so quickly and why hadn't she noticed? The anxious features of both men told her nothing. She agreed to their suggestion with a nod of the head.

Except, the Nephrite granted her a grainy image of Olsen and his unit, camped close to a line of trees she recognised. They weren't far behind. She'd wasted valuable time, though she had no idea how. They'd arrive in the morning and she needed to enter the castle before then. The reasons for that weren't clear either.

Lorcan delegated the task of finding supper to Tristan. He wanted to say something and, for reasons she didn't dare consider, she hoped it wasn't to offer explanations about her behaviour. After recovering from her temporary brain freeze – that was what she was calling it – he'd been super friendly and amusing. He'd provided the distraction she needed, even managed to make her laugh. Of course, he was being supportive and a good friend but that kiss and the hug hinted at other possibilities. They'd been in her head since meeting him in York, when she'd marvelled at his body and those dark and brooding good looks. Except nothing could happen between them. He was fae, with all the baggage that came with that definition. It was ridiculous to even think about them developing their relationship. The man would never be attracted to her, and she chided herself for thinking otherwise. It was a fantasy, a product of an over-active imagination. Yet, she could hope. With luck Tristan would take a long time to find food.

'You're feeling better,' Lorcan said as he sat next to her, relaxed now.

'Yeah, thanks to you.' She hated expressing her feelings, it didn't come easily but she needed to show her appreciation. 'I feel like you're the only one who understands me. You don't see me as some scary freak.'

He patted her knee and grinned at her. 'You're nothing of the kind. You've lived a shitty life. I used to think mine was bad until I met you.'

He laughed but she sensed the awkwardness in his confession. It was so tempting to break into his mind to discover what was really going on there, but she stopped herself. That broke a layer of trust that could never be reclaimed, so she relied on good, old-fashioned curiosity.

'Why was yours bad? Your father was a lovely man.'

The deepening twilight made it difficult to read his expression but his face turned as dark as the sky.

He shook his head and patted her knee again. 'We were different people. But that's not important. I just wanted to make sure you understood how much you can depend on me. You're not on your own, Frida, I'm your friend and there is still my debt.'

He chuckled and she joined in. She hadn't been this relaxed in a long time; the Nephrite had taken the night off. For the first time, she wasn't surrounded by a bunch of soldiers who hated her, and even the warm night air calmed her.

'I never told you but when I was with you and your father, I felt the happiest I've ever been. It was like I'd come home. I know that sounds stupid ...'

'Father would have loved to hear you say that.'

'Would you, Lorcan?'

'Of course, I would. I've told you how important you are to me.'

He hadn't, not in so many words, but it sounded nice to hear them now. Tristan came back and the moment vanished. Thanks to his resourcefulness, and courtesy of a patch of broad-leafed plants which had gathered enough moisture to sustain them, they could have a drink. He'd been unlucky with food. In fact, when it came to the realm's fauna, there was no sign of anything beyond a few insects. Tristan's grumpy mood led him to voice a string of complaints. The place was slowly dying; it would never be any good as a new Eden for humanity to colonise. Frida listened to the two men debate the issue as night pulled its darkest, warmest blanket over them. Their camp was little more than a square of weedy saplings, but positioned at the top of the river valley, it caught a balmy breeze which freshened the humid air. Exhausted, she lay back to watch the reeling constellations, replaying her conversation with Lorcan until sleep overcame her.

She woke, enveloped in darkness, to muffled noises and occasional soft grunts. She reached out, running her fingers along the ground for snaking tree roots. Nothing. Someone whispered something. She stretched her arm out, to where Lorcan had made his bed. He wasn't there. She couldn't find Tristan either. Another grunt.

They'd been captured.

Frida struggled to her feet, unsure what to do. Why hadn't their captors taken her? Perhaps they'd hadn't realised she was there. It was a risk but she summoned a trickle of energy into one hand to shed a little light on her surroundings. Their attackers might notice her but she had to take that chance. Whoever their assailants were, she'd blast them.

She held up one arm and splayed her fingers as energy rippled along her veins to generate an eerie green glow. She stifled a cry of shock at the sight of tangled naked bodies, writhing in passion. Two faces turned toward her with surprised expressions that rapidly turned into embarrassment. Frida doused her light and stood up, her legs buckling as the image of the two men refused to leave her mind's eye. She stumbled back to where she'd been sleeping to the soundtrack of rustling clothes and whispered regrets. A moment later, Lorcan appeared in front of her.

'I'm sorry. I'm so sorry.'

Waves of remorse and shame flowed off him. They threatened to overwhelm her, but she couldn't cope with his emotions, not while she had her own to purge. She burst past him, pushing him so hard he stumbled and fell. She stifled a snort of contempt and strode down the incline. He called after her.

'If you come anywhere near me, either of you, you saw what I did to Salann.'

There was no reply. She nodded to herself. They knew better than to doubt her.

She marched into the darkness, only halting when she heard the river. The distance was enough for her tempest to fade so it left her mired in a swamp of regret. Earlier on, she'd told herself how stupid she was to think Lorcan could be attracted to her. Well, he'd proved it, in the most humiliating way possible. She had indulged in a fantasy about a man who had no interest in women. A crushing loss of self-respect, greater than any she had ever known, overwhelmed her.

Frida stared into the darkness where she hoped there might be answers to how she could have misread the situation so badly. If she had used any common sense, she realised, she would have known Lorcan was fulfilling his debt, meeting the obligations established by fae society. He'd been kind so he could keep her calm, to stop her turning into a dangerous maniac that blasted the landscape. She'd been so desperate for another person's affection, she'd overlooked her guiding principle; she was a freak.

The word echoed in her head. Once a constant insult, the word defined her now. The darkness triggered a memory of another night, in a different realm, where someone else had defined himself in the same way. Jonas. Originally, he'd befriended her out of his commitment to politicians but he'd risked his life to accompany her to the university. He and Lorcan might share a similar goal but Jonas was different, he considered himself a freak as well.

Even then, that brought little comfort. Her bizarre behaviour made men afraid, including Jonas. It was obvious what she had to do, she needed to return to her hermit-like existence and stop deluding herself into thinking she had any other choice.

Except there was one alternative.

She sat down by the edge of the river and wondered if it was deep enough to lose herself in its depths. Knowing her luck, it wouldn't cover her feet. After scrabbling in the dirt, she found a stone and tossed it into the river. It didn't sound very deep. She let out a heavy sigh.

'You mustn't consider doing anything so rash. I can give you purpose.'

The voice made her jump, almost causing her to topple into the river. She raised her hands, energy arced across them and she peered into the darkness until her panic subsided. The voice had been in her head. For a moment she hoped it was the Nephrite, but the hollow tone and abject solitude made it obvious. The thing that had woken up and surveyed her mind was talking directly to her. Not only that, it sensed her thoughts.

'What purpose is that?' she said out loud.

The voice chuckled, making her shiver.

'It's why I had you brought here. We will escape this prison. Once we are free, we will bring those we hate to their knees. Because that's what you want now, isn't it? You want to make them suffer. All those who have treated you so badly.'

She wanted to say no, but her dark mood matched the offer a little too well. She'd considered ending her life in the river to eliminate her misery, but what if she could be the one to make everyone suffer?

'It's an attractive possibility, isn't it?'

'Who are you?'

The chuckle again. *'You know who I am.'*

'Njord.'

No reply came, but the sense of smug satisfaction was all too evident in her head. Their communication went beyond simple words. Suddenly his earlier statement struck her like a body blow.

'What do you mean, you had me brought here?'

'My representative will arrive in the morning and escort you into the castle.'

'But the expedition team will be here. They will want to come with me.'

Whoever this representative was, they had to be in the expedition team – there was no one else. Who were

211

they? How could they have led her here when no one had been to this world before?

'Your erstwhile friends will be too preoccupied. I have planned for this moment, Frida. Together we are going to make a lot of people suffer for our indignities.'

'I'm not sure I want people to suffer.'

'Really? Are you sure? Because your mood says otherwise. You are an exceptionally angry young woman. Your destruction of the dodder forest and those fools who tried to kill you proves it.'

'But he murdered my mother ...'

'And he deserved his fate. I would have done the same. But you are missing my point. The fury you unleashed was very impressive.'

Frida wasn't sure if that was a compliment, the others certainly wouldn't think so.

'You don't care what happens to the others. Why should you? They threaten and insult you, treat you as something to be pitied or feared. These are the reactions of all lesser beings who encounter people like us.'

'What do you mean, "people like us"?'

'Surely you have realised you are not like any of them. You have a different heritage. You have the potential to be so much more than you are now. I will show you just how much when we meet. You have spent your time amongst insects. You feel bad that you are not an insect too. Wait until you see what we can achieve together.'

'They said you would create havoc if you escaped this world.'

'Mere lies. Did you not learn in your education that it is the victors who define history? My failure to oust a

cruel tyrant left me imprisoned here. To guarantee no one would ever free me, they created stories which painted me as a madman. They demeaned my efforts to achieve equality in our society, forced my friends to abandon me, turned me into something to be ridiculed. I'm sure, by now, I've been blamed for every crime that has ever been committed.'

She could hear the bitterness in his voice even though he was trying to sound like he didn't care. He didn't speak for a moment. When the voice returned, it was calm again.

'From what I can discern from your mind, we share a common injustice. We have both been shunned by others, condemned to a personal dimension of isolation and loneliness. Would you agree?'

She didn't want to answer, but her agreement must have registered in his head.

'I thought so. I couldn't have asked for a better ally, Frida. I know this is new to you, you have lived among these insects for too long. It's time we joined together to free ourselves from our imprisonment and celebrate our freedom together. Now, get some sleep. Tomorrow offers much. Together we will start an exciting new chapter in our lives.'

The presence in her mind vanished. Like a switch turned off.

Frida stared into the darkness. With so many questions swirling around her head, not least what he expected her to do in this partnership, the possibility of sleep was zero. She laid down and tried to empty her mind. The last thing she remembered, before exhaustion finally claimed her, was the apparent similarity in their lives. They were both lonely and angry outcasts.

It would be good to have a friend who understood exactly what that was like.

Chapter 18

"It must not be overlooked we had encountered a situation unlike any of us had experienced before. None of our training prepared us for it. As a result, certain individuals failed to cope with the strain. It led to heated confrontation at times but nothing we could not overcome."

Major Sven Olsen, QGM, speaking at a military hearing

Frida woke to the sound of voices raised in argument. She was no longer on her own. The day's heat told her she'd overslept, and that was the last thing she wanted. Without moving, she scanned her immediate surroundings. The expedition team were everywhere and, on the edge of the group stood Lorcan and Tristan, awkward and silent. Layla knelt at her side.

She only had to dip her head slightly to whisper, her tone urgent. 'Keep silent. Your life is in danger.'

Frida followed the woman's line of sight through a loose gathering of people, all of them focused on two men. Olsen and Animal faced each other in a stand-off which generated so much tension, it washed over her in waves. For the majority it arose from pure dread, fear born of uncertainty. In comparison, Animal's allies emanated an excitement triggered by impending violence. It didn't take a detective to work out the topic of conversation.

Something awful had happened to fuel the eruption of discontent. The two sides might be facing each other with weapons drawn but they shared the same misery and the gory marks of battle. No one was spared ripped and blood-stained clothes, bloody wounds and the look of sheer exhaustion. Animal's beard dripped blood from his jaw where it looked like something had tried to rip it off, and more blood flowed from a wide gash on his bicep.

He looked down at her laid on the ground, noticed she was awake, and pointed a bloody finger at her. 'She's the cause.'

Those behind him nodded with an insistence, glaring at her with earnest and angry faces.

Animal shifted his attention back to Olsen. His voice was a growl, without any of the respect or hesitation he'd displayed earlier. 'You heard what those fucking creatures told us. To go home. Leave her here. Well, I say we do that. We leave this fucking shithole. We can't live in this place, its worse than the one we're trying to escape! We go back and tell them. And we leave that bitch here!'

Olsen wiped away blood trickling from a head wound with the back of his hand, before it dripped into his eye. 'And when the enemy tells you to run away, that's what you do, is it?'

Animal growled again. 'Yes! Because the cause isn't worth dying for!'

His words provoked more grunts of support from his allies.

'If we don't leave now, we're all going to die here,' Lofty called out.

'No one will find out what a shit hole this place is, if we don't get back to tell them.' A declaration from a man called Taffy, with a Welsh accent and nearly as much wild hair as his friend.

Others, including some of Olsen's non-military experts, nodded their heads in agreement. The rest looked hesitant, the idea of running away piercing professional pride. If the extent of the revolt came as a surprise to Olsen, he hid it by looking at Frida.

'Whatever is trying to scare us away wants this woman. You all heard Salann's warning. The entity trapped in this world will slaughter everything in its path. Its influence infiltrated and corrupted the fairies' home world, we saw that first-hand. We cannot let that happen in ours.'

He had everyone's attention now. They were scared. They needed purpose and Olsen was ready to provide it.

'This has stopped being a straightforward reconnaissance mission. We've encountered something that poses a significant threat to our families, our friends. If we abandon the fight now, we risk the prospect of another war at home. Is that what you all want? We need to find out what this thing is, then stop it.'

Animal laughed. It wasn't a sound born of humour, its source was a darker place and it matched the sour expression hidden behind the hair and the blood. 'Fair enough. We all heard that professor tell us the only way to defeat this thing was to kill that bitch. He tried and she murdered him. I say, what are we waiting for?'

Agreement swiftly swelled from a murmur to something louder and more ominous. It gave Animal the confidence to draw his gun and point it at Frida. He wasn't alone. Six others did the same. Jonas, his gory head and shoulders visible above the rest of the crowd, moved to stand next to Olsen.

With astonishing speed, Olsen levelled his gun at Animal's head. 'I told you before. No one under my command kills a comrade.'

Animal chuckled a second time, not taking his eyes off Frida as she carefully got to her knees and splayed her fingers. His laughter had a manic quality, one that drew worried looks from others in the crowd who watched each other nervously.

'She's part fucking fairy. And we all know what we do to them, don't we?'

Loud, coarse agreement erupted from Lofty and Taffy, a few others shared the same gleeful, murderous looks. The threat forced Frida's anger back to the surface where it fed off Njord's message; these people would always see her as a freak and a menace. She had no connection to most of these people, not anymore. As she tried to get to her feet, to issue her own threats, Jonas discreetly shook his head at her. A firm hand on her shoulder reinforced the message, and Layla hissed for her to keep still. Help was on the way.

Animal turned his head enough to take in Olsen but kept his attention on his intended victim. 'You shoot me, you won't save her. My mates will take you out, Olsen. You're outnumbered. If it's fight you want, we'll win. This is how it's going to work. We kill the bitch. Go home. Leave this shithole for good.'

It brought murmured agreement but his support had ebbed. Murder was a big step beyond desertion and most of them knew it. The moment lingered as pairs of eyes searched others to find agreement or, at the very least, hesitation.

'Look!' Layla pointed a shaking finger.

Cresting a hillock, a short distance away, a huge crowd approached. Huge in number but not in height.

'Trolls,' Layla whispered into Frida's ear. 'Just in time.'

She would have turned to ask the woman what she meant and how she'd known to expect them, but their arrival changed everything. With the possibility of an imminent attack, weapons swivelled to face the new enemy.

The approaching trolls made no attempt to hide nor move with any great speed but neither did they look friendly. The distraction allowed Frida to get up and search for cover. This was not her fight.

Her gaze told her the river was deeper than she'd imagined, interspersed with small boulders that explained the gurgling noises as it flowed downhill toward a rocky pass in the distance. Beyond it, a short walk away, a dilapidated wooden jetty stretched out from the riverbank, leading to the castle's lowered drawbridge and its rusty portcullis. Towers stood like stone rockets, pointing up at the sky with coned turrets and narrow windows. High walls surrounded the castle, though their appalling condition suggested a strong wind would bring them down. At its base, covered in grass and thorny briars, lay large blocks of grey stone. Like everything else in this realm, it was a picture of decay.

With no cover to be found, facing the oncoming troll horde was going to be her problem as well. Except the closer they came, the more the danger faded. The trolls appeared as a sorry bunch of haunted expressions and malnourished bodies: a pathetic rabble.

They came to a halt, maintaining a diplomatic distance. The troll front line comprised men of different ages, the tallest no higher than Frida's waist. Behind them, women in ragged and filthy clothes sheltered a handful of gaunt, wide-eyed children who clung to their mothers' bony bodies. Out of the crowd stepped a shrivelled husk of an old man. He grasped a large, wooden staff, as though it was the only thing keeping him upright. His filthy and wrinkled clothes looked to have belonged to a younger and fitter man, as did his skin. He took a couple of stumbling steps forward, ignoring Olsen as he moved to intercept him. His rheumy eyes remained firmly focused on Frida, glittering with a fierce intelligence. When he spoke, his voice showed none of the signs of advanced age.

'We have waited so long for you, Redeemer. Praised be to the Nephrite, they told us you had arrived.'

With almost comic timing, every head of the expedition swivelled to stare at Frida with the same bewildered expression. She flushed at their sudden attention. She didn't reply, and even Olsen appeared uncertain how to respond.

Lorcan stepped forward. 'You are trolls, am I correct?'

The old man glanced in his direction but turned back to Frida as though everyone else was superfluous. He bowed, the pain of doing so making him scowl.

'I am Ehlagron, chieftain of the troll clan which inhabit and mine this land.'

Lorcan took another step forward, into the old man's line of sight. 'My father told me of a being exiled to this realm as a prisoner. Is he still here?'

The troll chieftain didn't react immediately but the rest of his clan did. Fear leapt across their faces and bodies tensed as they muttered to each other in the same guttural language as the vættir. Slowly, as though deliberately taking in the others in the expedition for the first time, the old man turned his attention back to Lorcan.

'You speak of Njord. Yes, he remains.' A gnarled and filthy finger pointed at the castle. 'He awaits the Redeemer. She will negotiate with him as to the fate of this world, and perhaps others beyond our gates.'

His words provoked Olsen into joining in the conversation. 'What do you mean, negotiate?'

The old man turned back to Frida and sighed heavily, suddenly looking exhausted, as though clutching his staff wasn't going to be enough. 'He seeks to escape our world. He has drained its life force to sustain his own. If the Redeemer agrees to his terms, they will depart and no doubt rule the cosmos.'

'And if she doesn't agree?' Lorcan asked.

The old man shook his head sadly. 'Who knows? They may argue. Perhaps even do battle. The result will not matter. What little remains to support us in this world, will be destroyed by them.'

Frida flushed as two dozen pairs of eyes judged her. The old troll's words provided less of a favourable picture of what awaited her visit to his castle, compared to Njord's version. He'd chosen to highlight the advantages, rather than the drawbacks. He'd deliberately overlooked the scale of consequences if she refused to cooperate as well.

Olsen's face appeared in front of her, startling her. 'Is this true? Did you know about all this?'

She turned to walk away, refusing to be interrogated, certainly not in public and not when she didn't fully comprehend all the detail anyway. He grabbed her arm but she wrestled it free, instinctively raising both her hands and pointed glowing fingers at him. He took a nervous backward step.

'Touch me again and I'll blast your fucking red-faced head off your shoulders.'

She hardly recognised her voice; it sounded savage and vicious. His frightened response quickly lent her confidence, giving her the satisfaction of knowing she could intimidate him. A quick peek over his shoulder showed how Lorcan's expression wasn't all that different, and she didn't need any further incentive to publicise her new perspective.

'I don't know what the guy in the castle wants. I'm going to find out. Better not get in my way either. Apparently he's ready to stop you.'

Perhaps it was the mention of his name, or the arrival of the crowd of trolls, but whatever it was, she felt his cold and empty presence in her head again. His joy at hearing her words rippled through her synapses, their mutual resentment giving Frida renewed energy.

'My representative will bring you to me.'

The trolls scrutinised her, as though they knew about their secret communication. She peered back at them, expecting one of their number to step forward to act as her guide. The voice at her side startled her.

'I'll show you the way,' said Layla.

A tsunami of fear and trepidation mixed with something else, excitement possibly, reached Frida. The shock of the woman's role, as Njord's representative, silenced Frida, preventing her from demanding an explanation. There wasn't a chance anyway, her new guide calmly walked toward the jetty. Frida was left to follow.

'Frida, don't go!' Jonas called out. 'You're making a mistake. At least let us talk.'

Uncertainty and confusion slowed Frida as she followed Layla. Jonas' plea struck a chord. Of all the people she'd met, his kindness and courage hadn't wavered. But he was the only person, in a lifetime of persecution. She caught sight of Lorcan, at the back of the crowd, it triggered a mixture of embarrassment and resentment. Emotions cascaded inside her and left her confused and uncertain. Njord's words from the night before made sense. These people didn't trust her, he offered freedom from their threats and intimidation. The opportunity was tempting, prompting her to picture a future where she could be powerful enough to stand up for herself. Sure, Njord wanted her for his own reasons, but the troll chieftain had talked about negotiations. If she didn't like the deal, she would walk away.

Frida stole a swift glance over her shoulder. Jonas stood at the front of the crowd, which had returned to squabbling. He watched her as he repeatedly shook his head. That night in York he'd labelled himself a freak. If he'd truly understood what that meant, he would have understood, not judged her.

That was the final straw.

Layla reached the jetty and waited, the woman's fear rolling toward Frida in huge waves as she drew closer.

'You need to explain yourself,' Frida said, taking hold of the woman's arm.

Tears filled Layla's eyes. She gazed at Frida's tight grip and then into her face, signalling she would cooperate. She took a shaky breath.

'I'm sorry, Frida. I couldn't tell you before. It was difficult enough getting you here. If you'd known the truth … the penalty for failure was too high.'

She lost her breath for a second, grasped her chest, and closed her eyes. Across the drawbridge and at the other end of a short tunnel, a large wooden door swung open without any visible means. Layla noticed it, tension tightening every line on the woman's handsome features.

'We have a moment or two before you meet him.'

The woman who'd been so self-assured when they'd first met, as confident as Elsa but more stylish and sophisticated, looked like a frightened mouse now.

She trembled and her voice shook. 'He ordered me to find you and bring you back.'

Each word consumed her breath as she placed a hand on her chest, looking ready to collapse. Her final word suddenly struck Frida's addled brain.

'What do you mean? Bring me back? I've never been here before.'

'Not you. Your ancestor. Your bloodline.'

After a quick glance over her shoulder at the empty doorway, she continued. 'After the civil war in Asgard, Odin exiled Njord and his followers here. He sequenced their DNA into the portals to prevent them from leaving. It meant rehoming this realm's indigenous population to other worlds, a matriarchal society of warriors. Odin recruited the best. They became his Valkyries.'

The other woman watched Frida's reaction. She'd calmed a little, lost in the retelling of her story.

'Not all of the population left. Odin only cared about those he could use for this own ends. The rest became Njord's slaves.' Tears continued to tumble down Layla's dirty cheeks but something about her grief hinted at a deeper, more personal pain.

'Are you a slave too?' Frida asked.

'Yes, in a way. My torment began much later. On a foolish expedition, like this one. Doomed from the moment we arrived. You met my comrades in the entrance to the cave which housed the portal.'

'Then who ...?'

'The Order of Freyja. We were a team sent to discover the truth behind our goal.'

Jonas' voice rang out from the other side of the river, calling for Frida to come back and talk to them. It looked like Olsen had won the argument; Animal stood at the rear of the group, head bowed. The trolls remained nearby too, passive observers.

'We need to go,' Layla said, her breathlessness returning suddenly. 'Before he releases the draugr.'

Without any hesitation she fled across the drawbridge and waited at the entrance to the tunnel. Where she'd hoped Layla might answer questions, she'd added even more. Ignoring Jonas' pleas, Frida strode over the rotting wooden planks of the drawbridge and stared up at the castle's mouldering turrets. She'd never felt at home amidst the people she'd abandoned. Whatever waited for inside the castle offered something else, she wished she knew what it was.

A gunshot made her stop, instinctively crouching in a defensive position. After a second shot, Frida turned to blast whoever was responsible. She halted, hands partly raised. Awkward, dislocated things clawed their way out of the ground close to the jetty.

'Frida! We need to go!' Layla called.

'What are those things?'

Frida stared in horror as bodies struggled to free themselves from the compacted earth, and so did the rest of the team. Jonas, who'd been hurrying toward her, backed away from the skeletal remains which deliberately blocked his path.

'They're draugr,' Layla hissed. 'I told you. Now, hurry!'

'But they're dead bodies and they've come alive.'

The expedition team shifted to take up defensive positions. The dead advanced on them, stumbling and shuffling their way forward. They appeared to be the remains of normal men, women, and even some children. Rotten and ragged clothes flapped in the breeze which ruffled wisps of hair and carried the stench of decay. They didn't hurry to attack the team, a few could hardly walk, but their intention was obvious. Bony fingers bent into claws and jaws opened to reveal rotting teeth eager to bite flesh. Most unnatural of all, they approached in silence. Frida hesitated as her conscience fought with her desire to follow Layla, to solve the mystery finally. Dead bodies weren't much of a threat, she told herself, the team had guns.

Typically, the moment she thought it, everything changed.

From the base of the hill, more bodies thrust themselves out of the earth, sandwiching the group. Together they attacked, arms raised, jaws open. The first gunshots blasted arms and legs from bodies but did little to stop them. The fallen draugr dragged their bodies forward, now they raged and roared at their enemies. They threw themselves against anything living, biting, clawing and ripping apart anything within their reach.

'Aim for their skulls!' Olsen called out as a woman in a long, flowing gown launched herself at him, almost knocking him to the ground with enormous force. The woman wasn't easy to dislodge. She clawed at his chest and sank teeth into one arm before Olsen could level a gun at her head and blow it to pieces. Gunshots echoed along the river valley. One of Olsen's soldiers stumbled on a patch of mud and instantly three draugr leapt on him, his screams ending abruptly with a wet slurping noise that turned Frida's stomach.

Layla grabbed her arm. 'They're not your friends remember. We need to go. Now.'

Frida turned to the woman, ready to dispute the sentiment but didn't get chance.

'Frida, you must remember that you've saved these people repeatedly. At the dodder forest, did they thank you? No. What did they do instead? They treated you as a monster, something to be killed or imprisoned. Let them fight for their own survival now.'

Animal's willingness to kill her loomed large and provided the justification she needed. Frida nodded her head. 'You're right. Take me to him.'

They hurried through the open door. It slammed shut behind them, silencing the screams and calls for help from outside.

Chapter 19

'Draugr: an undead creature from Scandinavian folklore'
Norse Mythology: Creatures, Monsters and Gods by Alison
Miller

Layla led Frida out of the darkness of the castle's barbican into a large courtyard. It had been a garden, patches of cultivated soil remained, now little more than baked mud. Pathways wound in circular patterns, to arrive at a decaying statue she recognised: a vatnavættir. Its billowing costume looked exactly like the three sisters who'd attacked her in the Dubh's garden. Hollow fingertips reached up to the copper-coloured sky, long ago life-giving water might've spouted from them. Neglect permeated every leaf-filled corner, amidst the desiccated corpses of small birds and rodents, and trees which had once provided shade were now bone-white skeletons.

As Frida walked through the courtyard, she felt a tingling she recognised immediately. It was the same sensation she'd felt in the tree-lined dell. In the furthest corner of the courtyard, shaded from sunlight, green images shimmered.

The Nephrite had another story to tell.

She knew what to look for this time, to find the narrative presented in the looped sequences of holographic action. It began with a crowd gathering around a woman. Frida recognised her instantly; she'd said goodbye to the grandmother and the little girl in the dell. Her impassioned speech did little to convince those around her. They looked too frightened to do anything beyond shake their heads and nervously slink away. The next sequence showed the same woman in earnest conversation with another, before they shook hands and hurried out of the castle. The fear on the faces of both women was written large but it was her ancestor whose expression intrigued Frida most. She'd seen it on her own mother on several occasions, the set of her face when she was determined to succeed, when her stoic nature meant she'd see it through, no matter what.

Frida watched uniformed guards hurry across the courtyard in different directions, eventually discovering footprints in the entrance to the barbican. They were searching for the missing women.

The final part of the montage proved the most difficult to watch. A cloaked creature, face hidden amidst its folds of heavy woollen material, entered the courtyard. The terrified crowd waited for him. It wasn't only the hooded figure provoking their panic but also the handful of vættir standing reluctantly at his side. The dark figure said something to the assembled crowd and as one they shook their heads, nervous eyes glanced furtively at the barbican. Frida had no trouble working out what the figure wanted, the details of the escapees' destination. She had a good idea who was underneath the cloak too. The man she was about to meet.

The gathered men, women and children cowered at the prospect of what awaited them. Some tried to run, only to be driven back by guards and herded into a tight knot of panic. What happened next was a protracted display of torment as the cloaked figure singled out families and couples to suffer at the hands of the reluctant vættir. Some suffocated, deprived of air as disir strolled

230

amongst them, their hands gesturing like the creature in the crypt in York. Tree branches strangled others. A handful, close enough to the fountain, drowned as water twisted through the air to envelope them, an experience she remembered vividly.

As the sequence repeated, Frida recognised some of the victims. They were outside now, attacking the expedition team. They were what Njord meant by his preparations.

The fragile defences of her motivation collapsed. This man was a monster. She couldn't ally herself with a murderer. His speech about being the misunderstood victim in history was a ruse, intended to coax her into the castle. He'd almost succeeded too. Thanks to the Nephrite, she'd learned the truth about him. He'd assumed her ignorance would make it easier for Layla to lead her to him.

Frida peered at the woman, watching her with a suspicious frown. She probably didn't know about the Nephrite and she had to keep it that way. They were the only ally she had left. The trolls' warning reminded her of what awaited if she refused to cooperate with the man she was about to meet. No matter what she did next, people would die. The dilemma left her paralysed.

Once again, she was on her own.

'Frida! Wait!'

Jonas burst into the courtyard, followed by Lorcan, Tristan and the rest. They were all soaked in fresh blood, some so exhausted they were supported by friends. There was no time for Frida to share her doubts. On the opposite side of the courtyard, and with astonishing speed, more draugr burst out from another doorway. Except these weren't the murdered civilians. They were soldiers, armed with long pikes and rusty swords, and death hadn't robbed them of their ferocity. They ran past Frida to strike at the shambles of the expedition team, corralled into a tight defensive knot.

'Frida! You need to come with me!' The desperation in Layla's voice made it sound more like a whining plea than a command.

Frida watched the desperate fight in front of her. If she intervened, it would be obvious she'd chosen a side. Her one hope had been to approach this man with the impression of being an ally. She had no idea what would follow, just hoping she could retain the element of surprise. Layla clutched her arm, emitting waves of terror that made the prospect of refusing this man even scarier.

'We mustn't anger him. He will be waiting.'

A scream, high-pitched with pain, drew Frida's attention back to the battle. Lofty, one of Animal's pals, stared down at the pike buried in his chest before crumpling into a bloody mess on the courtyard floor. Animal, with a roar that befitted his nickname, hurled his enormous frame at the pike wielder who couldn't withdraw his weapon fast enough to defend itself. The big man grabbed the skeleton's skull, yanked it from the spine and smashed it on the stone slabs with another roar. He kicked at the legs of another attacker, breaking bones so it tumbled at his feet, then heaved the pike from Lofty's chest and skewered two draugr soldiers on it.

Yet still they came.

Four draugr soldiers rugby tackled Lorcan to the ground. As one raised its sword to kill him, Jonas caught its arm and flung it hard against three others eager to join in, shattering bones of all four. Another attacked with its pike thrust forward, ready to impale the giant. With the grace of a dancer, he side-stepped the weapon, grabbed a bony arm and hurled the corpse against the courtyard wall, smashing it into pieces. No sooner was Lorcan back on his feet, he drove a knife into a draugr's skull as it tried to decapitate Tristan. The two men gave each other a grim smile before dealing with the next threat.

Frida felt a hand grab her arm. So lost in the events of the battle, she recoiled instinctively, her fingers arcing green energy.

Layla appeared oblivious. 'Please, we must leave here.'

'I can't leave them, not like this.'

Suddenly, the older woman stood in front of Frida, imperious and stern. 'They are not your friends. I am. They want to kill you. We must leave now.'

'You're not my friend either. You brought me here for Njord. You're his servant.'

Frida turned her attention away from Layla's incomprehension in time to find Billy fighting for his life. He stood in front of a petrified Agnes, slashing wildly with one of the draugr's swords, his arms and face covered in blood. Olsen was no different. One of the twins, Maggie or Martha, Frida never knew which was which, had been wounded. As her sister fought to protect her while getting her back on her feet, Olsen defended them both with a pike he'd acquired. They'd all run out of ammunition now and survival was a matter of quick-witted adaptation.

It was Agnes' face that tipped the scales. Frida remembered her as the entitled rich girl who'd taken her in and given her a home, bought her clothes and acted like a friend. Now she watched her boyfriend do his best to save her life, knowing he was about to be overwhelmed. She wasn't worried about herself; her eyes remained firmly focused on Billy and her fears for his safety.

'I'm not leaving them.' Frida raised an arm, ready to blast the two draugr soldiers who were about to overwhelm Billy.

Layla grabbed it, pinned her with an expression that screamed desperation. 'You will anger him. He will make you suffer, Frida. Suffer like you cannot imagine.'

'Let him!'

That provoked a furious shake of the head. 'You don't understand. This ...' She flung out an arm to encompass the mêlée in front of them, '... is nothing compared to what he will do. Not only to your so-called friends but to you as well.'

'He needs me to escape this place. He won't kill me.'

Frida couldn't miss the terror escaping from the woman but with it came a bitterness she'd never seen before. It was intense and it fed her snort of contempt.

'He won't need to kill you.' Layla let her words sink in as her eyes drilled into Frida's, desperate to be understood. 'Do not think you can withstand his power. You can't. He is a demi-god, Frida. I beg you, please, leave them and come with me.'

A vicious slash to his arm drove Billy to the ground and the two draugr readied their swords. The young man's freckled face paled as he waited for the killing blow. Agnes screamed. Frida didn't hesitate, wrenching her arm free and blasting the two draugr into dust.

As one, the remaining draugr turned their empty eye sockets at Frida. The expedition team's astonishment lasted only a second before making the most of the distraction to hack and smash the bewildered corpses.

She had chosen her side. It was her decision, not one triggered by other people's actions or her headstrong emotions. In front of her, the bloody faces of Jonas, Lorcan, Tristan and Agnes looked at her with relief. The moment reminded her of something Elsa had said shortly after they'd met. She'd described her first encounter with the fae. Her unit had been outnumbered yet somehow had won the day.

'We'd all been to hell and back,' Elsa told her. 'There were some who annoyed me, others I'd once tried to get transferred. Yet, as we stood there, having recaptured the city, every one of them became my friend and I would have done anything for them.'

At the time Frida had never understood that kind of loyalty. She wasn't certain even now. One thing mattered. If they were going to survive, they needed each other. With that realisation clear in her mind, Frida stretched out her fingers, her energy eager for release.

'Everybody? Duck!'

They all obliged without hesitation Even the blood-soaked Animal dropped to his knees. Frida splayed her fingers into their widest angle and released her energy in a strafing movement that exploded skulls and felled bodies. She surveyed the carnage, blackened and blasted bones lay scattered across the courtyard. The team sagged with exhaustion, some looked at her with obvious relief. Frida heaved a heavy sigh, it came from the knowledge she'd made her decision, she'd chosen a side. She knew worse awaited her but, for now, it felt good to have reacted in the way that felt right to her.

She turned to Layla. 'Take us to him.'

Tears ran down the woman's filthy cheeks as she shook her head. 'You have condemned all of us.'

'Yeah, well, we'll see, won't we?'

The rest of the team looked around at the broken bodies, then over at the woman who stood upright and defiant. Slowly, exhaustion kicking in as adrenalin faded, they gathered themselves together. Jonas was quickest to respond, striding over to Frida, a hesitant smile on his blood-spattered face.

'Thank you, Frida. I knew you wouldn't desert us.'

Olsen joined them, Lorcan and Tristan just behind him. Frida read their faces, sensed their fear and determination. She was surprised when the recrimination she'd expected never came. She jerked a thumb at Layla, who waited behind her, frightened beyond belief, looking around as though she expected another attack at any moment.

'She's the traitor. Njord sent her to bring me here. She's a member of the Order of Freyja, but I don't think she's doing any of this willingly.'

The team's animosity was enough to make the woman forget her fear for a moment and stand up straight, step forward until she was level with Frida.

'You are all dead. You just don't know it yet. He will use you against her.' She nodded at Frida. 'You will all be his puppets. You will plead for him to end your life. He won't. He enjoys playing with people, making them suffer in a hundred ways. You should have listened to the warning you were given earlier and gone home.'

'What does Njord want?' Olsen snapped.

'Her!' Layla bit back. 'She is his means of escape. He cannot leave this world through the portals, his DNA prevents it. Over time, he found a way to inhabit the bodies of others, to control them. I told you, puppets. Her pure bloodline makes this easier.'

'Why does it?' Lorcan's eyes switched from Layla to Frida and back again.

'She is descended from one of the elite families of this world.'

By now the rest of the team had gathered themselves together and listened to Layla's story.

'Njord was exiled here with his allies. One of them was a woman called Freyja. She followed her husband into exile but Njord killed him for challenging his decisions. In Asgard Freyja had been a brilliant scientist. After her husband's murder, Njord forced her into finding a way to bypass the DNA issue with the portals. She succeeded.'

'How?' Frida asked.

'I told you that Odin called the indigenous people of this realm Valkyries.'

The whole team blinked and gasped as one.

'In Asgard, scientists possessed the means to merge one person into another. The host retained their identity but the second person could control the body. Freyja had worked on this principle before the civil war.'

Agnes stepped forward, pale and shaky with tear streaks on her filthy face. She stared at Layla, not hiding her animosity. But when she spoke, it was directed to

Frida. 'I read about this. There's a story in the thirteenth century Ynglinga Saga by Snorri Sturluson. It credits Freyja with this ability, though it describes it as magic, of course. The Vikings called this process *seiðr*. There could be some truth to what she's saying.'

The implied slur made Layla curl her lip and glare at the younger woman but she continued her story. 'Freyja persuaded a woman, a Valkyrie, to merge with her in this way. It was how she was able to escape Vanaheim. She merged with the other woman so her DNA wasn't recognised and travelled to the fae realm Alfheim. Freyja hated Njord for murdering her husband. She made sure he could not use the same method of escape by destroying all her notes and equipment before leaving. She established the Order with a single goal, to ensure Njord remained imprisoned here.'

Lorcan shook his head and frowned. 'I don't understand. If Frida's ancestor, or at least the person in her body, created the Order, why would they try to kill her and anyone with her bloodline?'

Layla's impatience showed in the way she shook her head, as though the man hadn't been listening to her. 'The fae in Alfheim were simpler folk. They didn't understand how two people could exist in one body. All they saw was an ally of Njord who had escaped from prison. We're not sure what happened. The story suggests she fled to Midgard and hid there, amongst the uncivilised humans.'

'And the Order retained its obsession with ensuring Njord remained in Vanaheim?'

'Yes.' Layla's energy vanished with the word, suddenly she looked defeated and old. 'Centuries later, and with the impending invasion of the human realm looking more and more likely, we thought Njord would be dead. We worried that if the invasion went wrong and the humans discovered the portal technology, there was a chance he might try to escape again. If Njord was dead, we had no reason to worry. We could abandon the Order. Our expedition was intended to assess any remaining threat. We found he had drained the life force of the flora and fauna of the entire planet so he could stay alive. He captured us before we could return with the news.'

Silence. All eyes turned on Frida.

It should have made her feel awkward and self-conscious. It didn't. She glanced at the scar on her wrist, the symbol of the Valkyrie, a ritual which had been passed down the generations until its meaning had been lost.

Olsen stirred. 'Let me get this right. This man wants to merge with this young woman so he can pass through the portal. Presumably to drain whatever world he inhabits so he can stay alive.'

Layla laughed, a sound empty of anything other than scorn. 'He is a powerful demi-god. He will do more than drain energy. He is angry and bitter at his incarceration. He wants revenge.'

Agnes frowned and shook her head. 'But the Asgardians are all dead.'

Layla looked at her with a mixture of pity and contempt. 'Their descendants in Alfheim aren't. But it goes beyond that. He craves power. There is nothing to stop him grabbing it either. The fae have grown lazy and complacent. Human beings are recovering from the war and global catastrophe. He will sow seeds of dissension between the races, set them against each other and then destroy whatever remains. The survivors will be his slaves.'

The Valkyrie of Vanaheim

Olsen searched the faces of his exhausted and badly wounded team. They watched him with the same forlorn expression. 'We can't let that happen,' he said.

Lorcan's voice echoed in the stone corridor, possessing much greater energy than Olsen's. It matched his smile. 'You're forgetting one thing. The trolls talked about it. Frida can resist him. They talked about a battle, one we might not survive, it's true. They understand this world better than us, they called her the Redeemer. She could be a real threat to him. After all, she's a Valkyrie.'

Everyone's eyes focused on her a second time. This time, Lorcan's confidence did make her feel awkward. He'd placed a huge responsibility on her broad shoulders with his message of hope.

In the awkward silence that followed, Frida turned to her guide. 'Take me to him.'

There was no hesitation or comment as Layla limped ahead of the group, silent and stoic. A quick scan of the woman's mind reassured Frida there was no further treachery planned, though she couldn't be certain.

Lorcan's message of hope niggled at Frida. She needed better command of her abilities to fight a demi-god but Salann had put an end to that by murdering her mother. Lorcan might have lifted the spirits of most of the others but that was all he'd done. She'd caught sight of Animal's reactions to Lorcan's words – nothing had changed where he was concerned. He remained at the back of the procession; she knew what solution he had in mind.

She pushed her anxieties aside as Lorcan jogged forward to walk alongside her, sensing his anxiety even before he arrived. His smile was there as usual but it lacked conviction. It surprised her to find she no longer held a grudge against him. The misunderstanding had been her own; she'd been stupid and misread his intentions. She returned the smile, causing his to falter, but he recovered quickly.

'Thank you for helping us back there. I know it's not been easy … to say the least … I've made matters worse too. I should have told you.'

She gave him a casual shrug. The new version of Frida hadn't come to terms with finding the right words for such moments of embarrassment, so gestures would suffice.

He lowered his voice to the smallest of whispers. 'Do you think they can help?'

'I don't know. They dumped a load of information in my head yesterday. That's stopped now. I can think clearer, but I have no idea how to use it or what it means. I can't communicate with them either. Even when I was asleep it was just a bunch of weird sensations and images.'

Jonas, Tristan and Olsen marched behind them, no doubt trying to listen in on their conversation. There was every chance Njord would be eavesdropping too, though Frida couldn't sense his cold and empty presence in her head. They marched in silence for a moment before Lorcan continued, his awkwardness lingering.

'You've undergone quite a conversion since I first met you in York.' His smile widened, 'Despite our earlier problem Frida, nothing has changed about my debt.'

Such silly fae traditions felt out of place here, in this remote outpost where survival was all that mattered and would never be guaranteed. Since she hadn't the words to say such things, the concept was reduced to four words.

'Fae protocols are stupid.'

'You're not the only one who's been on a journey, you know. There was a time when I'd have agreed with you. Fae society meant little to me, causing so many arguments at home. Dad believed they sustained our race's values, helped us retain some of the civilisation our complacency and endless wars eroded. I didn't appreciate that. I saw myself as an outcast because I was different to other men. Dad did nothing to change that perception. I embarrassed him when I was younger.' His expression darkened. 'I realise now he was right. I never got to tell him that. He brought you and I together for one reason. He couldn't protect you when you were young and needed to honour the obligation he'd made to your mother.'

'You lost your father to Salann, I lost my mother. We're even.'

His sadness washed over her. She took his hand and squeezed it, something the old Frida would never have done. Lorcan's steely determination drove away the sadness as he spoke.

'No, we're not. I must honour my family's debt, Frida.'

His words made her wish she hadn't been so blind to the attempts he'd made to be her friend. Things would have been so different. She didn't get chance to reply. Layla halted as the corridor opened into a small antechamber. A thin and filthy carpet covered the floor, tatty and moth-eaten tapestries hung from the walls. They stood in front of a large double door, twice their height and black with filth.

Layla turned to face them. 'He will know what has happened in the courtyard. I suggest you expect the worst and prepare to meet your deaths.'

Frida took a deep breath and hoped she sounded confident. 'Let's get this over with.'

Chapter 20

'The architecture of a castle required three things: security, status and comfort. Its walls might keep you safe but their size showed how powerful you were. Once inside, the interior design made the same bold statements.'

How to Build a Castle by Reginald Addison

The castle architect would have labelled the room a hall, though if they'd described it as the Grand Hall, it wouldn't have been an exaggeration. More of an understatement.

Instinctively, everyone raised their eyes to take in its height, to stare up at a black ceiling flecked with silver stars, illustrating the night sky and its constellations. Except, like everywhere else, the scale of dilapidation matched the size of the room. Huge damp patches turned parts of the ceiling brown, while weirdly shaped fungi sprouted out of corners and buttresses. Elsewhere, paint had flaked off to reveal the original wood, white with rot.

Like the anteroom, tapestries hung over the walls, depicting epic battles and heroic deeds. In most instances, the warriors wore stern expressions and were, without exception, women. The woven works of art suffered from the same neglect, suffering holes, tears and burns.

Inevitably, everyone's attention shifted to the figure at the farthest end of the hall.

He sat casually, one leg crooked over an arm rest, sipping from a glass filled with red liquid. It was a throne on a raised dais, gold in colour and ornately carved. The attention he gave his drink showed he was deliberately ignoring them.

With a nervous hobble, head down, Layla led them to stand in front of the wooden stage before shuffling sideways, as if to prove she wanted no part of their fate. Their host was nothing like the demi-gods Agnes had shown Frida in her books, no flowing locks, muscles or handsome face. Njord looked like a middle-aged businessman, bald, flabby and with a significant gut. He wore a pair of trousers like any fae man and a dirty smock, covered in a palette of coloured stains. As he drank, his jowls wobbled. When he finally acknowledged their arrival, Layla was his centre of attention, and he smiled at her with a predatory expression.

'You were gone a long time.'

The woman kept her head down, her voice trembling. 'I humbly apologise, my lord. There were so many drawbacks. Mainly at the hands of the Order. Their efforts to frustrate your ambitions have not lessened over time, in fact, they have increased. Their influence—' She halted the instant he raised a flabby hand and swallowed the rest of her words.

'You realise that the presence of your loving Carwyn in here,' – he tapped his head – 'has faded because of your tardiness. I haven't heard his bleating complaints for years now. Not so much as a word in fact. But I did warn you, didn't I? Take too long, I said, and your lover may not be here when you get back.' He waited for a reply, prompting Layla to look up, tears tumbling down her cheeks. 'I did warn you, didn't I?' A question delivered with a bite.

'Yes. Yes, my lord. You warned me.'

'Good. I don't want you thinking I'd reneged on our bargain.'

Layla's head dropped again and her shoulders shook as she sobbed silently.

Njord's attention shifted with oily ease to Frida. 'But, finally, here you are. The last Valkyrie.'

His examination of her was no different to other men who'd been equally demeaning; she'd kicked the last guy in the crotch but she bit her lip this time and waited. Like all the others, his nose wrinkled and he shook his head.

'Nothing to look at, are you? Plain is a polite description. Hardly the appearance I'd like for the rest of eternity, but beggars can't be choosers.' He pointed a finger at his flabby body. 'It's no better than this. Though Carwyn was in better condition when I took him over, wasn't he Layla?'

The woman's cries turned into a howl.

Njord chuckled. 'Are you as emotional as the rest of your gender? Your masculine physique suggests otherwise. Though, once I'm installed, it won't matter. Carwyn soon learned to stay quiet.' He grinned at Frida, eager to see the effect of his taunts. 'Of course, had you agreed to cooperate, as I discussed with you outside the castle, your involvement would have been less ... passive. But you chose to reject my offer. Such a shame. For you, of course. For me, all I want is your body so I can escape this prison.'

Frida thrust her shoulders back, stuck out her chest and tried to quell the butterflies performing aerial acrobatics in her stomach. 'You like the sound of your own voice, don't you?'

Njord's grin widened. 'I suppose you want to kill me. Go ahead, see how impossible that's going to be.'

His scorn and complacency provoked the obvious reaction; no doubt he wanted to see what level of threat she posed. Frida knew all that but didn't care – she wanted to hurt him. Bolts of green, incandescent energy leapt from her fingertips to form a wall of blistering hot flame. It struck an invisible barrier and flared in all directions. The man on the other side of the barrier chuckled. The hall around her didn't fare so well. Wall tapestries burned and fell into smouldering heaps.

'Quite a temper you've got there!'

A second energy bolt, forged with greater intensity and power than the first, met the same invisible obstacle. Flames flared and heat billowed around the huge hall as the team dropped to the floor to avoid its fiery backlash. Even before it had cleared, Njord's voice rang out.

'That's going to be a useful weapon to add to my repertoire.'

Frida bunched her fists in frustration, only now beginning to wonder if Layla had been right all along. A quick glance at the woman's expression, as she cowered on the floor, reinforced the theory.

Frida waited until the air cleared and she could see properly. 'You're not going to control me.'

Njord's smile vanished, the lightness in his voice too. 'And how are you going to stop me? I offered you a partnership but you turned it down and destroyed the draugr. Did you think your abilities would be enough? Such arrogance.'

'I mean it. I'd sooner kill myself.'

'Haven't my draugr shown you how little that matters?'

Robbed of any other reply, Frida could only glare. His chuckle returned.

'I do appreciate you bringing me more volunteers for my army. That's kind.'

He pointed behind her. The entire expedition slowly got to their feet, blank-eyed and with vacant expressions.

'Your human friends will prove useful. Some of them really hate you, don't they?'

Animal turned his bearded face toward Frida.

'There's something feral about this one. Let's have some fun, shall we?'

Animal stirred and moved awkwardly in her direction, like a child learning how to walk.

Frida pointed her fingers at him. 'Don't come any closer.'

'You're wasting your time, he can't hear you. The only thing in his mind is the need to kill you. All I had to do was give him permission.'

Frida glanced over at Lorcan and Jonas, standing like shop mannequins, as did the whole of the team. Layla had spoken the truth; the others were puppets. Njord's mind control went beyond anything she could do. Animal marched closer, inexorable, silent, unblinking eyes focused on her, features which scared her more than anything he'd done before.

'What are you waiting for? Kill him. Use your firepower.'

Frida glared at her tormentor in frustration. She wasn't a murderer but the man moving toward her was. She wasn't going to satisfy Njord's need for gladiatorial combat either.

That left her one option.

The risk was enormous. If she got it wrong and her assumption was incorrect, she'd fry everyone in the room. Njord held the others in thrall, they'd stay like that if she didn't act. Animal drew closer, this wasn't a moment for indecision. Frida pointed her fingers at the floor in front of Animal. Her gamble involved the castle architects building cellars or dungeons beneath where they now stood. If she could blast the floorboards and create a hole, Animal would fall into it, overcoming her immediate threat. The idea involved using the word 'if' a lot but she had no choice. With a deep breath Frida pointed her fingers at the floor directly in front of the big man and released a bolt of energy.

A ball of fire struck the floor, smoke billowed around the man advancing toward her. She waited for the smoke to clear. There was no sign of her assailant, just a hole in the floorboards. Frida heaved a sigh of relief and smirked at the surprise on the demi-god's face.

Her satisfaction was short-lived. The smell of rotten wood invaded her nostrils and loud creaks and cracks reached her ears. The floor shook. The thin carpet bunched around her feet, covering the tops of her boots. Before she knew what had happened, the carpet sagged even further and threads of yarn snaked around her boots and her ankles, shackling her. She tried to step backward, to escape the expanding hole, only to find she couldn't move. Struggling against the living carpet, she squealed, and with windmilling arms, she landed on her backside.

Her forced landing smashed the rotten wood beneath her. It surrendered to the laws of physics with another loud crack. The carpet wrapped itself around her, pinning arms and legs together as she tumbled into the hole.

Something heavy struck her head and darkness claimed her.

She woke and tried to get up. Except she couldn't, chunks of wood, heavy planks and the carpet had all but mummified her. Somewhere in the shadows something moved and cursed.

Animal.

Frida held her breath, not easy when clouds of dust clogged her throat and made the need to cough eye-wateringly vital. The movement and the cursing drew closer. His voice drifted through the near-darkness.

'Should have killed you a while back.'

Wherever they were, it had to be a confined space, his words echoing from one wall to another, making it impossible to work out his location. He might be only a few steps away, and he'd locate her easily if she tried to free herself now. He was a powerful man and, with her arms pinned, blasting him was out of the question. Her only hope was to act like a mouse hiding from an owl, lying perfectly still under the wreckage.

'Where are you? You fucking fairy hybrid? Show yourself and I'll make it quick.'

Animal's fall might have broken Njord's hold over his mind but it hadn't changed anything. He still wanted her dead. His next words came from directly above her and she fought to stifle a gasp.

'Show yourself, you fucking bitch.'

The need to cough burned her throat. She'd been holding her breath for too long. She closed her eyes to help her relax, forcing tears that quickly cooled as they ran down her cheeks. She opened them to see Animal's eyes fixed on her and a smile amidst the forest of beard. He reached down a bloody hand.

'What have we got here? All tied up like a turkey at Christmas. Even better. We can have some fun before I finish you off. I doubt a fucking ugly bitch like you has ever known a man. About time we put that straight.'

'I'll roast you if you come near me.'

The big man lifted a knee and stomped it down on the wreckage surrounding her. Frida squealed in pain.

'Who says you've got to be awake to enjoy it, eh?'

Another stomp, heavier this time, something snapped.

In desperation, Frida reached out with her senses and located the man's mind. She entered a dark maze full of childhood trauma and violence, a towering sense of injustice and entitlement driven by his size and strength. Like wading through sewage, Frida gritted her teeth as she drove deeper into the man's will. She wrapped her own mind around it, tightening the grip to curb his thought processes.

A third stomp broke her concentration and more of the pieces of wood around her, leaving her head clear enough for the man's fist to pound her face. Light exploded behind her eyes. Pain ricocheted around her skull as he stood on top of the debris that pinned her in place. A desperate attempt to control his mind again ended with another punch which almost dislocated her jaw. She cried out, bringing more laughter, a sound which turned into a wet, gargling noise.

Animal tumbled forward, to lie at her side, wide staring eyes locked on hers and a long shaft of wood sticking out of his throat.

'Frida? Are you all right? Can you move?'

Layla's face swam into view.

'Yes, but I'm trapped. Can you get this shit off me?'

Layla obliged, hauling away chunks of wood with surprising energy. Frida watched her work as relief and astonishment chased each other around her head. She'd convinced herself she was about to die, a demeaning and painful experience at the hands of a man she detested. She couldn't believe her luck at being spared, by Layla especially. Until she felt the cool presence in her head, monitoring her situation. Her enemy always knew what she was doing. Layla reached down a hand and yanked Frida to her feet.

'Come with me.'

A cacophony of heavy thuds and crashes drowned out the woman's words. The ground beneath her feet shook and Njord's presence wavered, then returned with a sense of panic. His presence vanished from her head. The floor beneath her shivered, large cracks formed, widened and turned into a spider's web before gravity performed its next trick. The floor vanished and Frida dropped so suddenly her stomach took a second or two to catch up.

Darkness was everywhere, so deep it was palpable. Her descent had been so sudden she was still standing by the time she found something solid beneath her feet. Pieces of wood continued to tumble and land around her but the seismic shuddering had stopped.

'Layla? Are you all right?'

No answer.

Frida summoned a ball of energy in the palm of her hand, lighting up her surroundings in an eerie green glow which did nothing to reassure her. She was in a land of nightmare. She clamped her mouth shut to contain her scream.

Layla lay in an unnaturally twisted position, spreadeagled over a lump of rock. A chunk of it protruded through her abdomen and blood trickled down one leg. Frida knelt at her side, took her hand and squeezed it. Despite leading her to this nightmare realm like a Judas goat, Layla had just saved her life. It left Frida feeling empty and helpless.

The woman's eyes fluttered open. 'Promise me, you will destroy him.'

'I promise. Keep still, I'll get you out of here.'

Layla shook her head very slightly. 'Too late. Listen. His real body remains.' Breath left her for a moment. She winced, and her next words were no more than whispers. 'Destroy the body. Hidden in chamber.' The woman's face relaxed, the lines of pain eased and along with it came a sigh. 'I can be with Carwyn now.'

Frida sensed Layla's mind open and the barriers drop. In the remaining seconds of her life, she shared the horrors of the torture she and her lover had suffered before agreeing to their forced separation. Carwyn had known he wouldn't survive his imprisonment in Njord's crazed and addled mind, yet Layla had fulfilled her mission in the hope he would. She couldn't desert the man she loved.

Layla's life force ebbed away.

Her earlier rage rose up, enhanced by her frustration now. Not only had she failed to hurt Njord in spectacular fashion, she'd sabotaged her chances by falling into the bowels of the castle and likely getting trapped there. She looked around the space as her green glow lit up the surrounding darkness. Things moved, or rather, writhed. And they were everywhere, on each wall and stretched across what remained of the ceiling, some dangling from the gap where she'd crashed through.

With her nose wrinkling in the expectation of what she'd find, Frida approached the nearest wall. Her first thought was that she had fallen into somebody's colon. Its plumbing stretched in every direction, with pipes of all sizes, transparent tubes through which a yellow-brown substance sluggishly moved. She decided she'd fallen into the castle's sewage system until closer inspection showed the shitty stuff moving upwards.

She was looking at a complex root system. To be precise, a collection of taproots which widened the nearer they reached the surface. During her time working for Herr Müller, the old man had done his best to inspire her with a love of nature, specifically the crops he grew so successfully on his farm. Carrots, turnips, beetroot and the like were crops formed from a taproot, but they weren't the plants which offered answers now. The old man had grown salsify, purely for the family's consumption, Mrs Müller used its roots to create a meatball-style stew.

Frida stared at similar taproots now. They shared the same appearance as salsify by burrowing deep into the earth but they served a different purpose. They drained the planet of its energy. It was how Njord obtained his power. Their sluggishness showed how little there was of it too; like a battery, the planet's energy had been drained.

Finally, she had an advantage. Her descent into the bowels of the castle had been fortuitous after all. She looked over at Layla's body and nodded.

'I'm going to destroy the bastard.'

She chose the broadest tube in the centre of one wall. Smaller versions stretched out in all directions but always led to the floor where they disappeared through gaps in the stone slabs. She summoned all her anger and frustration and channelled it through her fingers, releasing her energy with a roar of vengeance.

Just like in the hall above, it flared up and out, without touching its target. The force of her assault rebounded and struck her like a hurricane, knocking her backward, smacking her hard against the opposite wall. The world shook again but only for the briefest of moments, and darkness overwhelmed her, removing the pain of the collision. It tipped her into another deep pit, one in which she expected to fall, but instead she floated, weightless. She had to be unconscious, she told herself, hitting the wall had knocked her out. A dim light approached her out of the blackness.

Green light.

Her instincts triggered a sense of elation. A primal part of her brain told her everything was going to be all right though she had no idea why or how. The euphoria grew and filled her mind, like a New Year's firework display.

'At last!'

The Nephrite's distinctive chorus. They were the ones whose elation she could feel. And understand, no more weird sensations and images but actual words.

'You must activate us, Redeemer.'

255

'I don't know what that means.'

She spoke the words aloud before deciding the Nephrite probably knew what was in her mind already.

The euphoria dimmed, though the voices filled with greater urgency. *'He does not know about us. Or what we can do. But urgency is everything.'*

'No shit!'

'Activate us!'

'I don't know how!'

The Nephrite paused. *'Are you ignorant of the process?'*

'I must be, otherwise I'd be activating you, wouldn't I?'

'You completed the ritual, did you not?'

'The ritual—' Long lost memories from her trip through the portal surfaced. She pictured her mother implanting something into her wrist and the pain it caused. 'The thing my mother did when I was a little girl? I only remember it hurt.'

'When your ancestor left this world, she carried us with her. It was intended for this occasion, to redeem that which was lost. Activate us now.'

'Hang on. Why didn't you tell me this before? Why wait till now?'

'You needed to be in physical contact with us.'

She had no idea where she was, or even if she was dreaming. If she'd been knocked out, how could she be in contact with the Nephrite?

'You are not dreaming. This is real.'

An electric shock surged through her body. She was awake and her body thrummed. The floor had cracked open to create a huge fissure. She sat in the middle of it on a solid foundation of green crystal. Every muscle felt like it was on fire, though without any pain. It was more like the sensation of releasing her energy, except it was everywhere within her. Her brain delivered a thousand messages per second, sensing everything around her. Beyond her. Somewhere above her, the expedition team's fear and pain threatened to swamp her. She stared at her hands. They glowed. So did her arms, her legs.

'What's happening to me?' she screamed.

'Activate us!'

Frida stared in bewilderment at the mark on her right wrist where the scar glowed with a deeper intensity, dark green wings fluttered under her skin. She pressed her left thumb down but nothing happened.

'We need entry to your bloodstream.'

Frida dug a fingernail into the scar. A trickle of blood welled up to the surface and she pressed her finger down hard on the tiny green crystal, pushing it into her vein. An instant of pain vanished as her body exploded. She looked down at her body to reassure herself she was still in one piece.

'Good. Now we can communicate more effectively. You must leave this place now.'

'How? I don't know where I am or how to get out.'

'You share our power now. Stop thinking in human terms. Use the elements of this world, they are yours to control.'

'I don't understand.'

'Use the air. Let it lift you, like a bird.'

The reality was harder than the theory. Maintaining her balance, as both hands projected the lift she needed, was difficult. After a collision with a wall and scraping a thigh against a ceiling, Frida rose into the air, albeit shakily. The cold presence in her head didn't help but she did her best to shut him out as she slowly floated upwards through the hole she'd created.

All the time the world demanded her attention. She could hear the smallest sounds, the creaks and grinding noises of the castle's slow disintegration, accompanied by the stench of mould and rot which stung her nostrils and defined everything that was wrong with the place. But strongest of all, almost unbearably, the projected emotions and thoughts of everyone around her, extending far beyond the castle. The trolls watched from the top of the valley. Their anxiety dominated their minds but they believed in her success, guided by the Nephrite. So many people depended on her defeating Njord and here she was practising how to float.

Surprise, astonishment and even awe greeted her as she rose out of the hole in the hall, like some resurrected saintly figure. There was no sign of Njord. The expedition team busied themselves healing injuries amidst the chaos of what remained of the hall. Each one of them stopping to gaze at her, open-mouthed.

'Frida! You're ... you're glowing!' Agnes gasped as she clung to Billy.

'You all need to get out of here! Now! This place is about to collapse!'

Some of the group looked around in panic but most couldn't tear their eyes away from the phenomenon hovering a few feet above the gaping cavity. Frida didn't want to attempt a landing. She needed them to have enough faith in her to leave the castle. Her plans involved a solo mission.

'What's happened to you?' Jonas called out.

'It doesn't matter. Get everyone out and to safety.'

'What about Njord?' Olsen's voice was like crunched gravel.

'Leave him to me.'

'No offence, but you didn't cause him any problem earlier.'

The expression on Olsen's bloodied face didn't match his anxiety. He was actually frightened of her and he wasn't the only one. With surprise fading, most of the team watched her with growing trepidation.

'Things have changed. As you can see.'

They didn't move but turned to look at each other with spiralling doubt. That needed to change. The image, unsolicited but welcome, sprang into her head along with the means to execute it. She didn't need her hands to carry it out. Thought was enough. Admittedly, most of the thought wasn't hers; the Nephrite were doing most of the thinking for her.

She conjured a bubble of air around the team. They stumbled and fell, their shouts of consternation dimmed by the bubble. They floated across the derelict hall and the chasm in its floor toward the entrance. She collapsed the bubble and they tumbled through the doorway.

'Now get out of here!' she called.

A few remained: Jonas, Tristan, Lorcan and Olsen, but she thrust them through the door with a strong wind and slammed the door shut. Frida turned, satisfied.

Njord stood on the dais, smiling at her.

'Look at you, showing off!' he chuckled.

Frida remained where she was, hovering in the air, content and proud in her newfound power. Despite his laconic tone, she sensed his unease. The smile on her face mirrored his but it came from a very different place.

Her fingertips crackled with lightning and the air in the hall chilled significantly.

Njord's smile faded.

'You haven't seen anything yet, fuck face!'

Chapter 21

"I used to think of myself as a brave man."
Interview with Major Sven Olsen, QGM

The Nephrite told her to think strategically.

That was all well and good but they weren't dealing with the millions of sensations flooding into body and mind every second. Thinking proved elusive. They were right, of course, she couldn't just blast Njord – that had failed abysmally. Headstrong and emotional didn't work.

'Stop using using your anger as an energy source,' she said to herself. Listening to her inner voice helped her maintain her focus, which was essential as the Nephrite were piling a shitload of information into her head at the same time. *'You need to stay in control.'*

Njord's voice disrupted all of that. 'This is your last chance, Frida. Surrender to me now and I'll overlook the earlier mistake of killing my draugr.'

'Over my dead body!' she yelled back, cringing the instant the words left her mouth.

Njord chuckled.

A hurricane struck her out of nowhere, flinging her against the rear wall of the hall with such force she collapsed into a heap, pain registering in every part of her body. The Nephrite reprimanded her for waiting too long before launching her attack and losing the initiative. It was tempting to tell her new allies to shut the fuck up but she held back.

'You need to limit your focus. Shut out the irrelevant data. Identify your goal and how to achieve it.'

'Thanks.'

She'd acquired a sports coach apparently, this voice triggered hazy memories of her mother saying something similar during her training. It instructed her in the construction of a mental barrier to prevent access to her mind.

At the other end of the hall, Njord watched her and grinned maliciously. 'It took a long time to learn how to manipulate air from the disir. They were so very reluctant, you've no idea how many I had to kill before they agreed. Did you like my defensive barrier, by the way? Mastering the ability to modify atmospheric density wasn't easy. That's what the disir called it. But I had nothing else to do and I assumed it would come in useful. And the first time we met, it did! All that practice paid off! Now, have you accepted I can't be beaten or do you want to continue our game?'

Frida struggled to her feet, trying to dismiss the ache in her back and head. Njord was right – blasting energy didn't work and she had no other weapon in her arsenal.

'An attacking strategy doesn't need to be direct. In your memories we found evidence of the fae invading your world from places the humans overlooked. The best attack comes from surprise.'

Knowing the Nephrite were using her memories as a library unsettled her but she'd deal with that issue later, assuming there would be a later. Mother's lesson with the egg for breakfast came back to her to remind her of the need for subtlety.

Frida closed her eyes and shut out all the sources demanding her attention and let her enhanced senses provide her with answers. She found what she needed and grinned.

Rock proved a lot more difficult to manipulate than air. She understood now why the two elderly landvættir suffered heart attacks when they'd done it. Her Nephrite sports coach formed an image in her head of a fault line in the rock beneath the castle and indicated how she needed to drive a wedge inside to force it to open further. She pushed, a strange sensation, detecting the textures and densities of each mineral and which ones could be moved easier than others. Even so, exerting such force tested her strength.

The hall shuddered, dust drifted down from the ceiling, followed by small pieces of plaster, then chunks of masonry. A crevice opened up on a wall and widened with astonishing speed.

On the opposite end of the hall, Njord stared up at the ceiling in panic. 'Is this you?'

Frida relinquished her grip of the castle's foundations and unleashed her own hurricane, following it up with a blast of energy. The throne burst into flames and exploded. Njord leapt out of the way of the firestorm, rolling into a wall in the process.

He hurled himself out of the way of her second bolt of energy and responded with a gust of air that wasn't enough to cause her a problem. Exhaustion did that. Manipulating solid rock drained her physically and mentally. Her legs wobbled and she grabbed hold of the wall, a structure which should have provided solidity but didn't. The entire room shook. The hole she'd created in the centre of the floor spewed dusty, foul-smelling air, followed quickly by smoke, filling the room in less than a minute.

'What have you done? You stupid bitch!'

Njord's voice was raspy and breathless and some distance away; she couldn't see him through the clouds of muck belching out of the floor. She asked herself the same question. She'd wanted to create a surprise. Well, she'd done that all right. She had no idea what was going to happen either. She'd made a mistake compromising the foundations of the castle. Except the Nephrite had helped her do it, so she couldn't be entirely to blame.

Frida groped her way along a wall toward where she hoped to find the door, before the hole in the floor grew any bigger and she fell into it again. Cracking and creaking grew in volume, like somebody chopping huge quantities of kindling wood.

'Where are you going? Is this part of your plan?'

The terse question halted her blind quest for escape. She didn't have a plan, despite her allies' insistence on needing one.

'I'm not used to all this,' she called out, flinging an arm into the billowing dust and smoke as though the Nephrite could see what she was doing.

'We are trying to help you. But you must listen to us.'

Her sports coach sounded exasperated with her.

'Your dead friend spoke of our enemy's body. The avatar is a distraction. We believe it may be below you.'

Layla had told her of the importance of Njord's real body and she'd forgotten about it in all the confusion. If she returned to the root system she'd found, destroying it would rob him of his strength. After that, well, she could search for his body and destroy that too. The trouble was going back into the hole. Having rocked the castle's foundation, the whole place was slowly collapsing. She risked being trapped and crushed.

'I have to go back, don't I?'

Frida didn't need a reply and the Nephrite didn't offer her one.

A quick glance around the anteroom showed no sign of the others. They'd taken her advice and run. That meant she could bring the whole place down. Njord and his avatar would be finished – she'd die in the process but it would be worth it. Frida straightened herself and took a breath. The others would escape, get home hopefully and likely place a sign saying 'Do Not Enter' on the Vanaheim portal. It was fitting to die on this world, the home of her ancestors. She was, after all, the last Valkyrie and now she was about to ride into battle.

But without a horse.

Turning the flattened palms of her hands to the trembling floor, Frida lifted herself into the air and drifted into the billowing clouds of smoke and dust. A symphony of destruction sounded in every direction, warning her time was running short. She descended through the breach in the floor and down through the storeroom where a fire hungrily consumed the abandoned furniture. On the next level, the air cleared. She kept her mind alert to Njord's presence but he'd vanished again.

The arrangement of sickly looking roots plastered across the walls remained unchanged, despite her attempt to incinerate them. Njord would have protected them somehow since they were so important to him. She stared at a particularly wide and ugly taproot, perplexed. The thing was impervious to her blasts of energy and without any tools, she was powerless against it.

'*Remember, you share our control of this world's flora. You are a skogvættir.*'

'Of course! Like Scholr. Thanks.'

The taproot's texture was smooth and cool, and with the slightest sensation of a pulse through its semi-transparent membrane she could make out sluggish movement. With guidance from her Nephrite coach, Frida closed her eyes and reached out her senses until they met something which gave her a welcoming buzz.

'Sorry about this,' she whispered.

The biological make-up of the taproot appeared in her head, a series of sliding scales allowing her to adjust its chemistry. Its profile was primarily alkali, so all she needed to do was ratchet up the acidity levels to lethal proportions. It turned dark brown almost instantly, the discolouration moving along the system so that some of the network started to shrivel. Frida moved along the wall, repeating the process to more and more of the large taproots. The whole time, the wall itself trembled and above her the noise of collapse grew louder.

Holding a ball of fiery energy in one hand, she moved into the darker shadows of the room. She edged along the rift where the Nephrite glowed. In her absence, they'd been busy, crystallised strands reaching out and penetrating the corners of the room to burrow between the flagstones. She followed the strands heading in one direction.

'*There is an alien form of energy beyond this wall.*'

One strand, the nearest to the wall in question, lit up. Frida pressed a palm against the surface. She could feel something, a sensation that felt deeply unnatural.

'This has to be where Njord's body is hidden.'

'*We concur.*'

The room shook so hard, Frida fell to her knees. Something heavy crashed through the hole at the other end of the cellar and made her jump.

'*The building's structure is severely compromised, Redeemer. It is collapsing.*'

By expanding the size of her ball of light, she could see the taproots had turned brown and shrivelled across two walls, a third was well on its way. On the nearest wall, the one place she hadn't infected, a crack ran down the middle of the wall with astonishing speed. It divided into a spider's web of mini fractures.

That was when she sensed Njord. The icy-cold presence made her shiver. He was close. At the same time, she heard voices. And her name. She recognised the voice.

'Jonas?'

'Yes! On the other side of the wall. We found your emblem.'

Splinters of stone fell to the ground as someone thumped the wall repeatedly.

'There was a door here once, Frida. It's been blocked with stone but it's starting to collapse. Can you open it up?'

'What are you doing here? I told you to get out.'

Another heavy thump.

'All right. Stand back.'

She counted to ten to give them chance to find cover before releasing a carefully controlled bolt of energy. The wall came down easily, dust billowing in all directions, and

through it stumbled three figures.

Jonas' hulking frame stepped out of the dust. He immediately threw his arms around her and hugged her tightly. 'I was worried I wouldn't find you. No more getting rid of me with bubbles. Agreed?'

Despite the situation, his words and anxiety made her smile. Thankfully Lorcan saved her from answering by telling them to get a room.

He beamed his trademark smile. 'I wasn't going to leave you here on your own. I have a debt to repay, remember? I've no idea why he's here, he just followed us.' Lorcan jerked a thumb at Olsen.

His stern and uncompromising expression didn't change until the moment he stood in front of her. He reached out his hand. 'I owe you an apology, Miss Ranson. You have proven yourself to be the saviour of this expedition and I've been blind to your strengths, saw them only as a threat. Elsa recognised them and I should have paid more attention to her judgement.'

The other two men's eyes widened in astonishment.

She took his hand and shook it. 'Where are the others?'

'Lieutenant Wheeler has escorted them out of the castle.'

Jonas looked around the room with a frown. 'What is this place?'

'The source of Njord's energy. I've cut most of it off.' Frida pointed to the wall at right angles to where they stood. 'I think his original body is in there. I expect he's waiting for me.'

Lorcan and Olsen examined the glowing green tendrils and the mass of crystal from which they grew.

Olsen knelt down to scrutinise them, illuminating his face in its ghostly light. 'And this is the sentient crystal?'

'Part of it, yes. But we don't have time for all this. The castle is collapsing.'

As if to punctuate her statement, the room rumbled ominously and dust flooded from the ceiling as cracks spread across its length and breadth.

'All the more reason to get in that room and finish this,' Olsen said with the kind of stoic determination she'd often resented.

'I may not be able to protect you,' Frida said.

'We're here to support you, Miss Ransom. We provide the distraction while you deal with our enemy.'

All three men projected the same levels of determination that told her she'd waste her time trying to dissuade them. She shrugged her acceptance and thanked them. There wasn't time for motivational speeches so Frida splayed her fingers and hoped she'd calculated the right amount of energy to blast through the wall. She could now gauge the required firepower to achieve the result she needed, thanks to the Nephrite doing the maths.

The wall collapsed in a billowing cloud of dust and the four of them rushed through it, ready for whatever

Njord wanted to throw at them. Except he didn't. He stood on the other side of a coffin-shaped box made of a material that glistened like wet tar. The room was small, no bigger than her hotel room in York. Stretched across each wall and across the ceiling was a sight which made Frida's heart sink.

More taproots. Dozens of them.

'Your pruning exercise outside was annoying. If I had any plans to stay here, I'd be really pissed off now.'

Impatience showed on his face, his brow marred by lines he didn't have last time she'd seen him. At least she hoped so.

He shook his head, as if he was talking to a stupid child. 'It proves you don't know what you're doing. You're a little girl with hedge clippers in a jungle. Time to show you how dangerous that jungle can be.'

Roots, big and small, snapped in her direction with the speed of a cobra, snagging wrists and ankles to imprison her against a wall. Frida reached out with her new skogvættir skills, but the roots continued to swarm across her body, just like in the dodder forest, climbing to her throat to throttle her.

Njord's laughter pealed in the limited space. 'These roots are my creation, not the planet's flora, you can't manipulate them. I assume Layla is the one to blame for your appreciation of this world's natural elements, but I've had a long time to make my preparations. Now, be a good girl and stop struggling, while we merge.'

In her peripheral vision Frida could just make out the three men standing expressionless and stationary again. She hadn't expected anything less but they'd been brave to try.

Njord ambled around the black box, smiling smugly. 'Your destruction of my home irritated me. My energies are imbued throughout the fabric of the castle. Sustaining its structure long enough to capture you was draining. Thankfully, you decided to come to me instead. We don't have time to waste.'

Suddenly she was in the air, held aloft by the roots that bound her tightly. They floated her over the black coffin, allowing her to see inside.

Njord's withered body lay wrapped in the black cloak she'd seen in her vision. Skin, the colour of chewed tobacco, looked like overstretched elastic. The jaw flopped, displaying a few brown pegs which had to be teeth. Worst of all, its eyes watched her and, though she couldn't be certain, the mouth seemed to stretch into a smile.

The roots rotated her body to lay her out, face down, then slowly lowered her. The whole time, the thing's eyes watched her hungrily. Her panicked struggling made no difference, the roots' grip was vice-like.

'Soon be over,' the Njord avatar cooed at the side of the coffin. 'Then I'll be able to leave this flesh sack and you and I will escape my prison and wreak havoc in the other eight realms.'

The Nephrite had gone silent, clearly out of ideas and unable to help. Tendrils erupted out of the brown skull, snaking toward her, tipped with disk-shaped suckers. She could guess what they were for.

'I'll never cooperate! I'll fight you all the way!' Frida's voice shook, making her sound like a frightened little girl and she hated herself for it.

The entire room juddered, dust tumbled from the ceiling.

'You might merge with me but this place is about to collapse. We'll all be trapped under it, unable to escape.'

'Silly girl! I built my castle directly over a portal.'

She lost sight of the avatar as the vine-like growths lowered her inside the coffin, more tendrils bursting from the skull, eager to connect with her. Its putrid stench invaded her nose, and the licking motion of the thing's leathery tongue made her stomach churn. The prospect of lying on top of its body as it performed some form of absorption process only added to the horror, she wanted to vomit. Her mind raced to find ways to use her new-found talents, but all she could do was stare into the eyes that watched her approach. The only other emotion left inside her was regret. She should have done more, fought harder, had a plan. Brought the castle down on all three of them sooner.

Something Njord's avatar had said earlier leapt into focus.

"My energies are imbued throughout the fabric of the castle. Sustaining its structure long enough to capture you, was draining."

Now it was too late. It wasn't just the taproots she should have destroyed; it was the castle itself. She had used hedge clippers to solve the problem. Her accidental destruction of the building had been the right idea all along, she just hadn't executed it with enough force. Only seconds remained. Time to think bigger. Much bigger.

As the first sucker caressed her face, Frida reached into the strata of rock on which the castle stood, found the crevice she'd adjusted earlier and, with all the strength she had left, opened it as wide as it would go.

The world shook.

The coffin wobbled on its plinth as the ground beneath it shuddered violently, each time increasing in force and scale. Njord's avatar peered into the coffin, humourless and malevolent now. Its skin sagged, like melted candle wax, almost obscuring its eyes that glared with so much ferocity.

'What have you done?' He gasped and grabbed the side of the coffin as another quake forced him to his knees. His weight and another, bigger quake, dragged the coffin onto its side, spilling Frida and Njord's remains onto the floor. The grip of the roots eased. With some of the panic clearing, Frida remembered the trick she'd used once before. She increased her body temperature until she lit up the dark room. Within seconds the roots shrivelled.

The noise of demolition was deafening.

The three men, freed from their mental stupor, regained their senses only to find it impossible to stand upright. Driven to their knees, they could only shout their warning as the Njord avatar launched himself at Frida, knife in hand, teeth bared in a frenzy of desperation. Still trapped in the decaying roots and too weak to fight, she threw herself sideways. He followed her to the floor, knife in hand as he tried to stab her, missing only because she managed to dodge him each time. Except the roots trapped her, prevented her from moving any further. Spotting his advantage the avatar roared his triumph and raised his knife. Lorcan flung himself on top of the avatar.

'Get out, Frida, quick!' Lorcan called out before yelling in pain.

With another animal-like growl the avatar brought his knife down into the centre of Lorcan's back, stabbing him repeatedly. The effort slowed as the avatar's strength waned. Lorcan bellowed, a wounded animal but not yet finished. He reared up with sudden and enormous force, his assailant's hands sliding off the blood-slick knife. Lorcan grabbed its shirt and pushed the avatar up against the coffin, pinning it against the side with one hand, and drew the knife out of his own back with a grimace. In one swift motion, he used it to slash the avatar's throat, covering them both in its blood.

Another quake and a crack formed on the floor, racing from one side of the room to the other. Then it opened. Wide.

The coffin wobbled then slipped into the yawning gap.

'No! I need to kill him!' Frida screamed as the coffin then its guest, disappeared into the darkness.

A groan dragged her attention back. With nothing to hold it upright, the avatar's dead body flopped onto the floor at the edge of the chasm, Lorcan slumped next to it, his breathing shallow and raspy.

'Debt repaid. As promised.'

Jonas and Olsen ripped away the wilting taproots wrapped around Frida, but her attention remained on Lorcan's eyes as she watched the light in them dim. The need to scream her grief reached up into her throat, and she didn't try to stop it leaving. Primal in its origins, it didn't just convey her grief, it vented her frustration at losing Njord.

'We need to get out of here!' Olsen called.

The ground beneath their feet shook, every step was a balancing act, and staying upright outweighed the need for speed. Another loud crack and the chasm widened even farther, taking up most of the small room's floorspace. Its edges crumbled. Frida, Jonah and Olsen staggered backward and fell to their knees, only able to watch as the avatar and Lorcan's body fell into the yawning hole. A network of cracks opened up above them, heralding the collapse of the ceiling. At its centre a huge mass of masonry dislodged itself, forcing the three to throw themselves into the gap Frida had created earlier. The chunk of ceiling dropped, slammed onto the floor and tipped into the chasm, directly in front of where they knelt.

Above them, a shaft of light lit up the room. Frida looked up into its swirling dust cloud. She turned to the two men.

'Grab hold of me.'

She fixed Jonas, bloody and battered, with a fierce look. Her strength was waning, rapidly but she was out of alternatives.

'Are you sure you can carry us?'

'Got any better ideas?'

He shook his head and put an arm around her waist, Olsen did the same. Frida took a deep breath, placed her palms face down and projected a blast of air with what little strength she had left. It was enough for them to wobble unsteadily and float up through the hole in the roof.

Chapter 22

*'Trolls have not fared well in the retelling of Norse tales.
They might not have favoured human beings but they
were rarely hostile, unless provoked.'*

From 'Scandinavian Folk Tales' by Ingrid Pedersen

A warm breeze manoeuvred Frida and the two men away
from the castle. They watched the entire building fold in
on itself; towers toppled, walls crumpled to form a pile of
smoking finality. The disturbed air brought a billowing
stench of decay and an acrid bite of smoke to their
nostrils.

Badly weakened and with the loss of Lorcan fresh
in her mind, the weight of the two men was too much. She
dropped them into the river sparkling below them.

'I hope you can swim!' she shouted.

She drifted with the help of the breeze and landed
on the riverbank as the two men swam toward her. A
short distance away the expedition team, Tristan at the
front, ran toward them. Frida reached out a helping hand
to Jonas.

'You need to get them away from here. As far as
you can.'

Both men flopped on the grass, heaving for breath.

'Why?' Olsen gasped.

'This isn't finished.'

Frida turned to stare at the columns of smoke
rising from the rubble. Something didn't feel right. She

276

couldn't say what, whether it was a smell, a wrongness in the air, the way the ground beneath her feet didn't react as it should.

'You need to get them away. Fast!'

They both nodded together, trusting her judgement now. They sprinted to the approaching and bedraggled group, arms raised, calling for them to get away from the castle.

A call from the top of the incline made Frida turn. The trolls. They were waving to her, but it was no victory salute. With legs like lead, she strode up the incline toward them. In places, the topsoil had slipped, making the meadow look like waves on the ocean. She went higher to where ridges had formed, the tell-tale green glow of Nephrite emanating from the furrows. Her senses told her what she'd find before she reached the summit of the hill. The crowd of trolls separated as she walked through their midst.

A shallow rift displayed a wide channel of Nephrite, lighting the trolls' faces with its green light. The old man, Ehlagron, leaned hard on his staff to join her.

'The final battle begins, Redeemer.'

As if in reply, the huge mound of rubble that had been the castle, jolted. The tremor reached them a second later.

'You need to get your people away from here,' Frida said.

The old man shook his head. 'You still do not understand, Redeemer. We are the Nephrite's caretakers, and we have maintained its existence for as long as we have lived in this realm. You are our saviour. You have made your choice, to fight the invader.' His leathery expression turned into a crooked smile. 'We are here to help you.'

'I don't understand.'

The ground jerked and the hillside appeared to ripple like water. Within the rubble, a huge explosion deafened them. The old man watched fire belch from the castle's remains as their hearing returned.

'You are weakened. Your energies are depleted. Come, join me.'

He held out a filthy hand, its skin looked and felt like leather. She placed her hand in his, he folded arthritic fingers around it and they stepped onto the strata of Nephrite.

'Kneel with me,' he said.

He bent a knee while clinging to his staff. Frida could feel his pain and yet he kept smiling.

'I have waited for this moment my whole life, Redeemer. I had begun to think I would never witness it but, here we are.'

As her knee reached the sun-warmed surface of the green crystal, she felt the energy surge as it entered her. She gasped for a second before her breath vanished.

The old man, squeezed her hand. 'Steady. Take your time.'

The world reeled but she took a breath again and the dizziness faded.

Ehlagron still smiled benignly. 'Feels good?'

She smiled back and nodded. It felt better than good. She felt alive. Not only that, but she could also hear the Nephrite again.

'He is on his way. Be ready. Remember what we have taught you.'

Ehlagron's smile remained fixed though his eyes held a distant look, perhaps like hers.

'Can you hear them too?' she asked.

'Of course.'

The rest of the trolls moved purposefully to surround the fissure. As one, holding hands to form a chain, they stepped onto the crystal, eyes closed.

Every cell in Frida's body ignited with something she couldn't label as energy; it was something bigger, grander than that. Suddenly she felt dwarfed by the scale of what moved through every vein and artery, and the ground beneath her knees shivered in time to the ripples of whatever it was flowing through her. Above everything, the joy, the exhilaration, there was so much power.

Ehlagron grinned. 'I told you. We are here to help. Do this for all of us, Redeemer.'

The castle exploded, lifting blocks of stone high into the air. Out of the midst of flame and smoke, soared a black shape. It hovered over the derelict building to take in the scale of destruction.

Its voice was in Frida's head, tone raw and visceral. 'Stupid girl. I offered you the world and look how you repay me.'

Frida got to her feet, renewed. The trolls hadn't moved, their eyes still closed, their hands still linked, wearing sublime smiles. Some distance away, Jonas, Olsen and the expedition team watched from the top of the bluff where she'd first spotted the castle. She needed to move the forthcoming battle away from all of them.

She rose up into the air and reworked the breeze to push her in the direction of the black shape.

Its voice filled her head. 'All this time and I knew nothing about the entity that supports you now. After I've dealt with you, I will absorb it as well.'

The shape drew closer, near enough to make out a billowing black cloak surrounding the corpse-like thing that was the real Njord.

Frida didn't feel frightened now, the panic this nightmare creature had evoked in her had vanished. She was nervous but it was nothing compared to the need to destroy the thing which had killed Lorcan and so many others.

'Fuck off and die!' she screamed.

Green energy exploded from every part of her body, not just her fingertips. She'd grown beyond those basic skills. In her head, the Nephrite, and she guessed the trolls as well, fed her with information. Details of air currents, sources of heat, water and even the geological structure of the ground itself. Yet she could think, no longer dominated by an influx of knowledge.

Whatever was happening, Frida felt different, in control. She had one goal. To defeat the creature floating in front of her.

Her energy bolt struck the black shape with the force of a speeding train. It sent it spinning over and over, the black cloak tangling the creature inside until it struck the ground on the opposite side of the river.

Frida reached out to manipulate water from the river and envelope the writhing black shape as it recovered. She drew in more and more water, working it into a pipeline which transported the thing into the river itself. It disappeared into its dark depths.

She could feel Njord's fury. She hadn't beaten it but she'd demonstrated she meant business. She floated to the ground, a short distance from the edge of the river, ready for the attack.

It came as Njord burst out of the water like a missile. Spiralling flumes of water surrounded him, extending to bend around Frida's body, enveloping her in a towering column. With an outward thrust of her arms, the water lost its shape and collapsed.

'Predictable,' she called.

Plant-life at her feet coiled and snapped but she was in the air before it could reach her.

'Is this the best you can do, old man?'

His fury multiplied as air struck her with the force of a hurricane. It drove her backward, faster than any plane could travel. No matter how hard she tried to arrest her momentum, the air around her shifted so quickly she couldn't control it to slow her down.

The hurricane stopped abruptly. Unhurt, Frida looked down to get her bearings. She recognised the copse of trees which had once contained the home of the grandmother and little girl.

She floated into the entrance to the dell. The montage had ended, its purpose served. She sighed all the same. She sensed Njord's arrival as well as his sudden curiosity and allowed him to approach. This place felt right for what she had in mind.

'I know this place,' said the voice in her head.

'Yes. The scene of one of your murders. My ancestors.'

The cold, dead eyes inside the cloak's cowl took in the scene. 'How do you know …?'

Frida chuckled and strolled into the darkened depths of the saucer-shaped depression ringed by trees. Njord followed. Once inside, she turned to face him.

'There's so much you don't know. You've said as much. I mean, you've lived here for millennia and you knew nothing about the Nephrite. How stupid you were. How blind. But that's what anger and resentment does to you.'

The eyes inside the cowl watched her, suspicious now.

'I used to be like that. Not as bad as you, of course. But I held onto anger and resentment, isolating myself, ready to blame everyone else. If you'd chosen not to kill everyone, you'd have had friends. Who knows? Perhaps, the Nephrite might have helped you, like they did me.'

'I was imprisoned here with no reprieve!'

'You drained the life force of the flora and fauna to fuel your need for power.'

'I had no other option. I wasn't going to be denied.'

'You still don't understand, do you?'

The black figure paused, raised its arms to unleash another attack.

Frida smiled. 'You're not fighting me. I'm channelling the energies of the entire planet. And it's angry about what you've done to it.'

'You cannot defeat me, girl. I am a god of Asgard. You are nothing.'

'Wrong again, old man. I've drained what energy you had left with our skirmish just now. The destruction of the castle has left you vulnerable.'

Anxiety surfaced in those cold and empty eyes.

'The planet and I have had enough of you.'

Frida raised her arms and looked up. She'd kept him distracted long enough to amass enough kinetic energy from hundreds of miles around, and it waited above her. She brought her arms down in one swift motion. Lightning bolts, hundreds of them, struck the cloaked figure from all directions, illuminating the shadowy space with incandescent beauty that earthed itself in Njord's body again and again and again.

Frida seized her opportunity and used her psychic energy to torpedo Njord's mind.

Focused on his efforts to withstand the lightning, entry proved easy, a mere matter of pushing against a heavy door that would once have been impassable. Once inside, she took hold of the man's will and shackled it with an iron grip. Njord's body collapsed. The lightning bolts ceased, leaving a pungent smell of ozone and a blackened shell of a body.

Frida could feel his consciousness, inert now. She wasted no time. She couldn't afford to be complacent with this creature. She raised the body on a current of air and dragged it behind her as she travelled back to where the trolls waited.

Grinning faces greeted her as they stepped back onto the meadow, still surrounding the fissure of Nephrite. She landed next to Ehlagron. He didn't look at all well. Two male trolls helped him remain upright but he managed to smile at her and nod his head.

'Lay the body on the fissure,' the Nephrite instructed.

She dragged the body on its cushion of air over the green crystal and lowered it carefully. The crystal opened, like a large mouth, to consume the body. The black shape receded until it was no more than a black speck. The opening closed back up again.

'What is the Nephrite going to do with him?'

Ehlagron cleared his throat. 'Absorb him. Nothing is ever wasted.' His voice was hoarse and only a dry whisper.

'Is he dead?'

'What remains of his life force will fuel the planet for as long as it exists. It is the fate awaiting us all. My own absorption is imminent. I await the honour of joining the Nephrite.'

'Will your life force be consumed as well?'

'Oh no. I told you. Having served the Nephrite loyally throughout my long life, I will be part of them. You may even hear my voice amidst all my friends who wait for me.'

The old man had been right, there was a lot she still didn't understand.

Their work done, the trolls ambled off. Frida stood on the edge of the bluff to look down on the destruction below. She spotted the expedition team making their way toward her. She had little time to get herself together before they arrived.

It wouldn't be enough. Grief demanded her attention.

There hadn't been time to deal with Lorcan's death, she couldn't delay it any longer. Her grief threatened to overwhelm her. He'd saved her life and had been her friend. She wished their relationship could have been straight forward. She'd misconstrued his kindness because she wanted someone to care for her, to end her loneliness. In his way, he'd done just that. Tears pricked her eyes and she fought to hold them back.

'Life comes in many forms, Frida. Death doesn't have to be so final.'

She recognised the voice instantly and, even though it was in her head, she couldn't stop herself from looking around to find its source. The voice chuckled. Frida knew there would be a million-megaton smile to go with it.

'Lorcan?'

'Don't ask me how they do it. All this is new to me too. But you heard what Ehlagron said. We Nephrite like to reward loyalty, even to guys who don't deserve it.'

His words made her sob and for a moment or two, she couldn't speak. When she could, her throat was raw. 'Will I always be able to speak to you?'

'Suppose so. I'm not going anywhere.'

It made her smile. She sat on the warm grass and looked out over the scene below to wait for the others to arrive. For the first time in her life, Frida felt peace and contentment.

She had come home.

Coda

'Headline: United Nations officials to visit the Queen of Vanaheim.'

Someone had pointed out that it was two months since she'd defeated Njord.

It might have been Agnes, during one of her visits. Or Jonas – he was the organised one – which was a good thing given all the work that needed to be done.

The dell looked nothing like it once had. The whole area was a building site, but she'd insisted on her home being in that location. She could do that now, insist. It hadn't come easily at first, certainly not when it came to dealing with government agencies. In the first month there had been a lot of that. Frida hated every second of it.

With summer coming to an end, the heat had eased. She'd got used to it anyway. So had everyone who worked here now. The concept of the Spanish siesta had quickly caught on, seeing as it was pointless to work in the hottest part of the day. She sat in her deckchair on what would soon be her front garden and watched butterflies dance around a patch of pink flowers. Nature's speedy return had surprised her; apparently the Nephrite had placed many species into a deep hibernation. Lorcan had tried to describe how it worked but she'd got bored with the explanation.

Jonas sauntered over to her from their tent, his grin as big as the man himself. The idiot had a permanent smile these days. What was worse, it was contagious. She smiled back at him.

'It's been two months,' she said as a greeting.

'I know. I told you that yesterday. I knew you weren't listening.'

She shrugged and giggled at his feigned irritation. At least she'd pinned down who'd told her. He stood in front of her, hands on hips, dressed in a pair of baggy shorts and a thin tee-shirt that emphasized the curves of his magnificent body. She knew what he was doing with that stance but pretended she didn't. It was a game they played.

'You do remember me saying Olsen is bringing members of the United Nations here tomorrow. It's going to be a big day for the Queen of Vanaheim.'

She snorted loudly. 'Oh, shut up!'

'That's what they're calling you, back home.' Those two words changed her mood. Jonas spotted it instantly and sat in front of her, legs crossed. 'That's what *they* call it. Not me.'

She saw his eyes twinkle and smiled. She had to ask, even though she thought she knew the answer. But she needed to be certain. 'Don't you want to go back? Now we've found more portals and opened them up, you can travel here whenever you like.'

He didn't reply straight away. 'Is that what you want?'

Small green tendrils sprouted from the ground, snagging the big man's ankles and wrists. He didn't move but allowed them to wrap around his limbs. Frida giggled.

Valkyrie of Vanaheim

'Are you ever going to get tired of doing this to me?' he laughed.

Frida moved off her deckchair and climbed on top of him, propping up her head with one hand as she gazed into his eyes. 'I never hear you complain.'

He reached up and kissed her. 'I know what follows.'

They both chuckled and kissed a second time, with greater urgency. Frida freed one of Jonas' wrists so he could move a wayward strand of her hair.

He searched her face. 'In that world, you and I were the freaks. Here, we can be ourselves. Why would I want to go back there?'

She nodded. He maintained eye contact.

'It's going to change though. Once the Prime Minister gets your consent, they'll start the migration process. In a few years' time, there will be cities and roads ...'

'I know. But it's going to be on my terms. I won't let them pollute this world or over populate it either. They need to rescue their home world as well. I'll give them locations to populate but they won't be allowed to go beyond them.'

'And if they ignore you?'

She chuckled. 'It's why I'm going to give them a special performance tomorrow. Not just me, the trolls and the Nephrite too. A combined effort. We've designed it to be sufficiently intimidating, in a friendly way.'

Movement from the shaded areas announced the end of the siesta. Frida got to her feet and released the big man from his imprisonment with a casual wave of her hand. With another gesture, a cool breeze stirred branches as it moved through the camp site, lowering the temperature just enough to make it welcoming. Nearby, a fountain of water leapt out from the ground, fed from an underground spring she'd sensed a week ago. A couple of the workers gave her a thumbs up as they drank from the dancing fountain.

'What are you going to do now?' Jonas asked.

'A few last-minute arrangements to make with the Nephrite.'

'OK. Say hello to Lorcan for me.' Jonas waved as he set off to supervise the marking out of another building.

'Will do,' she replied.

She made herself comfortable in her deckchair. She'd contact Lorcan in a little while, the view from this spot was too beautiful to ignore at this time of day. She sighed contentedly. Jonas was right, she could do what she liked. She was a Valkyrie, Queen of Vanaheim and this was her home.

Acknowledgements

I hope you enjoyed Frida's adventures. Thank you for choosing my story. I'd appreciate it if you would leave a review on sites like **Amazon** and **Goodreads**. They help bring the story to the attention of other people, reviews are the life blood to writers.

The completion of any novel is a team effort. Special thanks go to my beta readers for their support and honesty, particularly Damien, Annabel and Phil W.

I owe a huge debt of gratitude to my editor, **PS Livingstone**, for her perception and attention to detail. https://www.pslivingstone.com/editing-services/

Thanks to my brilliant cover artist, **Ken Dawson** at **Creative Covers**. - https://www.ccovers.co.uk/

If you want to read more of my stories, you can find them at: https://www.philparker-fantasywriter.com/philparkerbooks

Printed in Great Britain
by Amazon

43692856R00165